BARBARY TERROR

John Chudley

Grosvenor House
Publishing Limited

All rights reserved
Copyright © John Chudley, 2022

The right of John Chudley to be identified as the author of this
work has been asserted in accordance with Section 78
of the Copyright, Designs and Patents Act 1988

The book cover is copyright to John Chudley

This book is published by
Grosvenor House Publishing Ltd
Link House
140 The Broadway, Tolworth, Surrey, KT6 7HT.
www.grosvenorhousepublishing.co.uk

This book is sold subject to the conditions that it shall not, by way of
trade or otherwise, be lent, resold, hired out or otherwise circulated
without the author's or publisher's prior consent in any form of binding or
cover other than that in which it is published and
without a similar condition including this condition being imposed
on the subsequent purchaser.

This book is a work of fiction. Any resemblance to
people or events, past or present, is purely coincidental.

A CIP record for this book
is available from the British Library

ISBN 978-1-80381-212-0
eBook ISBN 978-1-80381-213-7

Chapter One

"Where's Mumma being taken to?"

"What?" Sir Antony looked at his daughter, Maribel, with concern. "Where?"

"Down at the landing." Crippled with palsy in a wheelchair, Maribel, nevertheless, had sharp eyes.

Sir Antony squinted in the direction indicated. "By Jove, that's Magistrate Brandon Travallyn's men. He turned to his father's steward. "Quick, take a platoon of our dragoons and bring her to me."

"But, m'lord, the magistrate."

"I'll explain to Magistrate Travallyn. He's a friend. Don't get into conflict with his men. Just say I need to look urgently into what's happened. Eleanor has a unique role in my household, which I might have to remind him of, making it essential I intervene today. He's a fair man who would not send anyone to trial without good evidence. But the problem is, I don't know what that evidence is regarding the woman my daughter thinks of as her mother, her birth mother having died not long after giving birth."

"Yes, m'lord."

Antony looked back to his daughter. Small for her age, she had a sensitive face with flowing golden locks. Ignorant people, some in his household, whispered that she was crippled as a punishment for being born out of wedlock, but Antony knew better in this age of enlightenment. It was just one of those unfortunate things. She was a lovely girl, and he loved her very much. She was also very intelligent with exceptional mathematical ability. Her mother had been an under-maid in their household who he had fallen in love with. Aristocrats were not supposed to have affairs with servants in their households, but it happened from time to time. Sadly, the maid, who Antony had become very fond of, died 10 days after Maribel was born. His father, the marquis, had appointed Eleanor, a seamstress in their household, to look after her, who Maribel thought of as her mother. Now she was 11, Antony felt it was time his daughter was told the truth. His father, at 65, was not in good health and unable to walk since developing a painful seized hip, leaving Antony to run everyday matters of household and estate.

"Don't worry, my darling, I'll have Eleanor back in no time."

Two hours later, Eleanor was bought before him. Antony ordered everyone out of his presence. As Maribel was being wheeled away, he motioned that she was to be left with him. He looked at Eleanor reproachfully, "How could you let me and Maribel down?"

Eleanor hung her head. She knew Sir Anthony was an unusually enlightened and very fair master, much influenced by the egalitarian and humanitarian pamphleteers of the civil war, which ended in 1651, forty years before he was born, in contrast to his traditional and authoritarian father. "I stole the tinderbox from the market for my mother and father. They only sell cheap ones in the market."

"You stole a tinderbox? That was a dangerous thing to do. You were risking your life. It wasn't a loaf of bread or some eggs. If I hadn't intervened in your arrest, you could have been hung for that or at least transported to the Americas. How would you being dead have helped your parents, not to mention devastating Maribel? If your parents have fallen on hard times, you should have asked to see me. You know that."

"I'm sorry, I acted on the spur of the moment."

"You've put me in a difficult position. In this modern age, manorial courts are a thing of the past. Magistrates and judges are deemed to be unbiased and implement the law fairly, irrespective of status or title. You were wrong to do what you did. I hope Magistrate Travallyn is not upset."

"I didn't mean to cause trouble, m'lord." Antony looked at Eleanor, concerned and considering. He had many problems on his mind. Since 1864, the weather had become progressively colder, bringing crop failure and causing peasants to die of starvation. The effects of the great storm of December 1703 were still visible on their West Dorset estate 27 years later. Barbary pirates continued to prove a problem on occasion, seizing men, women and children to sell as white slaves, causing tenant farmers along the coast to abandon their properties in fear. The estate relied on the dues from its tenant farmers.

Additionally, his father was becoming increasingly frustrated and angry by his reluctance, at the age of 39, to marry Lady Beatrice, the daughter of an earl, his father's best friend, whose dowry would make a considerable contribution to the flagging fortunes of the estate. The fact that he did not like the haughty and ill-tempered Lady Beatrice, who he had known since childhood, was of no consequence. It was his duty to marry well.

Lady Beatrice would not put up with Maribel for one moment. One thing it did prove was that Antony could father children. But such offspring were conveniently put aside. Antony's reluctance to do so and that he was demonstratively fond of Maribel was considered by all to be an embarrassment.

Everyone relied on the prosperity of the estate. Antony was very conscious of this and, with his ideals, wanted to do his best for all, to be a caring and enlightened lord of the manor when his father passed on. He did not want Eleanor to feel he did not appreciate the love and devotion she had put into the bringing up of his beloved daughter. On the other hand, he must be seen to be doing his duty when confronted with the facts. "I know you didn't mean to cause trouble, but nevertheless you broke the law, so, having taken you, I need to be seen to pass sentence. In your own time, you must do two pieces of table linen for the refectory tables featuring our household livery, understand?"

Eleanor curtsied. "Yes, m'lord."

"And while you're here, there's something else. This is why I've asked Maribel to stay."

"Yes, m'lord."

Antony drew Maribel's chair towards him and put an arm around her shoulder, looking at her fondly. "Now you're 11, there's something I need to tell you." He lifted her out of her chair and put her on his lap. "Eleanor's not your mother. Sadly, your birth mother died soon after giving birth to you. My father instructed

Eleanor to bring you up but not to talk about your mother. He would like me to have nothing to do with you, but I've insisted that I have to see you. This you need to know, and to know that you must keep your head down and be careful not to create any problem. When I'm the marquis, things will be different."

Maribel gave a sob and wiped away a tear. "I was beginning to feel that your being my father was creating difficulties now I'm growing older – you are my father?"

"Yes, dear, that's why it's becoming an increasing problem. I was very much in love with your mother. She was a wonderful person, though a serving girl in our household. I wasn't supposed to fall in love with serving girls. Before long, I will have to get married, but your mother I will always love."

"What was her name?"

"Mary, that's why I had you named Maribel, the first three letters of your name being the same as for Mary. I know you're a smart girl and would realise you were being treated differently from the children of other servants."

"People wouldn't answer my questions."

"Your origin wasn't to be talked about. Next month I have to marry Lady Beatrice for the good of the estate as she has a very large dowry. Her father, an earl, is my father's best friend. They were in the Lord General's Regiment of Foot Guards together. It is expected of me, after which you could be in considerable danger."

Antony turned to Eleanor. "Why are your parents in straitened circumstances?"

"My father, in partnership with another man, ran a printing press in Lyme Regis. His partner did not pull his weight but took more than his share of the profits.

Then my father's sight began to fail. He couldn't place the pieces accurately or the ink in the incised marks. The business had to be sold. He bought a small holding near the coast but knows nothing of farming and, with the bad weather and people leaving the coast, is struggling. He's sold many of his possessions to keep going, including his one tinderbox. When the fire goes out, he has to borrow one."

"That's why you can read and write and taught Maribel."

"Yes, m'lord."

Antony looked at Eleanor closely. She had an attractive open face, short flaxen hair and a trim figure. He liked her devotion to his daughter, putting more time into her by teaching her to read and write than she needed to, and also the fact that she was prepared to risk her life for her parents. "I'm grateful you taught Maribel to read and write. It's important for her to be literate."

"I like caring for her. I enjoy teaching her. She has a flair for arithmetic as well. She's a lovely and intelligent girl."

Antony considered his words carefully. "I think so. I have a proposition for you and your family that would enable you to live comfortably but would have an element of danger. I would like you to consult your parents and consider it carefully before you accept."

Eleanor glanced at her master wide-eyed. "Yes, m'lord?"

"I would like you and your family to change identities and move somewhere else, along with Maribel, for which you would be appropriately paid and live well. The condition is that it would be a strict secret between us. When I become marquis, I'll deal with Lady Beatrice and have my daughter at my side, whatever people might think."

"Yes, m'lord."

"You'd better go now, taking Maribel with you. Walls have ears. Make sure she keeps her mouth shut. My father is very much in favour of Lady Beatrice. After you've worked off your sentence, I'll dismiss you. You taking Maribel will please my father no end, but our time will come, mark my words." Antony gave Maribel a long kiss and hug before putting her back in her chair.

Chapter Two

Preparations for Sir Antony's wedding to Lady Beatrice were to commence. But what was on Sir Antony's mind before all else was the welfare and safety of his love child. His father, very much annoyed by what he considered his son's besotted behaviour, would not raise a finger to prevent Lady Beatrice hunting her down. This had to be avoided at all cost. To keep Maribel safe until he became the marquis was his first priority.

Daily, he rode out on the pretence of attending to estate matters. At lunch time he would leave his escort in a hostelry with money for a good meal and plenty to drink while he went off on his own to scout around for a possible hideaway. After three weeks, he found what he considered the best, after which he would need to attend to wedding preparations.

It was a watermill in a secluded valley, powered by a tumbling stream. It had a mill pond to regulate the flow of water into an overshot mill wheel, now frozen. It was not easily seen from afar, but those at the mill had sight of anyone approaching. The beauty of it was that dense bushes covered the valley floor, enabling anyone not wanting to be found at the mill to escape up or down the valley unnoticed. Dressed as a town burgher, he approached the mill, knocked on the door and asked for the miller. A tired old man opened the door. Antony introduced himself as a merchant and businessman from Lyme Regis, asking if he could come in and explain the purpose of his visit.

Dusting his hands on his leather apron, the miller motioned him inside, inviting him to sit down at a rough table. Looking around, he noticed the ground floor was threadbare with little comfortable furniture. A lean, white-haired woman eyed him suspiciously from an inglenook. The miller introduced the woman as his wife. Clearly the mill was not prospering owing to the severe winters affecting farming and, to a lesser extent, the fear of Barbary pirates bringing about the abandonment of some coastal properties.

Giving himself a fictitious name, Antony said he had a client wanting to invest in a water or windmill. Antony said he advised a watermill as windmills were frequently damaged and set alight in the increasingly severe gales. He said this was the sort of sheltered watermill his client had commissioned him to buy, and he was carrying 500 guineas in his saddle bags for the right property, the maximum his client was prepared to offer. He had the necessary paperwork with him. He said that perhaps he might like to go over to the inglenook out of his hearing to discuss the offer with his wife.

Looking astounded, the miller did as Antony suggested. Twenty minutes later, he was back, saying his wife agreed, but he would need a fortnight to buy a house in one of the local villages. Antony said he would give him half the value now and that he would be back in a fortnight to give him the remainder when the title deeds were in his possession. When the man shakily put his name on the document Antony produced, he realised the miller was, for all purposes, illiterate. Before he left, Antony said, upon exchange, he would like his client, wife and daughter to be shown how the mill operated, as formerly his client had been in another line of business.

Riding away, Antony was again forced into realising the devasting impact climate change was bringing about. Though only November, ponds and waterways were already freezing over, crops frosted, withering in the fields. What was happening to bring about such cold? A merchant in Lyme Regis had told him that his ships could no longer reach southern Greenland to buy ivory in exchange for fashionable clothing and household items owing to the southward movement of the pack ice. It was said that fairs were now being held on the frozen Thames in winter. When would it all end? Some preachers maintained it was due to God's wrath, now Puritan lifestyles and values were in decline, along with the restoration of a dissolute monarchy. Antony kept an open mind. What was important to him was his love child, now of considerable concern in view of his impending marriage.

Before picking up his escort at the hostelry where he left them, Antony packed away his burgher's disguise. His escort, rested and well-fed, with plenty of good ale under their belts supplied by a grateful landlord, were eager to return before nightfall. As always in hard times, the appearance of his livery brought out the inhabitants of the villages they passed through who wanted to petition Sir Antony about their concerns. He was popular, being known as a master who was prepared to listen and redress wrongs. Inevitably it was well after dark before they returned to their castle home on a prominence beside a silted-up inlet, the sea once coming up to their walls and filling the moat now two-thirds of a mile away.

As he cantered up to the front entrance, his elderly personal servant, Claude, was waiting with a stable lad carrying a message. His father wanted to see him at the evening meal, and would he make sure he was on time and not keep his father waiting. He knew what his father would be on about. He was to stop attending to estate matters and get on with the arrangements for his impending wedding. Fortunately, Antony needed to go out only one more time to pay the miller the balance and ensure that Eleanor's father got the agreed mill operating instructions. It would seem strange and draw attention if it became known that the new miller did not know how to work his own mill.

Joining his father at his dining table by the fire, he found that his sisters and their families would be joining them later. For the present, they were on their own. His father did not beat about the bush. He had no time for his son's idealism and negotiating manner, which he considered a sign of weakness. An estate owner should be autocratic at all times. Complete authoritarianism got respect and obedience. The fact the civil war had changed attitudes and that even the king now had to negotiate with Parliament was completely lost on him.

"Your father-in-law to be is playing his part in getting on with wedding preparations. It's high time we got going. Are you going to get a move on and play our part or, suffering as I am, do I have to do it all? Get your priorities right. I know you've never liked Lady Beatrice, but there's no other eligible heiress that I know of whose father is prepared to offer the size of dowry that my friend the earl is, so get on with it. Do you hear me? Get on with marrying Lady Beatrice. You need a male heir; keep at it till you get one. That's an order."

"Yes, Father," Antony muttered, thinking darkly what he would do with Lady Beatrice when he succeeded to the title. The marquis signalled to a servant who was standing respectfully in the background out of earshot of their conversation. "Call the rest of the household to dine now. Have the first course served. Another bottle of port. I'm tired."

After the formal evening meal, Antony went up to his quarters in the west tower. His father's irritability, made worse by his painful seized hip, left him depressed. Away from the roaring fire in the great hall, it was cold, not helped by the increasingly cold winters. His father indicated that he would use some of the dowry to build a modern, warm manor house nearby, progressively using the castle for storage and guest accommodation, possibly demolishing the outside workshops, bringing them into the castle. His father loved the old castle, considering it projected authority as it did when first built, but times had changed.

Sir Antony's marriage to Lady Beatrice was arranged for the twenty-fifth of November of this year, 1830, at Exeter Cathedral, which was about 35 miles from the castle. Allowing for changes of horses and meals, it would take at least 10 hours to get there, a long day's drive in the best of weathers. On a pretence of checking out the first stage of the journey, a fortnight since his last visit, Antony made his way to the mill, leaving his escort at a hostelry where they could hire a change of horses on the journey to Exeter Cathedral.

Arriving at the mill, he learnt that Eleanor and her parents had been there the day before and that Eleanor's father had been shown how the mill operated and the miller's primitive accounts. Antony felt that Maribel, with her flair for arithmetic, could progressively take over the accounts as, in a wheelchair, she could not help in other ways. Satisfied, he gave the miller the agreed balance, saying he would expect him to move out the next day to enable his client and his family to move in. He was not to take with him items like casement windows or the staircase to the first floor, as cased stairs and casement windows were expensive. If they were, his client would be suing him for their return. Despite what his father thought of him, Sir Antony could be authoritative if he wanted to. Though the miller did not know his true identity, he realised he was someone not to be trifled with.

"Yes, sir," the miller replied meekly.

"I'll be checking on behalf of my client. You got a very good price for the mill in these difficult times. Remember what I said. I'll be taking my leave." With that, Antony left, joining his troop at the hostelry half an hour later.

The next day Antony had to turn his mind to the logistics of getting his court to the wedding. Looking at it, with the snow down early, average travelling could be as slow as three miles an hour. Therefore, he had better plan for two days travelling, staying for a night at the market town of Sidmouth, leaving just 11 miles to cover the next day to Exeter. With that in mind, he would need to travel to Sidmouth to arrange accommodation. A week later, he felt driven to see Maribel and learn from Eleanor how they had settled in with their new identity in their new home, wondering what Eleanor's parents had opted for as a surname. He needed to be careful, even in his own household. Though liked, there were the sycophants who liked to curry favour with his father and would readily drop a hint that his son was off on some private business of his own.

His father commissioned two companies of dragoons, one of which was garrisoned at the castle for personal escort duties. The other was used to protect the estate, helping to combat smuggling and keeping a watch for Barbary corsairs, providing a quick response in the event of a slave seizing landing, thereby maintaining the morale of their coastal communities. They were not cavalry but mounted infantry, fighting on foot but, being mounted, could be moved quickly to where needed. A cavalry trooper cost six pence a day to maintain against a dragoon's four, a fact not lost on his father. His father had them in green uniforms to be less conspicuous, rather than the conventional red and blue. They got their name from their short carbines, dragons or dragoons, which were kept in a saddle holster.

Today's escort, Antony chose from men who had previously been in trouble to whom he had given a second chance. They were told that, for security reasons, they were not to discuss with the rest of the company where they went. They considered themselves lucky, being required to spend a long lunch period being well fed at a hostelry. Antony hoped he could rely on their discretion. They were instructed to wait out of sight of the castle.

He left as the pendulum clock in the hall struck 10. Telling time away from towns and villages not wealthy enough to have a community clock was a problem. The hostelry, on a coaching route, where Antony would leave his escort, had a pendulum clock as ostlers needed to know when to get teams of horses ready. But away from the sound of striking clocks, only the angle of the sun in the sky gave an indication of the passing of time, that is if the sun was shining. If you went as far as the next county, the time could be different anyway.

Out of sight of the hostelry, Antony once again adopted his burgher's disguise and rode across country to the mill, taking care not to lose his way, easily done, then he would be in difficulties. He came to the gorge-like valley, following it down to the watermill. Maribel and Eleanor were delighted to see him. Eleanor introduced her parents. Her father bowed, her mother curtsied, expressing their gratitude for his taking them out of poverty.

"The price you're paying is that if my father, or Lady Beatrice, found you were hiding my daughter, it might not fare well for you. My father's not a well man, being unable to walk owing to a seized hip. When I become marquis, it will be different. I want Maribel by my side. You and your wife will be welcome at my court. Lady Beatrice will accept my ways or leave."

"We understand, m'lord," Eleanor's father replied.

Antony turned to Eleanor. "I'd like a walk along the stream bed. I'll put Maribel on my horse."

"Yes, m'lord," Eleanor replied, leading the way down to the stream bed. The going was difficult. Rocks, big and small, pools and cascades, required careful negotiating. The horse with its four legs was doing better than the humans. Instinctively, Antony and Eleanor grabbed hands for support. Suddenly Eleanor slipped and swung round against Antony, who held her close to steady her. Her warmth and closeness impacted on Antony physically and emotionally. He did not let her loose immediately but, heaving a great sigh, kissed her neck, the horse standing still beside them. After a minute, he let her go.

"I'm sorry, I forgot myself. I've been under stress. There are few I can trust, few who would be on my side when it comes to currying favour with my father. I feel I can trust you. Maribel loves you."

Eleanor looked surprised but not alarmed. She continued to hold his hand. "That's all right, m'lord. I understand."

"You do?"

"Yes, I'm on your side, always have been."

"Antony drew her gently towards him and kissed her again. "Thank you."

"Do you love my mummy?" Maribel inquired from the horse.

Antony looked up at his daughter. The fact that Eleanor, though not her birth mother, had been so good to Maribel was very important. She had wonderful qualities that Antony was increasingly realising, and he was becoming attracted to her. "She's been kind and loyal, wonderful to you."

"Then you love her." Antony turned to go back, feeling Maribel had said it all, holding Eleanor's hand tightly until they were in sight of the mill.

On the way back to the hostelry, Antony turned over in his mind the events of the day. He had not planned to blurt out to Eleanor in the way he did, but he was under stress, hating the idea of having to marry Lady Beatrice for the benefit of all – except himself. When he did think about it, if he had a choice, he could think of no one better in mind to marry than Eleanor. Perhaps serving girls were preferable to grand ladies as their lives were harder, and they had greater notions of fundamental values? Antony felt a warm glow at the thought Eleanor was on his side, someone he could confide in. He put away his burgher's disguise out of sight of the hostelry.

Organising the journey to and from Exeter Cathedral was like moving an army. They needed a baggage train for support. There was not only their own company of dragoons, but there were cooks and their food, serving girls, farriers, blacksmiths, ostlers, grooms, footmen and a host of other essential camp followers. It was a logistic nightmare that Antony was expected to direct and make work. No wonder he felt stressed.

The whole affair was also expensive. Antony did not like his father's trusted chamberlain, an oily and obsequious fellow. Being in charge of the household and estate's finances, he did not know how much he siphoned off. His father thought the world of him, as the chamberlain always made sure he said the right thing, strutting about importantly, symbolic key jangling. He once dared to question his father about the fellow's integrity, for which he received a rebuke. When he inherited and Maribel was older, he would put her in charge of finance, contrary to current practice. He would make some big changes.

His father's friend, the earl, was known to be wealthy, owning land in Dorset and Devon, though even his income must be reduced in these harsh times. He could afford, nevertheless, in some way, to commission a whole cavalry regiment, a detachment of which would be providing colour at the wedding in resplendent uniforms, cuirasses shining. In comparison, his father's dragoons in their green uniforms would pale into insignificance.

Lady Beatrice did not want to marry Antony any more than he wanted to marry her. As her father was a wealthy earl, she felt that she should be marrying someone with the status of a duke, no less. It was her father's loyalty to his best friend, the marquis, cemented in some way when they were young together in the Lord General's Regiment of Foot Guards that made her father insist she marry Anthony.

Antony would like to find out more about the earl's past. Was there some reason? Was his daughter in possession of some secret that could be best concealed if she was married to his father's best friend? Arranged marriages did not bode well for a happy future. When it came to love, Antony's thoughts turned to Eleanor, who sheltered and guarded his beloved daughter.

Antony had to liaise with the chamberlain over the cost of travelling to and from Exeter Cathedral. With his egalitarian views, he felt all the staff, in whatever capacity, should have adequate food and a roof over their heads on route, not just the family, the cost of which was disputed by the chamberlain. This needed to be considered and resolved by his father, the marquis.

He reminded his father that he was made to serve time in his father's home dragoon company as a lieutenant in charge of a platoon to teach him responsibility, organisation and discipline. It was during that time he realised the importance of the baggage train to ensure the company had adequate food and shelter; otherwise, they would fall ill and be unable to do their duties. He said it would be the same with the many supporting servants to, from and at the wedding. His father saw the logic of this and ordered the chamberlain to provide the necessary funds. The chamberlain reluctantly did as he was bid, looking daggers at Antony, who knew he would do what he could to subtly undermine him behind his back.

While preparing for what amounted to an expedition, Antony contrived to visit the watermill for the last time before his marriage. He left his escort at the same hostelry he did on the last occasion, more confident of his route across country this time. Upon entering the watermill, Antony took Maribel in his arms and made a fuss of her. He did miss not seeing her daily. After half an hour, he turned to Eleanor, saying he would like to be shown more of the tortuous route up the valley floor unsuitable for a horse or a wheelchair.

Eleanor responded with alacrity, "Yes, m'lord."

Out of sight of the mill, Antony spread his riding cloak on a dry bank and motioned for Eleanor to sit beside him. "It's good to be with you, somebody on my side without a hidden agenda."

"It's good to be with you, m'lord. It's lonely out here in the country, especially as we need to keep ourselves to ourselves. I have no choice but to endure the life of a spinster."

Antony drew Eleanor down beside him, wrapping his cloak around them. "And I will have to endure life with a woman I detest. We need each other."

Eleanor sighed, snuggling in close, closing her eyes. "We do indeed." Antony felt her body relax and wrap around him. He kissed and stroked her. "We will keep together. One day I would like you by my side."

Eleanor responded, kissing and heaving with pleasure. "I would like to be with you, but I don't feel good enough to be a lady."

After 10 minutes, Antony got up, drawing Eleanor to her feet. "I could be with you all day and night, but for the present, I must get back to my escort and the castle, but I won't forget."

"Me either." Reluctantly they hurried back the way they had come.

Chapter Three

The day their court was to leave for the wedding had arrived. With a heavy heart, Antony got up early, ate the breakfast delivered to his quarters and went out into the great courtyard. It had been a cold night. Two inches of snow lay on the ground. In front of him was organised chaos. A platoon of dragoons was to lead. After which, the family coaches, resplendent and shiny, were being drawn into place, only for the horses to be taken away again to be kept rested and warm before near departure.

In this weather, the coaches would not remain clean for long. Once on the move, two dragoon platoons would take up position alongside as outriders. Then came the baggage train, three wagons carrying servants and support technicians, personnel who could repair coaches and harnesses, deal with sick or lame horses, set up tents, cook, repair firearms and deal with all manner of contingencies.

By 10.30 they were off, his father, the Maquis, carried into the leading coach, his disabled hip giving him great discomfort in the swaying, jolting coach. He had his head out of the window, swearing and cursing at footmen and any attendants in hearing, finally falling back inside exhausted. As Antony watched the cavalcade pass, it looked more like a small army on the move rather than a wedding party. He joined for a while the rear platoon of dragoons before feeling he had better check the convoy.

By mid-afternoon, snowflakes began falling from threatening skies, isolated, gently at first, then more intensely, finally ending in a blinding blizzard. Coaches and wagons began to get stuck in the accumulating drifts, requiring serving staff to get out and literally put their shoulders to the wheels. By nightfall, it was clear they were not going to make Sidmouth. They had ground to a halt. The marquis' orders were that they were to push on, but in reality, for the present, this was not possible. A decision had to be made. Should they set up emergency camp until morning, contrary to the marquis' orders, or exhaust themselves and the horses by trying to do the impossible, hoping for better conditions in the morning?

In Antony's experience, snow generally moved on if there was wind about, and there was plenty of that. His father did not agree with the fact that the climate was getting colder, though there was plenty of evidence to the contrary. They must go on. He ordered that he be carried out where he could direct operations himself but, in the intense cold and wind chill, had to be taken back inside his coach and revived. In his absence, Antony decided that setting up an emergency camp was the only realistic thing. To try to carry on in these conditions would invite exhaustion and collapse.

By midnight all was quiet, court members making the best of it in their carriages. Antony's coach was modern, suspended on steel springs, but high off the ground and only sat two, not room to lie down in, and was swinging disconcertingly in the strong wind. He was concerned about the horses. They obviously could not change horses for the journey next day as planned. The ones they had would have to be sheltered, watered and fed from what could be scavenged about them.

Antony directed that all coachmen, postillions grooms and ostlers get out, tend to the horses, keeping them close together in a sheltered copse, cutting forage and getting them water from a stream. Dragoons, other than the guard, were to cut brush from the roadsides as best they could and lie it along the first few miles of their route for the morning. The captain looked at him. He was countermanding his father's orders, but it was the only sensible choice. He ordered the dragoons to carry out Antony's directives.

After the court was served a cold gruel breakfast in their carriages, the whole convoy was packed up and by mid-morning was on the move directly to Exeter. It was a hellish journey, most of the servants and specialist attendants on foot, once again literally putting their shoulders to the wheels, but it was the only way if they were to make Exeter in the day. The coaches and wagons swayed about alarmingly, getting stuck only too often, but Antony's strategy of placing brushwood under the wheels made slow progress possible.

Passing his father's coach, he heard his father bellow after him, demanding who gave the order to stop for the night and the dragoons to cut brushwood ahead of the struggling convoy. Antony did not answer his father directly, calling back that he wanted the convoy to press on, and that was what was happening, at the same time urging his horse forward to inspect the hardworking dragoons in front, dragging brushwood onto the frozen quagmires as best they could. He felt his father, in time, would get over his insubordination.

The convoy finally arrived in Exeter as darkness was falling, his father and court members with their personal servants going to prebooked inns, the rest assigned to pitching tent on the nearest common land. He was to be with his father, his two sisters and their families in the Mermaid Inn between Preston and Coombe Streets. He would have to tolerate living in close quarters with them. His father's steward and chamberlain had been left behind in charge of the castle.

His father had four daughters, two of whom died during childhood, two survived. Antony, his only son, was conceived when his father was 30. He never saw his mother, who died giving birth. His father married again, but his stepmother showed little interest in him, giving him no real love or affection. His father had no further children by his second wife, who passed away five years ago. His older sisters fussed around their father, whose condition was made worse by the cold and discomfort of the previous night. His father blamed Antony for countermanding his orders. His sisters knew their young brother was right, but no one contradicted the marquis except Antony on occasions to his peril.

Fortunately for Antony, his father's hip was hurting him to the extent that he was unable to sit up at table for long but was forced to lie down. Grace, the younger of his two surviving sisters, was the more supporting of Antony than his older sister, Magdalene. Antony sometimes wondered if it was owing to her name of Grace, first used by Puritans the century before, his mother's wish, his father having no time for Puritans. His father was carried to the parlour and put beside the roaring fire while his sisters tried on their colourful dresses, others reading or playing cards, his cousin Deidre playing the harpsichord to those who would listen.

There were not rooms for them all. Antony had to share his with three of his nephews. When it was time for them to turn in, he told them to get in the big bed while he pulled the sofa nearer the fire and endeavoured to make himself comfortable for the night. It was not a wood fire but a coal fire, coal being used increasingly in cities these days. Antony preferred the smell of wood, which burned cleaner. The inn had a pendulum clock in the hall. Listening closely, he could just about hear it chiming the hours, halves and quarters. He did not sleep well. His nephews had plenty to drink. They snored their heads off other than when they had to stumble out of bed and noisily use the chamber pots. Antony was only a token drinker. He liked to have a clear head and know what he was doing at all times. Many were drink dependent and suffered withdrawal symptoms when alcohol was unavailable.

In his wakeful hours, he thought of his pending marriage. He and Beatrice had known each other since childhood. He did not like her. She was bad-tempered, dominating and arrogant. She had, however, his father's ear. Only in one area did he feel sorry for her. Her first duty was to provide a male heir. Giving birth was dangerous; one in three women died of sepsis. His mind finally turned to Maribel and Eleanor, Antony wishing he was with them until he eventually fell asleep.

Next morning everyone was wakened early by a servant sent by his father, saying none of them were to breakfast in their rooms, but all to come downstairs to the table. On doing so, Antony was summoned to where his father was eating breakfast on cushions accompanied by his physician, Horace. A haughty individual, conscious of his position. His father told Antony that he had instructed the Dean that he wanted his son to have a high church wedding but was not sure if the Dean favoured the old religion and commanded Antony to reinforce his request. Antony, a reluctant groom, privately thought that he would do no such thing. As far as he knew, the Dean was progressive thinking.

The wedding was to commence at midday, a significant time coinciding with the 12 strokes of the town bells, necessary at that time, too, as it would be dark by half-past four. Like all once brightly painted churches, Exeter Cathedral had suffered greatly by the Dissolution of the Monasteries. Further damage was done during the civil war when the cloisters were destroyed, but since the Restoration, it had a new pipe organ that would add to the grandeur of the music. This would please the marquis, who was carried into the church in a sedan chair. When all invited guests were assembled, a message was sent to the bridal party. Antony took up his position with his nephew Bruce as best man. The die was cast.

Even in these modern times, the Gothic cathedral looked impressive, having the longest uninterrupted vaulted ceiling in England. What it must have looked like brilliantly painted 400 years ago to the people of those times, Antony could not imagine. Mounted above the three-arch roodscreen were the pipes of the organ, a new technical innovation a congregation of former times would not have seen. Antony would have liked to have been able to find out more about the organ. He liked making and creating, something his father considered beneath what a gentleman should be concerned about.

As he looked at the assembled guests, the women in their vividly coloured dresses first caught his attention, not to be outdone by splendidly resplendent men, either in gold-braided uniforms or fine wool cutaway coats, waistcoats, exquisitely laced shirts and neckpieces. Each elaborately handmade women's dress would have cost more than a working man would earn in a year, one of the reasons why women of quality always had to have armed escorts as their dresses were so valuable. Such inequality Antony considered not right. Though privileged himself, he would like to see a fairer distribution of wealth, one of the ideals of some of the civil war revolutionaries. At that point, a fanfare announced the arrival of the bride on her father's arm, accompanied by her maids-in-waiting. The grand wedding ceremony was about to begin.

Antony felt uncomfortable during the wedding ceremony. It should have been a time of great gladness and happiness, but, being an arranged marriage, it was a showpiece that had to be endured, sooner over the better. Lady Beatrice, in dazzling red and gold, looked far from enchanted, staring defiantly about her as if challenging anyone to look her in the eye.

At the reception, when the savoury meat wedding cake was cut up, Antony's cousin Marigold found the traditional buried glass ring, indicating that she was the next woman to be married. She showed it around in delight. Antony heard his new wife, standing alongside him, sniff, "Who'd want to marry that shrew?" which remark incensed Antony as, like her name suggested, Marigold was a golden flower. On the other hand, when Antony thought about it, she was lucky as, not having a dowry, she would be able to have a man of her choice.

Antony hoped, for her sake, she chose wisely. All the while, the earl strode around as if he were someplace else, on occasions going over to talk to the marquis, whose sedan chair had been placed on three-foot blocks.

Back at the Mermaid Inn, Antony found he had been moved along with Beatrice to the bridal chamber, a small room created by flimsy partitions. It had a bed, a coal fire, two upright chairs and a small table, little else. Knowing the tradition of listening to hear the consummation, which Antony considered a disgusting tradition, he read a book by the light of his flickering candle, there were always draughts. Being ignored by Antony, Beatrice talked to and scolded her personal maid, finally dismissing her as it had been a long day and grumpily took herself to bed. When Antony was satisfied Beatrice was asleep, he snuffed his candle and gently got into bed, aware of the whisperings on the other side of the room partitions.

Next morning, Beatrice's maid bustled in at the appointed time and gently awakened her, to be again scolded and abused. Antony felt sorry for the girl. He, too, could have had his personal servant, Claude, in attendance but had quietly asked Claude the night before to bring him in the morning a lump of bleeding raw meat from the kitchens, wrapped in muslin. While Beatrice was being decked out for the day, using the small table and a hand mirror, Antony surreptitiously bloodied the under sheet, dumping the upper untidily on top of it. He then went quietly out the door and gave the meat back to Claude, waiting outside. The information the sheet would reveal would soon get back to his father, who would assume he was doing his duty in begetting an heir.

At half-past ten by the hall clock, the wedding convoy was ready to begin the return journey. It was expensive keeping the respective courts in inns, and both the marquis and the earl were anxious to be off. The day was clear and cold, but there were threatening clouds about. The sooner they made a start, the better. In the morning, they jingled and jangled along, making about four miles an hour. Their coach could only comfortably take two. Owing to its modern suspension, it swung about alarmingly in the ruts, making Antony and Beatrice feel seasick.

Suddenly the carriage lurched to the left like a ship striking a rock, throwing Antony and Beatrice violently forward. "Bloody hell!" Antony exclaimed, leaping out of the carriage, then helping Beatrice out, gently wiping a little blood off her forehead and putting her wig on straight. He looked at the carriage, sagging dangerously on the left front side.

Making a judgement, he turned to two of the footmen guards standing by. "Escort Lady Beatrice to one of the following carriages." The third guard footman, fallen off at the abrupt lurch, was covered in mud and limping. "Help me, the driver and postillion get this coach off the road," he ordered, going forward to calm the struggling horses.

"What are you doing, you fool! Leave all that to the coachman and postillion!" Lady Beatrice shouted.

Cheeky wench, Antony thought, ignoring her, signalling for the footmen to carry on. Once off the road, he examined the coach to see what had happened. The bracket on the spring holding the suspension shackle had sheered, the angle being too great to sustain the constant severe lurching of the coach. To him, it was a design fault. He would have loved to have been able to have worked as a master craftsman, creating and designing new inventions, not the thing for a gentleman in his position – according to his father.

So that he could not be seen by his father, who he could not keep ignoring, he untied his horse from the back of the coach. He rode across the fields behind the hedgerows to the maintenance wagon bringing up the rear to tell the blacksmith, with his portable forge, and the harness maker exactly what the problem was and what he had in mind to put it right.

The servants crammed into the maintenance wagon were surprised to see him, respecting the fact he was fair and considerate and liked to feel their working conditions were as tolerable as possible. With the leading coach off the road, the rest of the convoy struggled on at walking pace, the thawing roads becoming more treacherous.

The marquis ordered the convoy not to stop for lunch but to press on. At dusk, snow began falling, and progress became slower. Antony joined his new wife in her coach with her personal maid. She was in a foul mood. Antony asked her how she was and was sworn at. He caught the eye of her maid and raised his eyes. The maid, looking profoundly uncomfortable, gave him the faintest of smiles. Antony decided he was not going to give the order to stop for the night. The weather would do it for him, something his father could not overrule.

Sure enough, the leading dragoon platoon stopped, not being able to see the following coaches. Lady Beatrice was furious but realised they needed to keep together for security and support – and for the commissariat, no one had eaten since breakfast unless carrying cold food with them. Servants and dragoons could not carry on without food and drink. After two cold, bleak hours, during which Beatrice spent much of the time swearing, it became apparent the convoy could proceed no further. The only time Antony had any respite was when her personal maid took Beatrice out into the snow to relieve herself.

Eventually, servants brought hot food, indicating camp had been struck for the night. The marquis was nowhere to be seen. With his extremely painful hip, he could not ride to see what was going on. It was freezing outside, not much better in the coach. After a while, cushions and rugs were brought. Here they would be spending the night. Beatrice threw herself haughtily into a corner and, after much swearing at her maid, who struggled to make her comfortable, fell quiet.

Antony tried to make himself comfortable in the opposite corner. He had just got off to sleep when he heard a bump. The maid had fallen off the narrow seat in front onto the floor. Antony gave her one of his cushions and a rug. He gently squeezed her hand. She squeezed it back in gratitude. Where she was lying kept his feet warm. He would have liked to have snuggled down with her but did not want to get her into trouble if Beatrice awoke, which was more than likely.

In the early hours, Antony was woken by another bump, from outside this time. In silhouette, he could just make out a horse. As quietly as possible, he climbed out of the coach. It had stopped snowing with patches of clear sky but very cold. In a situation like this, without proper stabling, caring for the horses was a problem. They had to be kept secure, pacified, fed, watered and as warm as possible in the open. The continued progress of the convoy depended on them. Drivers, postillions, grooms and ostlers were out doing their best. They were having a busy night foraging, trying to keep the horses sheltered and close together for herd warmth. Fires had been lit. All were pleased to see him. Leading from the front, out with his servants, was much appreciated. He was offered what food and ale there was going, which he politely refused. Compared with them, he had been well fed. He stayed out, helping and directing, till dawn.

When he returned, Beatrice was awake, demanding to know where he had been. Antony did not reply to her question; it was none of her business, the impudent trollop. Instead, he politely asked her how she was and was sworn at. He raised his eyes to the roof, noticing the maid dare not look at him. A gruel breakfast with mulled wine was brought around, much the same as everyone else had except staff who had rationed ale – drinking water from any source but springs was dangerous. Beatrice would not eat gruel, complaining it was peasant food. It was the best that could be done out in the open. This was a campaign breakfast. It was not possible to stock up with much fine food before leaving. It was never intended they stop for the night once again.

It was this unprecedented cold weather that made travelling so unpredictable. The marquis would not accept that climate change existed. If he did, he might have reflected on the wisdom of undertaking a long journeying by road at this time of the year. But he was stubborn and opinionated. No one could tell him anything, especially Antony.

By mid-morning, the convoy was on its way, hoping to make the castle by evening. A messenger was sent ahead to tell the castle they hoped to be back by evening to ensure food and warmed accommodation would be there to welcome them. By midday, the horses, sensing they were nearing familiar territory, needed less urging. Beatrice was in an even fouler mood, if that were possible, having learnt that it was considered the marriage had been consummated, by some trickery of Antony's doing, no doubt to appease his father. Antony predicted that, out of the servants' hearing, she would have a right carry-on, and he would never hear the end of it. He realised that he would have to consummate the marriage sometime.

His buff riding trousers were smeared with horse dung, and his once white stockings were caked with mud after having attended the horses for the later part of the night. Beatrice complained he smelt. It was no big deal. She was out to find fault. Everyone smelt. Life was full of smells. Only the quality could afford baths, taken infrequently. He felt he needed to leave the carriage for a spell and ride with the lead dragoons, feeling sorry for the poor maid left alone with the dragon.

Mounting his horse, he rode ahead and drew up alongside the lieutenant out in front. Antony could see both horses and men were tired. "Had a difficult night?" he eventually inquired.

"A proportion of horses and men are in a bad way, m'lord. We're not equipped to withstand these increasingly cold winter nights in the open."

After some thought, Antony eventually replied. "That I've noted. Winter deployment only in extreme circumstances. The away company is in winter quarters."

"That's good, m'lord."

"I'll speak to the marquis." They rode on together in silence.

Unless conditions deteriorated, they should reach the castle by early evening, Antony felt. Turnpike trusts were significantly improving major routes, but parliamentary lobbying was needed in the first instance, then a company had to be convinced that there was sufficient traffic for a toll road investment to be profitable. Antony could not see that the traffic over the routes they travelled from down near the Devon/Dorset border to Exeter and back was sufficient to create a turnpike trust. Initially, these trusts were supposed to be for a twenty-year period, the roads then reverting to the parishes. In reality, the initial debt was rarely paid off, and the trusts were renewed as needed. The estate tried to improve the roads within its boundaries, but there were so many other costs involved in running the estate that the condition of the roads had a low priority. The increasingly cold winters were making everyone poorer. Travel by road was a problem in winter.

Night had fallen by an hour or more before the leading platoon reached the castle. Over the next hour, the remainder of the wedding convoy passed the entrance towers, castle staff hurrying outside to meet the carriages. After handing over his tired horse, Antony felt obliged to seek out his bride. She had gone straight to their converted draughty living quarters in the south tower. She was tired and out of sorts. Seeing Antony, she dismissed the servants and let rip. Antony let it all flow over his head. There was little use trying to talk reasonably against such a vitriolic flow of verbal abuse.

When Beatrice finally slumped exhausted into a chair, Antony said quietly, "We've known each other since childhood. We had an arranged marriage. This is what both our fathers wished. To keep them off our backs, I arranged that they were made aware by the conventional sign that the marriage had been consummated."

"Trickery, I might not be a virgin!" Beatrice shouted angrily.

"You might not be, but I bet your father thinks you are," Antony replied calmly. "I'll consummate the marriage when I'm ready if that's your wish, bearing in mind that childbirth is risky. While we're together, we may as well get along."

"Bloody hell!"

"If that's the way you want it, but I don't. We both know we're not in love. Now I'm going to have a bath. When the water's brought up, you can have it first while it's really hot."

"I've ordered a meal to be brought up. I'm not bathing. I'm tired and don't feel well." Beatrice replied. The first reasonable thing she had said since their wedding.

"As you wish, I'll bathe and dine later." He went out to the servants standing patiently outside the door.

Having a bath was a guilty pleasure that wealth and privilege made possible. Antony felt sorry for the bevy of maids who had to struggle up with heavy pails of hot water to fill the copper bath. But he did like to feel clean in a dirty and smelly world. He always liked plenty of fresh, sweet-smelling herbs in his living apartments. At the conclusion, he ordered the water be taken down to the servants' hall for children to be washed in the now lukewarm water as it was too cold at this time of the year to take children out under a pump. Beatrice said Antony was pandering to the servants. Antony's reply that they were human beings like they were but less privileged, at which response Beatrice snorted. Like many others, the night out in the cold carriage had taken its toll. Beatrice went to bed grumpily with a headache and a running nose with no desire that evening to consummate the marriage.

The next day, the consequence of the court's travelling to a winter wedding in these appreciably colder times became apparent. A number of servants and dragoons had died of exposure. A few dozen horses had to be put down, having broken bones in falls or become incurably sick. Many family members and servants alike had developed contagions, bilious fever, agues, coughs and breathing difficulties leading to asphyxia in a number of cases. Exeter people had many winter ills, which the wedding party had been exposed to as well as to the extreme weather. The wedding had proved costly in more ways than one. Without telling anyone, Antony decided to go down to the servants' hall and see conditions for himself. Most looked pleased to see him. The chamberlain, steward and butler did not.

He went into the outdated medieval kitchens to see what was being dished up to servants and found it to be a watery gruel and little more; no meat, greens or eggs, but a ration of coarse bread was available. It was the beginning of winter, and food should not be in short supply so early on. Antony turned to the head cook. "I think serving staff deserve better than this. Food's not short yet?"

"I can only buy in for them what the money allocated allows. I would like to be able to buy more in variety and quantity." Antony realised he could not openly criticise the man's superiors but made a note that the first thing he would do when he became marquis was to create a modern accounts system, managed by an accountant directly responsible to him, rather than the prevailing traditional, antiquated way of doing things. In the meantime, he would try to influence his father regarding his mistrust of the chamberlain's integrity. The fact that he was looking into the head cook's money allocation could well induce the chamberlain to allocate more before this was necessary. Antony would wait and see. With that in mind, he went back upstairs.

Court life for the next few days was not back to usual. Many family members were still struggling with coughs, colds, fevers and sore throats, not turning up for meals. His father was bad-tempered, complaining about the reduced numbers at formal mealtimes. Antony felt he only had himself to blame. He had been in no hurry to get married. A week later, well wrapped up against the winter cold, he felt he needed to check on the estate to see how their tenant farmers were managing. He was concerned for their welfare and wanted to promote new farming systems involving the rotation of turnips and clover. To produce more food, he felt that the present low-intensity farming system needed to be converted into a much higher-intensity system based on arable crops. It was little use moaning about the increasing cold weather affecting output. Something needed to be done about it. He also learnt that Beatrice, with the blessing of his father, was already sending out parties seeking the whereabouts of his beloved daughter, which concerned him greatly. He determined that, incognito, he needed to check on the watermill. Two days later, with his trusted escort, he went out to do just that.

He sent his escort ahead to meet out of sight of the castle, leaving later alone as if riding out locally for exercise. Glancing back, he saw Beatrice looking out of the top window of their tower. His movements were being watched and, no doubt, being relayed to his father. He wondered if it was already known he was meeting an escort out of sight of the castle, indicating he was going further as it was dangerous to go far without one. If that was the case, he knew they would be subtly interrogated.

He had no choice but to leave his escort at the same hostelry as on former occasions as anywhere else was too far from the watermill to be practical. That is why he had to go on alone, making sure he was not being followed. He watched out carefully, doubling back on one occasion behind hedgerows to put anyone following off the scent. When he finally reached the watermill, he found Eleanor's parents visibly shaken with no sign of Eleanor of Maribel.

He was told that two days ago, a posse of armed men wearing the marquis's livery was seen approaching the watermill. Eleanor immediately left carrying Maribel in a shawl, instructing her father to hoist her wheelchair, which Antony had a hand in designing and making, much to his father's disapproval, up to the loft and hide it underneath what was waiting to be ground. They did not know where Eleanor had gone. They were resentful and frightened that the posse demanded entry and the watermill roughly searched. Though they held a leasehold from the estate, they were not direct tenants.

Antony felt Eleanor and Maribel had probably left upstream rather than down. He tied his horse as the stream bed was too difficult for it and hurried upstream, slipping and stumbling over the rocks. After half an hour, he came across a rough path leading up the steep left-hand side of the gorge to one of his tenants' farms. He wondered if Eleanor and Maribel had taken refuge there. He scrambled up and knocked on the door. For a moment, he was not recognised, dressed as he was, but suddenly he was and was bowed inside. At the same time, Maribel, in the background in Eleanor's arms, cried, "Dadda!" Eleanor came forward, and he put his arms around them both.

Antony explained to the farmer that his daughter was under threat and in hiding. Until he became marquis, Antony said he was concerned to keep his beloved daughter, conceived out of wedlock, safe. The farmer, who had a strange accent Antony could not recognise, expressed concern. He also went on to say that he had information which His Lordship might find of great importance. Intrigued, Antony asked what that was.

Chapter Four

In his unusual but not unclear accent, the farmer directed Antony to a table, sitting down beside him, Eleanor seating herself on the other side. Maribel sat on the table, one arm about her father, the other around Eleanor. Antony put his arm about Eleanor's waist. He missed her genuine warmth and affection.

The tenant farmer said his name was Joao Pereira, a former sailing master in a Portuguese merchant ship captured at sea by a Barbary slaver. A sailing master was a responsible position. Along with the bosun, who maintained the structure of the vessel, the sailing master was in charge of the propulsion system, the sails, directing their setting according to the course given by the captain or watch officer. After his ship was taken, he had to work as a chained oarsman until the galley reached the Mediterranean, where he would have likely been sold as a white slave.

However, off the south-western Mediterranean coast, the galley was captured in turn by a patrolling British man-o-war. Joao was released, but when the captain learnt that he was a trained and experienced sailing master, he was pressed into that role in the British navy. Compared with a galley slave, this was luxury indeed, but he was not a free man. When his third-rated ship of the line arrived in a British home port three years later, he bought his way out of service with prize money due to the crew, which, because of his position, was considerable, enabling him also to acquire the farm he now ran.

While a galley slave, he learnt that, since the time of William of Orange, increasing Royal Navy attention had been given to the menace of Barbary pirates to merchant ships off the west coast of Europe and to the protection of isolated communities along the English south coast. Feeling the pressure, Barbary Atlantic xebecs had, in turn, resorted to acquiring intelligence from an unknown Dorset or Devonshire nobleman in exchange for a large amount of gold. Joao Pereira maintained that liaison was by means of a small fishing boat, or the like, from the busy port of Lyme Regis, making contact out of sight of land with the pirates' xebecs, using renegade English seamen. These turncoats were meeting elusive representatives of this Dorset or Devonshire nobleman to obtain details of ships' sailings, passenger lists and destinations, as well as to arrange for coastal protection patrols to be diverted elsewhere during projected raids. All this, according to Joao Pereira, for the handing over of substantial amounts of gold.

Antony felt this elusive nobleman could not be his father. Despite his failings, his father was an honourable man. But there were other landowners feeling the pinch of decreasing returns due to the increasingly cold weather or who were in massive debt brought about by the bursting of the South Seas Bubble, who Antony thought might not have the same principles. His father's friend, the earl, perhaps who always seemed well off? He would do his best, enlisting the aid of Magistrate Brandon Travallyn, to find out more.

Meantime the sun was getting lower. He had no means of knowing the exact time, but he knew that he had better get a move on. Saying he thought it was all right for Eleanor and Maribel to go back to the watermill, panting and slipping, he hurriedly returned to his horse, just calling in at the watermill long enough to inform Eleanor's parents that Eleanor and Maribel would be returning.

Dusk was falling when he got back to the hostelry, finding his escort more than a little drunk, having been drinking all afternoon. Normally this would have displeased him, but perhaps it was a good idea as, in their present state, they did not know where they were. When he eventually got back to the castle, well after dark, he was late for the evening meal. Beatrice asked him where he had been, to which Antony briefly replied, "Estate business."

She said that he had no need to go out so often on estate business. What did she know? It was none of her concern. What Antony knew was she had his father's ear and was causing trouble.

Antony appreciated that they so far had not consummated their marriage. This could not be put off indefinitely. Beatrice had recovered sufficiently from her cold and sore throat. She would soon be making demands he could not refuse. She had made the rude joke going about in fashionable circles the other night that it was not its length or its size, but how often a male could make it rise, to get Anthony to prove his manhood, which he ignored. If he did not act soon, she would be complaining to his father that he was not fulfilling his duty to produce a legitimate heir, which is why their fathers had brought them together. Antony could understand why this was important to his father, but for the earl? Eventually, that night he managed to get to bed on his own, thinking about his lovely daughter, Eleanor and the disturbing information he had received from Joao Pereira.

Next morning, he was up early as was his custom. The household tended to carouse of an evening, it was the good life, especially for the males. His father limited his drinking as his health did not permit much indulgence in alcohol these days. Some of the women followed the men's example, Beatrice being one of them, so they were not in a fit state to get up early. She had fallen asleep before her maid had fully prepared her for bed, her wig lying untidily on the floor beside her bed rather than being placed carefully on its usual stand. Getting up quietly, Antony put her wig on the stand, poured her a glass of port and put it on the side table of the bed as she liked to start the day with a glass. He then quickly dressed without the aid of his man. He did not wear a wig but had his shoulder-length dark hair tied tightly at the back. He put on his riding trousers, flared at the hip with leather on the inside leg and seam on the outside, which Beatrice complained he tended to live in, a fresh white laced shirt, which he liked, and a smart cutaway blue riding jacket, flared fashionably at the back. Carrying his calf-length riding boots, he crept out of the room. His mission today was to contact Magistrate Brandon, who he knew was staying for the next few days at the Castle Inn in the village.

Magistrate Brandon Travallyn was surprised to see him when word was sent that he was waiting downstairs. He invited Antony up to his chamber, the best room in the inn overlooking the square.

He was dressed in a long black coat, had his own hair tied back like Antony's and wore steel-rimmed spectacles. Antony wondered why he had his coat on as there was a log fire in the room. Maybe he had just come in from outside. He was a man with a mission – to fight corruption in high places. He was endeavouring to become a lawyer and eventually a judge but had not the resources at present to go up to Lincoln's Inn Fields for the long period of study required.

He stood up as Antony entered. "Good morning. I'm surprised to see you, m'lord. I wanted to have a word with you about interfering with my lawful arrest. If I did not know you as an enlightened friend, I would have taken issue at the time. We have known each other for a long time. I thought there must be some explanation. Take a seat. I'll order up some mild ale."

"There is. That's what I've come here about and more." Antony preferred spring or spar water when he could get it, but village or town water, pumped up from ground sodden with excretion from surrounding habitation, invariably brought illness. There was no choice but to drink mild ale. "I had to. She was a victim of circumstances not of her making and beyond her control. She acted on the spur of the moment. She admitted what she did was wrong. I punished her for it."

"You took a liberty. Manorial courts were superseded centuries ago."

"I know. We've both agreed we're against corruption in high places, which there's plenty of. I'll tell you why I had to protect Eleanor, the girl's name, and still have to though she's no longer with me, as she brought up Maribel, my illegitimate daughter who I'm very fond of. Maribel thinks of Eleanor as her mother. I also want to bring to your attention an extremely high placed conspiracy that is having awful consequences for many innocent people, including yourself if it were known you were making inquiries into this evil conspiracy."

"You intrigue me."

Antony began to explain to his friend the unique role Eleanor had in his and his daughter's lives and the disturbing corruption at Lyme Regis, that by chance had recently come to his attention.

Magistrate Brandon listened intently. "That is a story. I'm sorry for you and your daughter. I'm not married. I have a female companion. If true, what your farmer's maintaining is a monstrous treachery, something I must look into."

"Could be dangerous," Antony interrupted.

"I can see that, but nevertheless, now you've told me about it, I can't turn a blind eye."

"Even if these renegades only stay a day, they'd have to meet intermediaries somewhere like an inn, slipping in by fishing boat. There has to be a fishing boat prepared to do this for them, or they reside locally, living as fishermen and operating a boat, actively catching fish as a cover."

Magistrate Brandon looked thoughtful. "Whatever, I need to identify these renegade turncoats. They could lead us to who's responsible for the treachery. They are pawns in a dangerous game. Maybe your Portuguese tenant could be of assistance. I'd like to talk to him. With his sailing experience, he would be able to sail a small craft for us, knowing what to look out for. I'll keep him in mind. It would need your authorisation, of course, as he's your estate tenant."

"Technically, my father's. But I would unofficially. However, we will need to keep this strictly to ourselves.

If word got out, those responsible or connected would be on their guard. There're also people in my household I don't trust. One I know is actively working against me at the moment."

"It's a challenge."

"It certainly is," Antony agreed.

"Shall we meet here again in a fortnight's time?"

"In a fortnight," Antony confirmed. "After that we'd better change venues."

On his way back to the castle, Antony felt unsettled. He liked a quiet, organised life with events under control as far as possible. Lady Beatrice, his new arranged wife, was a problem. How best to deal with her was taxing his mind.

Later that evening, when she sent out her personal maid demanding he come to her, he said, "I know we've had this conversation before, but you don't have to put your life at risk having a child. Our fathers think the marriage was consummated, and they could think we were just unlucky regarding your not becoming pregnant."

"Trickery!"

"We won't go into that. But I've given you the chance to opt out. I couldn't be more reasonable than that. It's on your head."

"I want a child."

With that, Antony went ahead and found, as he expected, Beatrice was not a virgin but made no comment. It did not matter to him. He knew who he loved and felt secure in the relationship he had with her. But time was not on his side.

Later that night, Antony got to thinking. He had never got on with his father. He was sensitive and liberal by nature. In contrast, his father was the opposite, insensitive and utterly conservative, suspicious of change and innovation. Could it be that, if Beatrice had a boy, he would have a disposition and attitudes his father approved of, and he would contrive to make the estate over to him? When he thought about it in that way, he felt that he must do his best to make conception unlikely. He was also aware that Beatrice was unduly inquisitive about what he did by day out of her sight. A woman's role was to get on with traditional women's affairs and pursuits, not pry into her husband's. What was she up to? Antony felt he must tread warily.

His father always liked a traditional Christmas with friends and family gathered together with plenty to eat and drink. To that end, he had ordered his sisters' boys to go out hunting for venison. This was another bone of contention Antony had with his father. He felt there was no harm in commoners scavenging for firewood and taking small game in the forest, but his father was adamant that, dating back to Norman times, the forest was his exclusive domain and that he could vigorously hunt down and set traps for any trespassers.

Antony knew he would be expected to play a big part in events leading up to Christmas, owing to his father no longer being able to walk, which would conflict with his desire to protect Maribel and Eleanor, and to find out about how the Barbary pirates got their information.

Before he got too involved, he decided to go out and visit Maribel and Eleanor. He would take no chances. Three days later, with snow on the ground, he made careful preparations. He would not go to the hostelry the most convenient to the watermill but to another further away. It would be a greater trek for him on the last stage alone, but he felt the need to change his routine.

He detailed his escort to go down to the headland as if on a training and observation mission and then return and wait out of sight of the castle. Riding out later in a cold-weather cape, he could see Beatrice looking out at him from their top tower window.

It was not that Beatrice was without the ability and talent to satisfyingly fill her days. She could produce arresting tapestries if she wanted to. She was also a very good artist. She could draw exceptionally well. There was one thing the marquis, Beatrice and he all agreed on, and that was the need to build a warm, liveable mansion adjacent to the castle with modern kitchens and many chimneys for wood fires for every family room. A Norman castle was far too cold and expensive to live in these days. The civil war had proved that, with modern cannons, high towered castles were soon breached. Forts needed to be squat, star-shaped, shielded by bastions 20-feet deep or more. Antony had suggested that, consulting with his father, Beatrice sketch what their new mansion should look like for the architects to work on. He fancied the new Palladian style, but if they wanted the baroque, he would not object. It would give her something constructive to focus her mind on rather than pry on him.

Passing between the round gate towers into the chill wind beyond the courtyard, he got to wondering, not for the first time, the reason for the increasingly cold winters. He subscribed to the modern theory that the earth and planets revolved around the sun. Could it be something to do with the earth's orbit or inclination? He knew some astronomers were looking into that possibility. Could this be calculated? He abruptly felt he had better keep his mind on the matter in hand.

When he arrived at their prearranged rendezvous, his escort were off their horses, stamping around trying to keep warm, looking none too pleased. He knew they would change their tune when invited to undertake an extended lunch with plenty to drink at their master's expense. They started off, buffeted by the wind and occasional swirling snow showers. By midday, they arrived at their hostelry, further along the road than the last one.

Antony saw them in, talked to the inn keeper who was delighted to be in receipt of his custom, and continued his journey alone, a large riding cloak concealing his livery. Riding cross country, he had to take care not to lose his way. Nearing the watermill, something made him look up. There, on a knoll, a single sinister horseman in a dark cloak was pointing a cutlass his way. He felt uneasy. What did this mean?

Suddenly he thought he heard hoofbeats. He reined in, stopped and put his ear to the ground. He could hear thuds not far away but was not sure if they were riders or spooked cattle. The countryside being partially forested, he could not see far. As a precaution, he changed direction, almost doubling back. Abruptly he came across fresh hoof prints of two riders. He froze. He was carrying one flintlock pistol. He should have been carrying two, which was the custom. He got off his horse and carefully put a fresh amount of primer into the flash pan. Keeping the pistol in his hand, he remounted his horse, riding slowly through the trees, stopping and listening, his heart pounding.

There was an abrupt crashing. Two masked riders were bearing down on him, their pistols blazing. He felt a searing pain across his left upper arm. His horse reared, throwing him off, but he held onto the reins, firing a shot after them. He dragged his frightened horse into a copse and went shakily through the reloading process. Firstly, he had to undo his reloading pouch and fumble for powder, a ball, a patch and extract the ramrod. His left arm hurt terribly. He felt sick with the pain, and he was losing a lot of blood, but his arm was in a normal position. The ball had not hit the bone but passed through the flesh. He was lucky.

Barely able to measure out the black powder owing to uncontrollable trembling, he half-cocked and contrived to pour in the correct amount of black powder down the muzzle and tamp down. He then wrapped the ball in the patch and tamped that down with the ramrod. The trickiest part was to get the right amount of finely ground priming powder into the flash pan; filling the pan by a third would do.

By the time he had packed everything away into the reloading pouch, he felt exhausted. He listened. He could not be charged down while among dense trees. His assailants were not highwaymen, who were only just beginning to operate on the roads out of London carrying rich carriage folk. This was a targeted attack. It was not logical to think this had anything to do with Beatrice if she wanted to get pregnant. Who then? Did the assassins know who he was, or had they just picked up that he was someone on their trail? Was his conversation with Magistrate Trevallyn in the Castle Inn overheard? The waiter bringing up the mild ale could have been primed to hang around, appearing to be innocently clearing crumbs off or otherwise attending to the tables? He felt that the paid assassins, whoever they were, would not strike again today. If not killed on this occasion, it was a warning. They would likely be instructed to try again.

Warily, trembling, he struggled back on his horse, using a log as a mounting block, threading in and out of trees as much as he could to make it difficult to be charged down. He did not know where he was but felt any small stream would probably lead to the gorge. Following one down, he eventually came to the gorge and rode beside it until he could find a way down near the watermill. He was on the point of collapse as he approached.

He was seen. The mill door was flung open, and Eleanor flew towards him, crying out in concern. She carefully brought him down from his horse, calling for her father to take charge of it, and half carried him inside, lying him down on a couch, putting her arms about him. Then she jumped up, picked up Maribel and put her beside him and rushed outside.

Maribel stroked his head, kissing him. "What's happened, Dadda? You're hurt. Your arm's torn and bleeding. Oh, Dadda!" She began to cry.

Antony tried to put his good arm around her. "Don't worry, darling. I'll survive."

"Dadda, Dadda." She put her head beside him, stroking his hair. "Don't die."

"I'll be all right," Antony answered in what he hoped was a reassuring manner. "Don't worry, my dear." With his good arm, he patted her hand.

Abruptly the door was flung open. Eleanor appeared carrying sphagnum moss from a bog beside the stream and thyme. She grabbed a knife, cut off what remained of Antony's shirt sleeve, tired it tightly round his upper right arm to reduce the bleeding, wiped his arm with thyme leaves, then plastered thyme leaves fresh on the wound followed by sphagnum moss, all secured by a light scarf.

"What happened?" Eleanor asked.

"I was ambushed by two masked men firing pistols."

"Who were they?"

"I've no idea, paid assassins, it was a targeted attack."

"Who would have orchestrated it, Lady Beatrice?"

"I think not in this case,"

"Who then?"

"I learnt from your friend further up the gorge, Joao Pereira, one of my tenant farmers who you took refuge with, which he learnt while forced to work as a galley slave when captured by Atlantic Barbary pirates of a conspiracy involving a powerful south coast aristocrat. For a large amount of stolen gold, this seemingly respectable aristocrat provided information of merchant ship passenger lists and the whereabouts of vulnerable coastal communities. Magistrate Brandon and I were beginning an investigation to try and discover who this traitorous high-ranking person might be."

"You think this traitorous bigwig could be behind the attempted assassination?" Eleanor looked at Antony wide-eyed.

"It's a possibility. I must be getting back to the hostelry. I took too long getting here in the first place."

"You're in no state to go back alone."

"Don't leave us, Dadda. Mummy will look after you." Maribel held his good hand in concern, looking at her father imploringly.

"I'm so sorry, darling," Antony replied, attempting to struggle to his feet.

"I'll take you back," Eleanor said firmly. "Get our horse and His Lordship's, put my saddle on ours, please, Dad. Hurry!" Obediently Eleanor's father did as he was bid.

"But?" Antony replied weakly.

"No argument, m'lord."

Eleanor put her arm under Antony's good one, and half carried him outside.

Antony observed their horse to be a shaggy half shire horse; the saddle, seemly homemade, was for astride riding. Ladies always rode side-saddle; only brazen hussies rode astride. Then she threw up her skirts and mounted. "Give me the reins of His Lordship's horse and a hand for him to mount behind me," Eleanor commanded her father.

Her father cupped his hands for Antony to struggle up behind her. Then they were off, the old horse slow but sure-footed.

Antony put his good arm around Eleanor's waist, his bad arm dangling on her bare thigh. "Your legs will freeze in this weather." He contrived to pull her skirts more over her. He was glad she was not a lady. He liked her as she was, a brave, sincere maid.

"I know the way to the hostelry. My father and I have been there on occasions." Antony lay his head on Eleanor's shoulder, her warmth and closeness comforting him, making him feel stronger.

It was dark when they reached the inn. Dogs barked. Eleanor threw up her legs and slid to the ground, gently easing Antony off. He kissed her. "You're a wonderful girl. I won't forget."

Eleanor helped him mount his horse. She walked her horse back into the shadows, watching Antony ride forward, the house dogs barking madly. Eleanor watched the door open. The innkeeper came out, followed by six very drunk dragoons. Eleanor calculated that they were more likely to fall off their horses than Anthony. At least they only had to follow the road back to the castle. She hoped they were not persuaded to use their carbines as, in their present state, they were likely to shoot themselves. They seemed unaware of Antony's damaged shoulder.

Antony's man Claude was waiting for him in the darkened courtyard. "Open a side door for me, then help me slip into my apartment. Boil water and put it in my washing bowl, then fetch me honey, wine and vinegar."

"Yes, m'lord." His elderly manservant hurried away to do his bidding. He could see his master was deadly pale and in pain. Claude was a good, loyal man. As a young man, he was employed by an aristocratic French family living in Britain who backed the Royalist cause and fell out of favour, going back to France at the turn of the century, stripped of much of their wealth, abandoning Claude as a twenty-year-old. His father allocated him as his personal servant as he felt Claude, at his age, was not up to much else. Claude was devoted to Antony as Antony treated him well and took him into his confidence.

Claude returned as quickly as he could. "Is Lady Beatrice still at dinner?"

"She is drinking with the gentleman, m'lord."

"Good. Take this tourniquet off me; it's been on for too long. I can't feel my hand. Gently take the dressing off, clean the wound with wine, put on some honey, then replace the dressing. Cut away my shirt and use the other sleeve to keep the dressing in place."

"What happened, m'lord?"

"I had a ball through it, which fortunately missed the bone."

"Your escort came back very drunk, m'lord."

"It wasn't them."

Antony would have told Claude the details but felt, to protect him, he had better not. "Grab me a little supper and spring water. Don't say anything about my wound to anyone."

When Claude came back, he bade him sit with him, ate what he could, drinking spring water. He was very thirsty. He then undid his belt and, with the help of Claude, took out a key from a hidden compartment inside the buckle, asking Claude to unlock his bronze bound chest, where, along with rings, a pair of silver pistols and documents, he kept opium which only the rich could afford.

Opium was imported into England from Egypt and Turkey. It was a tenth-part of laudanum which he would need for the next few days for pain relief. He took the amount of laudanum he considered appropriate to ease the pain and allow him to sleep.

"I'll take a similar dose in the morning when we are on our own," he said to Claude, who was collecting up his outdoor clothes. "You keep it with you. I don't want Lady Beatrice to see it."

"As you wish, m'lord." Claude gave Antony his sleeping attire, carefully helping him put it on.

"There are people in this household you should not trust, the chamberlain being one of them, the steward most likely as well. If they appear to be friendly, it will be because they will be trying to find out about what you know."

"I'm aware of that, m'lord."

"I'm sure you are."

"You can trust me, m'lord." Claude stayed with Anthony, making sure his master was comfortable, only tiptoeing out when he heard Her Ladyship returning unsteadily.

When Claude returned in the morning, he found Her Ladyship's maid silently laying out Her Ladyship's day clothes, Antony sitting up awake, waiting for him, Lady Beatrice asleep, smelling of wine of the night before. On seeing Claude enter, Antony motioned the maid to leave the room, instructing Claude to pour him another dose of laudanum. After that, he asked Claude to adjust his dressing, help him dress, and arrange a sling before assisting him out of their tower chambers.

In the dining hall, the marquis, having breakfast as usual by the fire, called over to him, "We didn't see you at dinner last night. What have you done to your arm?" noting Antony had it in a sling.

"My horse spooked. I fell off and impaled my upper arm in the fall."

"I thought I had you taught you to ride when you were a boy. Horses get spooked; that's their nature. You need to pay a bit more attention."

Antony observed his father closely. He was his usual arrogant, insensitive self. He could see no shrewd scrutiny in his manner as if he suspected the explanation given. He felt, however, that his father could be manipulated by a clever person with a hidden agenda who he trusted. "I'll send over my physician later to look at it for you."

"Thank you, Father," Antony replied, feeling that the last thing he would do was let Physician Horace look at the injury. He was not that stupid that he would not be able to observe the difference between a ball wound and an impalement. He wanted no one to know that he was on his own at the time to protect Maribel and Eleanor. Additionally, by keeping the attack to himself, he might be better able to work out who was behind his attempted assassination. As he was in disguise at the time, his real identity would not have been known.

When Physician Horace came over to his quarters later, Antony said that fortunately a surgeon had seen to his injury soon after the incident and said it was not to be disturbed for a number of days to prevent the wound from becoming septic, as such injuries often did, ending up with the removal of the arm. Physician Horace seemed to be relieved at the explanation as he did not want to be responsible for the loss of the marquis' son's arm.

Lady Beatrice was awake when he returned to their bedroom, being dressed and made up by her personal maid who Antony pitied. She gave him a more searching look than his father, noting his pale, shocked state and observing his arm in a sling. He gave her the same explanation as he did his father. She looked at him keenly. Lady Beatrice was clever. Antony felt she could be dangerous.

By way of conversation, Antony asked her how the sketches for their new mansion were going. She said she was getting advice about drainage and ventilation, finding out how modern flues worked, all of which needed to be taken into account in the mansion's design.

Antony learnt from Claude that the company captain had questioned his escort about where they had been and His Lordship's horse being spooked, leading to his fall. According to Claude, the captain was disconcerted to discover that his escort were unaware that His Lordship had been injured or could remember where they had been.

This pleased Antony as he very much wanted Maribel and Eleanor's whereabout kept secret. He wondered, however, who gave the order for the captain to question his escort in the first place and looked searchingly at Beatrice for any sign. She was difficult to read from her body language, characteristically dismissive of his injury but shrewd enough to know it was more serious than he let on.

Antony was too unwell that day to do anything but get by. Claude gave him another dose of laudanum at his request. He went to sleep for the afternoon in the rather cold anti-room, warning Claude to be very wary of Lady Beatrice. Claude said he was on his guard. Antony knew he did not like her as she treated him like dirt. His arm smelt all right. If sepsis were to set in, it had not happened yet. Before long, he would need to get the wherewithal for a fresh dressing. That could prove difficult. He just wanted to get through the day.

In the evening, he felt a bit better. Though the marquis could no longer sit up to table, he liked standards to be kept. He expected the ladies to be dressed appropriately in a gown, under which there would be a corset, a bodice, petticoats, along with ruffles and pretty shoes. Lady Beatrice liked to have their main bedroom to herself with her maids when dressing, which suited Antony fine. As he had not been out, he did not have to change, but Claude put a little powder on his hair, which Antony never liked but knew was customary.

His father expected Antony to take his place as host, entering the dining room first with the most senior lady, who was his elder sister, Magdalene. She chose to sit at the head of the table, Lady Beatrice following, leaving Antony with Lady Grace at the foot of the table. Lady Grace was concerned for her younger brother's white appearance and his arm in a sling. When Lady Magdalen was finally settled, all could choose their seats and sit down. Antony had long decided that when he was marquis, he would do away with this stuffy protocol.

"What happened to your arm, Antony?"

Antony wondered if Grace had been primed to ask this question or, as he always had a good relationship with his next sibling up, was she just being kind? He told her the same story he told the rest. He did not want to disclose that he was on his own and particularly the reason why.

The meal consisted of two courses and a dessert, meats placed in the centre of the table with accompaniments like fish, vegetables, stewed soles, egg creations, custards, puddings with fruit dishes around the outside. The meal took two hours, during which Antony was expected to make conversation with Lady Grace's friends, which, this evening especially, he found an effort. He was never more pleased than when the last wine was served, drunk ceremoniously, after which Lady Magdalene rose and led the ladies to the drawing room, leaving the gentlemen to talk and drink. Motioning the men not to stand, Antony took his unobtrusive leave of the dining room, those noticing his sling understanding why he might not want to linger at dinner.

As usual, Lady Beatrice, along with some of his young nieces, joined the men until late in the evening, which they were traditionally not supposed to, dinking and flirting with the male guests. She knew Antony would never be with them; if not early to bed, he would be off somewhere around the castle, consorting with a few individuals he liked, disregarding their rank or role.

However, tonight Antony was in no fit state but to go to bed. Claude was in the anti-room waiting for him. The anti-room was originally a defensive space prior to entering their big round tower, now converted to living quarters, as were the other towers for family living at the castle. It was where servants waited but could be used for additional accommodation. It had a couch, table and two chairs but was cold and draughty with no fireplace. All family members were looking forward to living in a modern mansion nearby rather than a medieval castle, designed to subdue and overawe in former times.

"You look as if you've had enough, m'lord?"

"More than enough, Claude. Tomorrow you will need to get me fresh sphagnum moss.

"Where do I get that, m'lord?"

"Look to the north for a pool in a freshwater stream, as far away from cattle or human habitation as possible, and thyme, you'll find it in the walled kitchen garden, ask an undercook. But keep your quest as quiet as possible." He slipped Claude half a guinea. "Help me change to sleeping attire. I'll take a good swig of laudanum last thing."

Claude was a good soul. He gently helped Antony to bed as if he were his own son. When he was marquis, Antony intended to look after him if he had not family who could or wanted to do so.

Antony was not aware of Beatrice going to bed though lights would have been lit, and her long-suffering maid would, no doubt, have been subjected to a tirade as usual.

When Claude called in the morning, Beatrice was heavily asleep; Antony awake. There was little private space in a castle, even for a lord, let alone those of humbler birth. "Good morning, Claude."

"I hope you managed to get some sleep, m'lord?"

"The laudanum knocked me out. Got what I asked?"

"I was up early, m'lord."

"Good man. I forgot to ask for honey. Ask an undercook for honey for an abrasion on my horse, then make your way to where I stable my horses."

"Very good, m'lord."

"If you're asked where you're going with wound dressing material, say it's for my favourite horse."

"Yes, m'lord."

Antony was pleased Claude could get the wound dressing he knew to be the most effective in preventing sepsis which so often occurred. Antony was a worrier by nature. He wanted to protect Maribel and Eleanor. He also wanted to survive to run the estate when his father passed on in an enlightened and humanitarian manner, bearing in mind some of the best ideals floated in the civil war era. So, when Claude joined him in the stables, he sent out the grooms and looked at the wound anxiously. It had a degree of redness but did not look or smell as if gangrene had set in.

"It looks good, m'lord."

"You think so?"

"I've seen a lot of injury in my time."

Antony was most relieved. "Help me redress it. Honey on first, then a poultice of thyme leaves." Antony had brought with him a clean shirt. With the sphagnum moss on top, he asked Claude to cut off and use a shirt sleeve to hold the whole dressing in place. Handmade fine cotton shirts were expensive, but what else had he? He could see that Claude was appalled, as the cost of the shirt would have been more than a working man earnt in six months. "Can't be helped," he said to Claude. "Have you any ideas how such attacks could be avoided in the future."

"Spread misinformation to confuse those behind the attack."

Antony wrinkled his brow in thought. "You're smart, Claude. That's an idea."

"Thank you, m'lord. I'd do anything to help."

"That Magistrate Travallyn and I are looking for clues other than where we really are? I'll have to think how I'll go about it." Antony pondered while Claude carefully put on a fresh dressing.

Chapter Five

Antony contrived to get through the day quietly, trying to regain his strength. One of the things he would dearly have liked to do was to look through the estate's accounts, which the chamberlain jealously kept locked in a chest to which only he had the key. His father trusted him, but Antony did not.

Another thing that interested him was why the earl, his father's best friend, was so insistent his only daughter marry him, bringing to the marriage such a generous dowry. As a result of which, the mansion was being built, and other estate improvements and upgrades undertaken, like field drainage systems to control the water table by sluice gates and outfalls to make to the land more productive, less likely to flood.

Was his father being subtly bribed? Controlled by the earl, a friend and benefactor? Or was it the other way round, did his father have a hold over the earl through knowledge of some past event going back to their time together in the Lord General's Regiment of Foot Guards? But there was one thing Antony knew, though his father had his faults, he would never stoop to emotional or any other form of blackmail. He felt what might be of interest was to find out what went on in the past between them.

Antony had not seen Beatrice so far that day. When he did catch up with her, she was in the top of their tower in what had been converted into a spinster's room for the light but was also well suited to painting. She had up to dry a number of painted elevations of their new mansion on which the work was soon to begin. Antony had to admit she had ability. If only she had a nicer nature, he would be able to take to her better.

"You still look pasty. With all that riding about in the fresh air, you should be in better shape," was Beatrice's unsympathetic greeting when he entered.

"I hope to be when I've recovered from my injury," Antony replied.

"Fallen off your horse? You need riding lessons."

Antony chose to ignore her cynicism. "Your painted projections look very impressive. Have the architects seen them?"

"They're more useful than riding about the countryside," Beatrice indicated her paintings. Antony noticed that up in this tower room, Beatrice had a panoramic view as far as the eye could see. He also noticed a telescope. He left looking thoughtful to have a quiet lie down for an hour or so as he would be expected at dinner as usual this evening.

Three days later, he received a letter from Magistrate Brandon Travallyn. He looked at the seal carefully to see whether it had been tampered with. As far as he could tell, it had not, but some people were very clever. In it, he said that he had been to see Joao Pereira again and that the more he got to know him, the more he was impressed by his ability and resourcefulness. He also had news regarding Maribel and Eleanor. He asked if he could meet again with Antony at a rendezvous of his choice. After reading it carefully, Antony destroyed the letter.

Whatever he was going to do, he had better act quickly as it was now well into December, and his time would have to be increasingly spent organising Christmas. But how and where to meet Magistrate Brandon was a problem. He wanted to meet him unseen by prying eyes. After much thought, he decided to meet him after dark in a fishing hut on the inlet creek used when the sea trout were running. He put nothing else in the letter, asking Claude to leave it at the Castle Inn with the landlord for him to give to Magistrate Brandon when he next visited. Three days later, Antony got a reply. He would meet him in the unused hut at 10 that evening after they had both had dinner.

By now, Antony was feeling much better. Very luckily, his wound had not turned septic, thanks in the first instance to the prompt action of Eleanor. After the formal part of dinner, Antony excused himself, as he often did, having requested Claude to go to his stables and ask the grooms for his horse which he was to lead, as quietly as the cobbles would allow, to a dark part of the courtyard.

Antony emerged silently from an unlit doorway wearing a dark cloak with the hood well over his three-cornered cocked hat. He carried two recently primed pistols which he always had with when away from the castle since his attack, making sure they were ready for instant use. He walked his horse out through the tower gates, keeping in the shadows, feeling sure nobody would be watching out for him at this hour.

He made his way down the left bank of the stream, the moon creating a shining pathway on the water, keeping pace with his horse. He looked back towards the castle, built on a knoll. Not many lights shone from the ring of towers as most were still at dinner in the great hall of the keep. It was said that once the castle was right on the coast, seawater filling the moat, which was kept in by lock gates when the tide receded. But over the centuries, sediment built up the land and the sea was now two-thirds of a mile away.

The dark shadow of the hut appeared ahead. It had been constructed in recent times near a bend creating a deep pool on the inside where seatrout rested in season before continuing their journey upstream to spawn. By now, the run had finished and the hut was deserted. Antony hunted for the concealed key, opened the door which he left open, and sat on a chair near the door with his pistols beside him ready on a table. Before long, he saw the silhouette of his friend Magistrate Brandon on his horse, his well-formed shoulders, tied-back hair and fashionable cocked hat worn at an angle, creating a distinguished image.

"Magistrate Brandon?" he called softly.

"M'lord, why all the secrecy?"

"Feel your way inside. I'm not striking a light. I'll tell you."

Tying his horse, Magistrate Brandon stumbled inside. "Well?"

Antony told Brandon the whole account of his attack from the time he set out that fateful day to their meeting now.

"A targeted attack?"

"What else could it be in that remote place? It was not as if I were on Hampstead Heath? For an instant, I glimpsed a mounted figure in a dark cloak looking down at me as if directing operations. They were paid assassins. I must have been followed from the time I left the castle.

I know I have enemies in my own household, but would they want to assassinate me – to frighten me perhaps? My gut feeling is that my attempted assassination is part of a big conspiracy, the one you and I are trying to get evidence about involving Atlantic Barbary pirates substantially bribing a very high-ranking dignitary in the county or beyond. There're not many of them. We need to make a list and find out about their past history, what's known about them, for example, who lost a lot of money in the South Seas Bubble. If we had sufficient compelling evidence, and it would have to be compelling and irrefutable, you would be the person who would be presenting the evidence to obtain a prosecution. I feel that our conversation at the Castle Inn must have been deliberately listened into. I would watch your back. You could be the next to be targeted. That's why I invited you here; difficult to be followed in the darkness and no question of being overheard." Antony could sense Brandon pondering over what he had said.

"I'm most concerned by all you've told me. My movements have been, to date, in very public places. I see I'll need to look out in future. It shows that whoever's behind the conspiracy will stop at nothing."

"Desperate and determined," Antony agreed. "Watch out."

They rode back companionably alongside the stream, patches of high cloud casting shadows on the gently flowing water, the towers of the castle dominating the landscape as they drew nearer. "What's it like living in a castle?" Brandon asked.

"Cold and draughty, a community of family and servants with undercurrents and rivalries, not many of whom I can trust."

"My lifestyle is simple and uncomplicated by comparison, open to criticism perhaps, but that's all," Brandon remarked.

"Sounds preferable to me. As it's difficult getting messages to you, can we agree to meet at the same place at the same time five days after Christmas? That would be the thirtieth of December?" Antony proposed.

"After Christmas?" Brandon queried.

"As my father can't walk, he wants me to organise the build-up to Christmas. Christmas is an important occasion for him."

"All that advent ritual doesn't sound like your father? I didn't know he was religious?"

"He's not. He just likes the family around him on Christmas Day. Though I don't think many family members other than those living in the castle will be attending owing to the severe winters of late and our guest accommodation in the keep, which is sparse and cold. Not what folk like these days. They like comfortable living in modern homes with their own rooms, fires and privacy."

"You aristocrats all the same," Brandon observed, a product of the increasingly educated middle classes. "Think the best is your rightful heritage. Lost the civil war, but since the Restoration, thinking again you have God's ordained right to be on top and rule. It won't always be like that. As more of the less privileged get the right to vote, they'll become a force to be reckoned with."

"Don't tell me that," Antony replied, more than a little irritated. "You know quite well what I think. Many more should be able to vote. That's why we're friends."

"Yes, I know," Brandon apologised. "I just get impatient that change takes so long. We're getting near your castle. I'd better leave you. See you on the thirtieth. Good luck, God be with you."

"Same time and place on the thirtieth. Happy Christmas," Antony affirmed, looking around him on his guard, drawing one of his pistols. He came back the way he left, walking his horse in the shadows between the raised entry gate, which really should be closed at this hour, but night closure was not necessary in these peaceful times. Slave-snatching Barbary pirates only attacked soft targets. Antony's present concern was the noise of his horse's hooves on the cobbles as he walked it to where Claude was waiting near the stables.

Inside nobody seemed to have missed him. Beatrice was not yet in their room but still over in the keep. He felt tired. Though not down with sepsis, the wound had taken a lot out of him. He went straight to bed with some laudanum and fell instantly asleep.

Next morning Antony awoke with Claude standing patiently beside him. He thought about what Brandon had said. It was true; he was privileged. He always had a personal servant, something he took for granted. He imagined for the first time awakening in a poor home, with wife and children all cramped into one small room, children crying out for food when there was none. Many of his tenants were living on the brink of starvation, immensely grateful if he stopped and just greeted them.

"Have you ever felt hungry, Claude?"

"Many times, m'lord, when I was young before I was fortunate enough to get employment here," Claude replied, surprised to be asked such a question.

"My friend, Magistrate Brandon, said I was privileged."

Claude was obviously taken aback by the conversation. Finally, he said, "There's always been the rulers and the ruled."

Antony felt that said it all. Though of liberal disposition, wanting to do good in the world, Antony had always taken his position for granted, a member of the ruling class, the aristocracy, not really knowing what it was like to be anything else.

There was Claude, standing patiently before him, towel over his arm, glass of laudanum in his hand, old enough to be his father, waiting to help him wash and get dressed, ready to bring him all the good food he wanted for breakfast if he did not feel like going over to the keep.

"As soon as my arm feels tolerable, I'd better lay off the laudanum. It's very addictive," Antony observed.

"So I understand, m'lord." Antony realised that, unless he took a sip on the quiet, Claude would never have had such a painkiller, it being well beyond the price range of servants. Lady Beatrice was heavily asleep beside him, wig awry on its stand, her shaven head looking very unattractive in the light of morning.

"I'll wash and dress in the anteroom, then perhaps I'd better make an appearance over at the keep for breakfast. He could see Beatrice's maid looking curiously at him as she had overheard his conversation with Claude, perhaps wondering whether His Lordship had lost it this morning."

"Has the Christmas guest list been sent out, boy?" his father called from the fireside as soon as he entered the dining hall. By persisting in calling him *boy* in front of the servants, Antony felt was demeaning since he was no longer a boy. It did not help his respect.

"Yes, Father," Antony replied quietly, going over to him. "But I expect that few not living in the castle will attend owing to the increasingly cold winters."

"What's the matter with you, boy? Winters have always been cold."

"They're getting colder."

"Fiddlesticks! You're getting soft. The young people today are always whining, not like when I was young."

Antony felt there was little use arguing with his father. He was an old stubborn climate denier and would never change. Nevertheless, he felt compelled to say, "They say the sea ice has come so far south that Norwegian ships can no longer get through to their Greenland colony. Nobody knows what's happened to the poor colonists."

"Fiddlesticks. Rumours!"

"Ask ships' captains at Lyme Regis sailing to Norway and the Baltic."

"I wouldn't waste my time."

Antony shrugged his shoulders. His father's mind was closed on the subject, as it was on many others. He walked away.

After breakfast, still stung by Magistrate Brandon's remark that aristocrats like him took for granted what they considered was their God-ordained place in the world as the ruling class, decided for his morning exercise he would ride as far end of the castle road where it met the through highway and visit his nearest tenant farmer. He decided to take an escort of six dragoons from the castle company and marshal in the castle courtyard in full sight.

Beatrice, noticing the troop assembling, asked where he was going. Antony told her. She queried whether his going was necessary so near Christmas with all that he had to do. Antony replied politely that estate visits were none of her business, knowing she would report his intentions to his father and have him followed. When the troop assembled, he inspected them. They looked happy and relaxed, anticipating a long lunch at a hostelry with plenty of ale.

It was a comparatively short ride to the end of the road. At the farmhouse, he dismounted, asking his escort to wait. The farmer and his wife, alerted by their dogs, rushed outside in welcome, asking their children to make themselves respectable and help with ale and scones. Antony said that was appreciated but not necessary, that this was a brief pre-Christmas call to wish them a happy Christmas and to see how they all were.

Inside, on a settle near the fire, he said he wanted to know how they were faring in times made difficult by increasingly cold weather and economic decline. The tenant farmer replied that what his wife was getting for geese and eggs at the local market was good, but the main farm crops, which, by their tenancy agreement, were sold by the estate, were unrewarding, hardly enough, when the farmer felt, in a time for food shortage, prices should be higher. Privately, Antony thought the farmer had a point.

He looked around the farmhouse. Basically, it was of good quality but threadbare. The tenant was not prospering. He called the children over, who were hovering in the background, and asked to be introduced. The farmer said he was concerned for their future. As they grew older, the farm would not be able to support them all. Some would join the drift to the towns but being illiterate, they could not make progress among the merchant classes. They had no access to schooling out in the country. There were no dame schools, and if there were, the tenant farmer could not afford them.

Antony held the hands of the two youngest. They were sweet children. He thought of his Maribel. Though crippled, she was literate and numerate, as was Eleanor. All children should have access to education. The farmer himself was no doubt illiterate and could not understand contracts and therefore was at the mercy of estate owners such as his father and one day himself. Magistrate Brandon's observation was quite right. Being privileged, he needed to find out how ordinary people lived. He got up and thanked the farmer for speaking to him in a frank manner, saying it was his aim to improve the lot of all on the estate by advocating rotational cropping and improving land drainage. He finally gave the farmer a guinea, wishing him and his family a happy Christmas.

Outside, his escort were waiting restlessly, looking very cold. To their surprise, he said that was all for today and directed them back to the castle, leading them through into the courtyard, dismounted and walked his horse with theirs through into the stables.

"Back so soon?" Beatrice observed in surprise when she saw him. She clearly did not believe him when he had said where he was going.

"I'm concerned for the welfare of our people," Antony replied.

"A waste of your time. The steward and chamberlain attend to all that."

Cheeky, privileged shrew, were Antony's thoughts. He felt that he would love to be able to wave a magic wand and have Beatrice change places for a month with one of their most menial serving maids. Such an experience would teach her not to take her position for granted and have more thought for others less fortunate than herself. He also thought ruefully that if he were to do the same, it would be a wake-up call.

Claude brought him a late lunch in his room, after which he felt compelled to put his feet up for an hour or so. Though his arm seemed to be all right, he felt that he must be combating a degree of sepsis to make him feel so usually tired. He also learnt from Claude that Lady Beatrice had directed a rider from within the household, riding one of her horses, to follow Antony and his escort this morning, not a dragoon from the castle company garrisoned on the third floor of the keep.

Claude did not know who this person was as the speaker fell silent when he saw Claude. Later in the day, he found out that the rider was one of Lady Magdalene's sons, his elder sister being very friendly with Lady Beatrice. Antony's suspicion was growing that Beatrice's motive in getting pregnant was to conceive a son for his father to will the estate to this son and cut him out of his inheritance, though he was sure he could not do this to his title when he passed on. He would ask his friend Magistrate Brandon, who had training in law, when he next saw him.

That evening after dinner, the marquis instructed Antony to make sure that holly, ivy, mountain laurel, mistletoe and a large yule log were gathered ready to decorate the great hall on Christmas Eve but not before, as this was considered unlucky. He wanted rosemary with bay and lavender hung about the pillars in the hall and organised the giving of presents before Christmas according to custom. A donation to the local church on Christmas Eve was to be prepared, which the chamberlain liked to keep to a minimum.

Though second to his father, Antony felt lonely in the busy castle community. With Maribel and Eleanor gone, he did not feel sure of anyone except Claude. Though many, especially the serving staff, liked his liberal and humanitarian views, few would stand up for him in their own self-interest. Only Claude, small, thin, with only a few strands of dark hair left, he felt he could really trust. Not even torture would make him betray what he knew in confidence.

"I've got much to do before Christmas," he observed to Claude, who was helping him change owing to his still painful arm.

"If I might suggest, m'lord, before dinner, in front of the others, put Lady Beatrice in charge of, say, the decorations; she considers herself artistic. She couldn't really refuse."

Antony considered what Claude suggested. He was right. So far, he had acted negatively towards her in response to her attitude. He needed to be cleverer than that.

"By Jove, I think you're right, Claude. Why hadn't I thought of that?"

"I'm sure you would have, m'lord," Claude replied diplomatically.

"By the way, when you leave, tell the court barber I want a shave at 10 tomorrow."

"Very good, m'lord."

Antony smiled ruefully to himself. There he was again, taking his position for granted. Only the rich could be clean-shaven. It was dangerous to try and shave oneself with a cut-throat razor which the majority could not afford in any case. That night he tried to cut down on his use of laudanum but consequently did not sleep well, being haunted by bad dreams, such as losing his way then being captured by demons from whom he could not escape, whatever he attempted.

He woke up feeling thoroughly frustrated, the nightmare mirroring his life at the present time. He felt like lying in; however, there was much to do. The few gifts to each other had been given out on December the sixth, St Nicholas Day. He had given his sisters silver pins for their wigs and for his father a unique pair of Miquelet flintlock ball butt pocket-sized pistols with pierced brass inlaid butts from the late seventeenth century for his pistol collection, which was his pride and joy. He had yet to organise gifts for tradesmen, servants and the poor in the form of blankets, food and money on St Stephen's Day on the twenty-sixth of December.

That evening before dinner, he announced loudly to his father in the hearing of everyone that Lady Beatrice would be in charge of the Christmas Eve decorating owing to her well-known artistic ability. His wife looked daggers at him but could not publicly refuse. That evening in the apartment she blazed at him that he should have asked her first before he made the announcement that she would organise the Christmas decorations. Antony blandly countered, saying that, as part of their marriage ceremony, she swore that, along with other things, she would obey her husband. Antony said that to date in their marriage she had shown no inclination either to obey or even consult him in anything. He let her go on yelling her head off until she grew tired and called for her maid.

As Christmas Eve approached, Beatrice found she could speak to Antony to the extent of asking him where she could direct the servants to collect the traditional decorative requirements. Antony replied that she could start with their own walled kitchen garden for sweet-smelling herbs like lavender; everyone liked the sweet smell of Christmas, which was all part of the themed tradition. Also, Michelle's Wood, five miles north, was a good source of holly and ivy. He said the servants would know. Just tell them what she wanted and the quantities and send them off. Clearly, Beatrice had been given little responsibility when with her father, the earl. She did not thank Antony but stamped off, still in a huff.

During decorating on Christmas Eve, Antony kept in the background. He could only reach up with his uninjured arm. The servants scurried about, unhappy with Lady Beatrice's imperious commands. A few looked at Antony as if to say that they would have been much happier had he been in charge.

On Christmas Day, they assembled at noon. An hour later, they were led by Lady Magdalene into the great dining hall with its flags, shields and statues under which innumerable generations had sat and dined before them, giving all within a sense of timeless security. When she sat down, the company milled about to sit with friends. As usual, Antony sat with Lady Grace and her family.

He looked around him. There were not many extended family members who were not residents of the castle. Christmas, Yule, the old Saxon word which originally meant midwinter, was one of many festivals throughout the year. People looked forward to it as a good feast during the hard times of winter and a reminder that the days from now on would gradually get longer once more. While waiting on the first course to be served, carol singers from the local church sang "Joy to the World" and "O Tannenbaum". It was all very reassuring, confirming they were members of the exclusive ruling class, which Antony, like the others, had until recently taken for granted.

He began to sense that great changes were coming that would affect the social order forever. At the sight of his complacent relatives looking forward to eating on one afternoon more than a poor man would consume in a week, confident that life would always be this way, foreboding thoughts came over him at the start of what should be a carefree occasion.

Already there were rumblings in France among the mercantile classes about the corruption and extravagance of Louis XV's despotic regime while common people starved, which the ruling elite of England could well take note of. There was also growing evidence that Jacobite Scots were planning to put James Stuart on the English throne, by force if necessary, raising the spectre of a Catholic sovereign, rekindling the divisions of the past, which were also ignored by his class.

Antony tried to put these thoughts out of his mind, along with those of his growing concern for Maribel and Eleanor, and to listen to the traditional reassuring carols. But he could not. He excused himself and went up to his apartment, where he found Claude going over his clothes.

Claude looked up, surprised to see him. "Wound troubling you, m'lord?"

"Do you think the present state of the nation will go on like this?" he asked Claude, to his surprise.

"The life of a nation is like the life of a person; always changing whether you like it or not," Claude replied simply, having seen much change in his long life.

"That's what I thought, but my class seem not to think that way."

"Need a little laudanum?" Claude asked, concerned at his master's depressed state of mind.

"That might make me nod off over Christmas dinner."

"Would that matter too much?"

"Well, just a swig then." With that, Antony went back to an afternoon of courses interspersed with music from their own musicians playing a guitar, trumpet, harp, kettle drums, and a pochette, a small violin, in a happier frame of mind induced by a little opium.

It was not until the afternoon of Boxing Day, while the family were assembling the traditional gifts, particularly of food to thank their servants for their services, especially on Christmas Day, when devastating news was brought to them.

Twenty-seven young people had been snatched from the village of Limbeley on Christmas morning walking on a minor road in a group to the village of Shertonham, which they had been doing as far back as anyone could remember, to join the young people there to celebrate Christmas together. They were ambushed by Barbary Coast pirates, according to the few who escaped, who seemed to have first-hand knowledge of the fact that there would be a group of unprotected young people travelling on this road on this day at this time. It could not have been a coincidence.

Antony looked over at his father. He was visibly shaken and outraged. Antony knew his father well. He was a blunt man, incapable of putting on an act. He looked across to Beatrice. Her face was inscrutable. He had no way of knowing whether the news came as a shock or otherwise. All the rest of his family were as amazed and outraged as his father. From what he had learned to date, Antony realised it was a carefully targeted snatch based on precise intelligence. Joao Pereira was right.

It was Antony's father who spoke first. "The pirates had to have inside information. They only want healthy young people. How would they know they were all walking together at that time and at that place? It's too much of a coincidence."

His daughters, Lady Magdalene and Grace, nodded in agreement, as did many other family members within hearing. Antony looked again at his wife. Her face remained inscrutable. Did she know something the others did not? Antony could not tell. All he knew for sure was that she was instrumental in the search for the whereabouts of Eleanor and Maribel, owing to jealousy and not wanting Maribel in later years having any claim to the estate which she felt should pass to the child she hoped to bear. For that reason, she particularly wanted a boy. The atmosphere in the great hall was subdued as the family continued packing the servants' boxes and those of the village considered in need, each absorbed in their own thoughts.

When Antony went over to his father by the fire, propped on his soft cushions, the marquis said, "Those bastards had to have precise information about where and when unescorted youngsters were on their own in a lonely spot. Who would do such a treacherous thing, obviously for a pot of gold? Had we any idea Barbary pirates were off our coast, the youngsters would have been escorted by our dragoon company."

"I'll ride out tomorrow, give our condolences to the people of the village of Limbeley and tell them that Magistrate Travallyn and I are going to find out who's behind this treachery," Antony replied.

"Good for you, boy. I'm glad for once you've got your priorities right." Antony was relieved to hear his father's reaction. He obviously was not in any way a party to the atrocity. His father's concern would make it easier for him to be away from the castle for periods of time, investigating how the pirates were getting their information. The estate very much needed their healthy young people. He was due to meet Magistrate Brandon Travallyn in four days' time. Tomorrow he would visit the devastated village people. But for today, they all needed to get on and finish packing and then start distributing the Boxing Day gifts.

The next day, with a platoon of dragoons, he left not long after daybreak for the village. It was cold, with occasional snow showers, the ground frozen underfoot. They needed to ride carefully to prevent horses from falling. It took two hours to reach the village.

To their dismay, instead of the usual enthusiastic, loyal reception, they were greeted with hostility. 'Where were the dragoons? Why were the young people not protected? How could they carry on as a viable village without them? They were their insurance for the future,' were some of their complaints.

Antony tried to explain that no one knew the Barbary pirates were in the offing, especially in midwinter. It was generally a summer incursion, rare these days. If they had any idea, the dragoons would have been there in force to annihilate them as soon as they came ashore. That is what they were maintained for at considerable expense.

But the surviving populace was not to be placated. They were hissed and spat at. To avoid further provocation, Antony and the dragoons sadly withdrew, riding back in silence. When he told his father, the marquis was obviously perturbed. It was something he had not experienced before, a tenants' revolt. He agreed something had to be done to ensure such an audacious incursion never occurred again.

On the evening of the thirtieth, while everyone was still at evening meal, Antony once again led his horse quietly out of the courtyard, keeping in the shadows, two pistols newly primed in his holsters, to ride to the small fishing hut halfway down the creek leading to the open sea. He wanted Beatrice not to know of his mission to meet his friend, Magistrate Brandon, as he was uncertain of her loyalty and did not wish to be ambushed a second time, if indeed she was behind his ambush last time, which he doubted.

There was little moon showing under heavy clouds, making it very dark. It was easier to let his horse find its way down the path beside the tidal waters, the lapping of the wavelets merging with the wind sighing across the marches. He wondered if Brandon was ahead or behind him or even remembered. Arriving at the hut, he tied his horse, felt for the key and stumbled inside, leaving the door propped open. He had not sat for long, facing the door, pistols at the ready, when he heard a horseman approach.

"Brandon?" he called softly.

"M'lord."

They recognised each other's voices. "Feel your way inside if you can. I don't want to strike a light." Antony saw Brandon's shadow in the doorway and heard him feel his way in. He took his pistols and held them above his head as he did not want them knocked into or fumbled in the dark as, fully cocked, they could fire and injure one of them.

"Shocking news," Brandon said with feeling. "All those young people. "The community is doomed for the future."

"It will have a devastating effect. It can't go on. We will have to do something about it. My father, along with the rest of us, recognised that the pirates had to have very precise intelligence, gained in some way from a well-informed source. But how and from whom is the question?"

"The last throw of a desperate breed whose traditional way of life is coming to an end in the North Atlantic owing to the range and efficiency of our navy," Brandon agreed, shifting his position and knocking a chair over. "How do we make a start?"

"I suggest we see our tenant, Joao Pereira. He's a surprisingly intelligent and resilient man. He must be, having been captured by them and enslaved as a rower. The life expectancy of a galley oarsman is only a few months before they're worn out and thrown overboard. Nobody could know more about how the pirates operate than him. And he knows a great deal about the sea, ships and sailing as well. A sailing master, along with a bosun, is the most senior of non-commissioned naval ranks."

"He could sail a boat," Brandon observed.

"Must be an expert, I would think," Antony affirmed. "I'll tell my father that I'll be away with you for a few weeks, investigating how the pirates are getting their information, starting with interviewing Joao Pereira on the third of January. Can you arrange an escort? An escort of my dragoons would get us nowhere. We'll need to operate incognito to have any success."

"I could hire locally. There's an abundance of unemployed ex-sailors and marines."

"It'll be a start. I know there's plenty of that sort around, eager for any kind of employment."

Brandon took a while to reply further. Antony could not see his face in the darkness to get a clue to his reaction. "I'm not well off. I would need financial assistance. There's no provision in law for financial assistance while seeking evidence of wrongdoing. The victim has to provide this himself if he's ever going to get to justice. Courts won't convict without indisputable evidence if the person accused is of high rank, which he could well be in this case."

Antony replied after a long pause. "I only get an allowance. I don't have control of the estate finances, but I have saved up quite a number of gold guineas over the years which should be enough for our present needs, working together. I'd better be getting back before I'm missed."

Antony could hear Brandon fumbling his way to the door. Outside, their horses moved restlessly in the darkness. Few people went out at night other than watchmen in the towns. The uneducated believed that imps, goblins and malevolent spirits haunted lonely places at night and stayed safely indoors. Even those enlightened and educated like Antony and Brandon felt uneasy as the wind moaned eerily over the inlet, rising and falling like wailing lost souls. Their horse caught their mood and shied at shadows. They were both relieved when they neared the lit castle towers.

"Sounded like banshees out there on the inlet. Irish folk believe the wailing of a female banshee warns of imminent death in a home. Not good. We'll meet in the Castle Inn yard at dawn on the third," Antony said on parting at the landing.

"Agreed, good luck with your arm," Brandon affirmed, hurrying on to the Castle Arms.

Leading his horse into the castle yard, Antony felt relieved to be back within the security of the castle. He left the stables by the rear door and made his way into the great hall in the keep. Late dining was still in progress, some of the family looking a little drunk. His father had retired. "You're always up and down," his sister Grace said on his re-entrance. "You look cold."

"It's cold in our tower," Antony replied.

"I'm looking forward to our new home. I see a start has been made on the foundations. Will we be dining in the great hall in the keep still?" Grace asked.

"Only on special occasions, I think, is our father's idea," Antony replied.

"Will you be making changes when you become marquis?"

"I certainly will," Antony replied with feeling.

"Some may not like it," Grace observed.

"I'm sure some won't," was Antony's brief reply.

He had always wanted to be a humanitarian estate owner, secure as he was in his own comfortable lifestyle, which he had not questioned but took for granted. Now he had seen something of the poverty and insecurity that was the lot of the vast majority, he was troubled. But for an accident of birth, that could have been him. He had not thought of it in that light before. More than ever, he felt that, when he inherited, he must improve the lot of the people if he could. Grace looked at her young brother as if she was not quite sure what he meant. Ever since he was young, he tended to have his head in the clouds. She hoped he would not do anything rash.

"Waste of your time," Beatrice said when he told her he would be away with Magistrate Travallyn for a period to investigate the abduction of the 27 young people. "Why don't you stay here and do something worthwhile?"

"My father is of the opinion that bringing the informants to justice is of great importance."

"We'll see about that," was Beatrice's arrogant reply, as if she would soon change his father's mind.

It was Antony's experience that, when his straight-talking father had a conviction, he was not easily persuaded out of it.

"That's your opinion," Antony replied and closed the subject. However, Beatrice's outburst made him question once again where her real loyalties lay. He felt she was not to be trusted.

It was a cold dark morning when he met Magistrate Brandon at seven on the third of January in the courtyard. Their escort would be waiting for them at the Castle Inn. There was little wind but mist in places. In a particularly dense bank in a hollow, Antony drew Brandon aside to wait with him in silence behind some bushes just off the road. Sure enough, they could hear approaching hoofbeats. "Our shadow," Antony whispered cynically as the hoofbeats, muffled in the mist, drew on ahead.

"I guess he will come across us at Castle Village."

"What after that?" Brandon asked.

"I'm sure the escort you've engaged could persuade him, for health reasons, that it's in his own interests for him to go back home. I shouldn't doubt he'll tell the person who instructed him to follow us that, unfortunately, he lost us."

"You think so?" Brandon questioned.

"I'm sure so. I don't feel he's the heroic sort, especially when I consider who the person might be."

"I guess you know your people."

"After interviewing our tenant, I'd like to drop in at the watermill to see if Maribel and Eleanor are all right. After that, we'd better go to Lyme Regis or nearby. The informants must spend time in that area. When away from a village clock or coaching inn, it's always difficult to know the time. We need to be at an inn by nightfall. The days are short this time of the year. One of these days, an entirely different sort of clock will be invented that can be carried around. We'll just have to judge time by the angle of the sun unless we can hear a village clock. Who have you got for an escort? Roads are dangerous places?"

"Two ex-marines and four sailors. When that sort leave service and come ashore, they easily get into trouble, especially if they have too much to drink. They all would have been hung but for me. There are too many hanging offences. Their crimes were minor, crimes of poverty. When they were discharged from their ships, the sailors had been pressed, they had no idea where their villages were in relation to their discharged port. They couldn't get home, had no work. I got them off hanging, for which they're eternally grateful and will do anything for me, especially when I pay them for escort. As you said, in my job, I must make enemies. So I've taken your advice to watch my back," Brandon explained.

"They seem excellent."

"I feel I can rely on them."

"When we come to Castle Village, I'll point out who our follower is. As I said, if your escort could have a little word with him to convince him that it is in his interests to go back home, I don't doubt that he'll make up a convincing explanation of how he came to lose who he was sent to follow," Antony reminded Brandon.

They did not have anything to eat at the inn. Time was getting on. Their escort looked a formidable lot as they sat their restless horses in the castle forecourt, the ex-seamen armed with Spanish seagoing cutlasses and the ex-marines with espingoles, French blunderbusses, their weather-beaten faces disfigured with scars.

Brandon had hired for them quality horses, as they could not be slowed down by their having poor mounts, the ex-sailors especially looking uncomfortable in the saddle but, hopefully, they would soon become experienced. Compared with his smart dragoons in livery, they looked like bandits. Such men needed firm handling, respecting their employer, something Brandon seemed able to achieve.

They set off in a cool light breeze from the north with the possibility, it appeared, of a light shower. Brandon and Antony rode together, their escort 10 yards behind, just out of earshot. They met several parties going in the opposite direction; no one from behind caught up with them.

After the inn where Antony intended to stay the night, having booked and paid for their two main rooms, they headed south across country, Antony taking careful note of their route. It was important to stay in a coaching hostelry where their horses were looked after and could be exchanged if necessary. Reliable means of transport was of the essence.

Picking their way, Antony recognised a feature reminding him it was in this area, when he was on his own, that he was waylaid and injured. On this occasion, Antony was carrying a small fortune in gold guineas which, at 30 ounces for every hundred, was quite weighty and difficult to disguise. He looked up to see if he could see a sinister mounted figure on an eminence in a dark cloak looking down at them but observed no such figure. He was glad of his cut-throat escort. Nevertheless, he looked around uneasily. His arm, injured in the ambush, still hurt.

Alerted by his dogs, Joao Pereira was both wary and surprised to see Antony and Magistrate Travallyn approaching with their motley escort. Antony introduced his friend.

"I've seen a lot of your people lately. A young man with a dragoon sergeant and six of your dragoons have been searching properties in this area with a fine-toothed comb. By their questioning, it seems they think that your daughter and whoever is caring for her are hiding out in this area. They said they wanted to bring the child back to the castle to care for her."

"None of my doing," Antony replied. "The young man has been authorised by my father. My wife wants to get her hands on my daughter as she sees her as a threat. I hate to think what would happen to her. That's why I'm having her, along with the woman she considers her mother, safeguarded in a secret location.

"Magistrate Travallyn and I are visiting you today because we'd like to learn from you all that you know about how Barbary pirates operate in the Atlantic. You probably have heard by now of the tragic abduction of the 27 young people on a minor public road about 20 miles from here. The abduction was very precisely carried out. The Barbary pirates knew exactly where they would be on that day and time. It could not have been a coincidence. Magistrate Travallyn and I are trying to find out how they got their information. The navy has been informed and are out to rescue them if possible if they knew where temporarily they might be held before being spirited away to the Mediterranean to be sold as white slaves."

Joao Pereira looked relieved. "Come in, m'lord and good sir, and I'll tell you what I know." Joao went over in detail what he had found out as a galley slave. He did not know as much as he would have liked as he was chained, ate and slept where he rowed. Antony thought it remarkable that he had survived the ordeal until rescued by the navy, who then pressed him into serving with them at warrant officer level as a sailing master. He must be very tough indeed. Antony felt he would have been broken physically and mentally after 24 hours.

He went on further to explain that Magistrate Travallyn and he were going down to Lyme Regis to stay in the town or in a nearby fishing village to try to discover how agents ashore were getting information out to Barbary galleys waiting offshore out of sight of land and where the captives might temporarily be held.

Joao Pereira thought for a while. "Best to acquire a handy small craft to check local estuaries without delay to find where they might be concealed before they're spirited away by a fast-sailing craft under a foreign flag to a south-western Mediterranean port."

"That would mean we would need to hire a suitable small craft. It might be difficult to conceal who we were and our purpose if we tried to hire," Antony mused.

"I can see it might," Joao replied. "I'll tell you what, there's not much going on here in midwinter. My wife and Jimmy, our farmhand, can manage without me for a while. I've got a score to settle with those bastards. I can sail, with the help of Magistrate Travallyn's escort of ex-seamen and two marines, a small coastal craft. If you were to buy some sort of fishing boat or, better still, an ex-pilot sloop at Lyme Regis, we could scout south along the coast, selling the craft when we are finished with it. I've picked up coastal navigation, but only officers and gentlemen know how to navigate out of sight of land, needing mathematics, trigonometry and all that. You are a gentleman, m'lord?"

"It doesn't mean I know navigation, but I suppose I could find out from ex-captain friends," Antony mused. "We're staying overnight at the nearby Friar and Flagon Coaching Inn on the main road. Could you meet us there as early as possible tomorrow to make the most of the daylight hours?"

"I certainly will. I've been waiting for years for an opportunity like this. Thank you, m'lord. I'm your man," Joao replied enthusiastically.

Antony looked at Joao, large, expansive, swarthy in appearance, always optimistic and cheerful, despite his hard life, having to adapt to life in a foreign country, and admired him. Without rank or title, he felt that he was a better man than he was. He turned to Brandon, "We need to get moving quickly downriver to the watermill to check on Maribel and Eleanor."

Tom Kelly, Eleanor's father's new identity name, came rushing out to see them, concerned and puzzled by Antony appearing with a friend and bandit escort, "I'm so pleased to see you, m'lord. The heat's on here. The watermill was searched again yesterday by a young man and a party of your dragoons. They found a pretty quality lace handkerchief with the initial M sewn on it. They knew it must belong to Maribel. Fortunately, Eleanor saw them coming, took a warm cloak, said she would build a brush shelter and is hiding out not far upstream. They'll catch their death of cold. They can't stay here any longer. The net is closing in."

"All right, I'll look after them both and make other arrangements. I'll keep them safe."

He turned to Brandon. "Follow me upstream. You'll need to lead the horses." Antony led his party through the undergrowth, calling Eleanor's name.

After half an hour, stopping and listening, he heard Eleanor answer, recognising his voice. "We're here!"

In deep undergrowth beneath the stunted forest growing on either side of the stream, he found Eleanor with Maribel wrapped in a dark cloak. They both looked cold and frightened.

"Dadda," Maribel cried, stretching out an arm to Antony. "Don't leave us again." Antony took her in his arms. She was shaking with the cold. He wrapped his riding cloak about her. Holding her in one arm, he put the other out for Eleanor, pulling her to her feet.

"Take Maribel," he said to Brandon, who looked awkward, probably never having held a child in his life.

"Hold up your skirts," he commanded Eleanor, "while I get you on my horse."

He gave her a leg up, then wrapped her cloak about her, after which he took Maribel from Brandon and gave her to Eleanor to hold. "Right, let's get going. It's getting dark. I hope we can find our way in the twilight to the Friar and Flagon."

Once out of the gorge, he mounted up behind Eleanor. His heavily laden horse complained, showing his displeasure by shaking his head about. After half an hour, the moon rose, taking the place of the fading twilight. It was cold. Bad fairies and goblins stalking the shadows were common knowledge. The party was silent, on its guard. Antony heard the two ex-marines cock their blunderbusses. They looked to Antony to find the way. He was not sure. Everything seemed different after nightfall.

Eleanor sensed Antony hesitate. "There's Perkins Rise under the moon," she whispered. "Head for that."

Antony peered into the darkness. On the horizon was a knoll like a hump on a camelback. He gave her a squeeze with his bad arm around her waist in acknowledgement.

"Elves of the dark are coming closer," Maribel announced.

"Our vibes are stronger," Antony reassured her. "They surround us like an invisible shield. Denizens of dark places are kept at bay. They can't hurt us. We'll soon be at the inn."

"They're all around us! I can feel them getting closer. I'm very hungry."

"Plenty of good food will be waiting for us. We'll get you warm and comfy soon. The inn can't be far away." Antony was concerned at her weak, frightened state.

Mounting Perkins Rise, Antony was relieved to see the lights of the Friar and Flagon in the shallow valley below. But for Eleanor, he might never have found it in the dark. The horses sensed they were near stabling and increased their pace. Dogs barked at their approach. The innkeeper hurried out to meet them.

"Make sure there's a good fire in the main bedroom. Get water up for a bath. We'll dine in our room in an hour, my lady, my daughter and I."

"I didn't know Her Ladyship was with you, m'lord," the innkeeper answered in surprise.

"Now you know. We haven't eaten all day. Magistrate Travallyn and our escort either. Get your staff going."

"Yes, m'lord, straight away." The Landlord hurried inside urgently, calling for ostlers who ran out and held their horses' heads while they dismounted stiffly and went inside to be met with warmth and curtsying maids. They were led upstairs.

In the larger upstairs bedroom, maids were scurrying to light the fire and room lights. "All the wall and ceiling lights lit," Antony commanded. "They'll make the room warmer."

A copper bath was brought up, followed by a bevy of maids carrying jugs of hot water, their feet scampering on the stairs. Eleanor put Maribel carefully in the large bed away from the warming pans. "Bathe Maribel first, then wrap her in a bathrobe," Antony said to Eleanor. "Then yourself. The maid will help you." Antony indicated the maid left standing by with towels and a bathing robe. "As soon as I've arranged the guard rota for the night, I'll take a bath."

Eleanor looked at Antony in despair. "I can't be a lady. I don't know how."

"It's just a state of mind. You're educated and speak well. I'll be back soon."

He went downstairs to arrange that three of the escort remain on duty through the night, one outside each room and one downstairs, taking two or three-hour turns. When he came back up, he found Eleanor finishing, looking awkward as she was not used to being waited on. He turned to the maid, "My left arm must be kept dry. It's been injured and has a dressing." The maid curtsied in response.

Antony then took his turn in the bath, Eleanor watching to see his arm was kept dry. When he was in his bathing robe, she looked at his dressing carefully. For the present, there was no way of renewing it. He needed to be careful. While maids scurried up and down, emptying the bath before eventually carrying it off, they both went over to examine Maribel. She was warmer but flushed with shallow hurried breathing. "Ague?" Antony whispered.

"I hope not." Eleanor stroked her brow. "Her humours are not in balance due to having spent the night hiding in the brushwood. It was perishingly cold."

Maribel smiled at them weakly. "Mamma, Dadda." Antony had given up telling her that Eleanor was not her birth mother. To Maribel, Eleanor was her mother. She was so pleased to have them near her, both together.

"Our meal should be up in a short while," he said, smiling at his daughter he had not seen for so long. He turned to the duty maid. "Get the bed warmers renewed and tell the landlord we're ready for our meal."

Before the clock downstairs had struck another quarter-hour, the meal was brought up, the landlord himself carrying roast venison, obviously most pleased to have such a distinguished guest as Antony and his lady. He carefully cut the venison himself, asking Antony if it was to his liking. Eleanor looked awkward, not used to her new role as a lady.

They ate the meal at their leisure, warming up in the heated room. Outside, the wind howled. In the gusts, they could hear the smoke jack rattling away in the kitchen chimney downstairs. It was luxury to be in the warm. On such an occasion, Antony put egalitarian aspirations aside. He was glad of his rank and privilege, glad especially he could share it with those he loved. He went out the door to see if his guard was on the landing. He turned to the duty maid. "When our evening meal is cleared away, wait outside but come in through the night to stoke the fire and keep six candles burning." The maid curtsied in acknowledgement.

When the bed warmers were removed, they joined Maribel beneath the warm sheets, only Antony having night attire to change into. Maribel looked so happy between them, putting an arm out to them both. Antony was concerned how thin and frail her arms were for a girl of her age.

"Bad elves are dancing in the shadow," Maribel said nervously.

"There aren't any bad elves in the room," Antony maintained reassuringly, holding her close. "It's just the candles flickering in the draughts casting moving shadows." He gave her a kiss.

"If you say so, Dadda." Smiling contentedly, Maribel fell asleep.

"I never thought last night our next night would be like this," Eleanor whispered. "I wish it could go on forever, warm and safe."

Antony felt the same but apprehensive. There was much danger ahead. Somehow, he had to keep them safe until he succeeded to his title.

Morning came only too soon. They had to be up, organised and out. Brandon greeted them on the landing. He had slept well and was eager to be off. Antony ordered breakfast in their room. He would eat on the go. He called for the landlord. "I need a light, sprung, two-seater carriage with a driver for one or two days."

"That will be 15 shillings a day, m'lord."

"In it, I want a number of rugs, and it must have a good driver and guard,"

"It will be available in half an hour, m'lord. Henry is a good driver. This is a quality inn for the quality."

When the landlord had gone, Eleanor said she did not need a carriage, only a horse to ride. Antony explained that a lady rode side-saddle, which was awkward, difficult to learn and a difficult way to manage a horse. Maribel needed shelter and care. A carriage it had to be.

Barking dogs announced an arrival. It was Joao Pereira, larger than life, keen and eager, sporting a pair of what he said were Persian pistols, awarded to him as prize money. Antony said he would need a better horse which the landlord arranged. They left as the clock in the hall was striking nine thirty with the aim of getting near Lyme Regis in daylight hours. Brandon was none too pleased a carriage was being hired as he felt it would slow progress. Antony pointed out that half of all children died before reaching adulthood, and he intended to give Maribel every chance of survival. He also reminded Brandon who was funding the expedition.

Eleanor looked awkward as she was handed into the neat, sprung four-wheeled carriage, painted ruby red with gilt around the windows. A high dashboard shielded the driver and guard seated up in front. It was completely closed in with seating for two. Antony handed her Maribel wrapped in a rug. "You'll get used to being a lady," Antony said in a low voice. "I'll be riding nearby. If you want the driver to stop, tap on the window. The rest of the party will stop in the vicinity until you're ready to go on. Keep Maribel warm and comfortable. At Lyme Regis, I will get you more suitable clothes in keeping with your status, good luck." He gave Eleanor a gentle kiss on the cheek in encouragement and shut the door. The second day of their journey had begun.

Chapter Six

The roads, as usual, were a problem, particularly at this time of the year. For the horsemen, it was easier at times to ride into the adjacent fields and heathland, but the coach had to stagger along on the road, Eleanor holding Maribel in her arms for safety. They were rounding a bend, fortunately all on the road quite close together, when six riders approached. Their appearance made Antony uneasy. He could not place them. Not many travelled at this time of year. They did not look like local market traders. Few markets were open. Owning horses came at a cost. Horses had to be fed and stabled. The assorted bunch did not look as if they could afford much. Somebody must be paying for the horses. Something made him look upward at the adjacent hillside. In a small clearing, a sinister mounted figure in a dark cloak was looking down at them.

Coming closer, the riders showed interest in the coach, peering inside. They could see little as the windows were steamed up. Antony led his horse to a stop, pulled out his pistols and cocked them. Henry, the coachman and his guard cocked their blunderbusses, as did their ex-marines, their ex-sailors drawing their cutlasses. The horsemen, noting their defensive stance, slowly rode on, looking back meanly as they did so.

"What was all that about?" Brandon asked.

"Your guess is as good as mine. They're being directed by a sinister figure in a dark riding cloak. Militia have been banned since Oliver Cromwell's time. His employer must be a powerful person," Antony observed. "I've a feeling the horseman in the dark cloak could well be the Barbary pirates' principal agent ashore. I don't think he knows who I am."

"Somebody must be paying them."

"Clearly, but who? Hopefully our investigation will come up with answers." Antony was pleased to put his pistols back in their holsters as his damaged left arm was aching with the weight.

"Leave that!" Brandon snapped to his escort, who were looking back after the departing riders in a challenging manner. Follow at your usual distance. We're moving on."

"Aye, aye, sir," they acknowledged, Joao included, doing promptly what they were told.

"How do you get their respect?" Antony asked admiringly.

"My father was a vicar. Through his calling, he had titled friends. One of them got me a commission in the navy, my father thought it would be a good, steady career but I never got further than sub-lieutenant. One of the things I had to learn was how to control and lead seamen, gain their respect. You had to be fair but very firm. If you couldn't control them, you stood no chance. The escort, by my manner, including Joao, know I've been a naval officer."

"I never knew that. You never told me," Antony said in surprise.

"No, I blotted my copybook, after which I stood little chance of being promoted to a full lieutenant. Now I want to train as a lawyer when I can afford it."

"How come you left the navy?" Antony asked, intrigued.

"Coming up the Channel in the third-rate *Monmouth* from the Azores, the captain overheard a seaman saying to his mates that they were approaching Falmouth whereas he had announced that they would be off Bembridge Point at dawn, Portsmouth by dusk. The seaman was sure they were off Falmouth as he came from Falmouth and had seen before nightfall a skein of migratory geese fly overhead such as he had witnessed at this time of the year since childhood.

"The captain had him severely flogged for offering a contrary opinion, saying he was lucky he did not have him hung from the yardarm. But as dawn rose, they found themselves east of the Lizard with the Manacles reef 200 yards off their larboard bow. It took frantic emergency action to bear away just in time. As they were so near Falmouth, the captain stopped there briefly to take in food and water before proceeding up channel with land in sight.

"After the event, I was unwise enough to observe in confidence to whom I thought was a friend that the captain should apologise to the seaman. My friend seemed to tell others what I said. This eventually got me before the captain. He told me, in no uncertain terms, that if I were not an officer, he would have me flogged as well. As you might expect, I never got further promotion and eventually left the navy. Navy captains apologise to no one."

"I understand determining longitude is very difficult?" Antony queried.

"Yes, it is; latitude is not a problem. It is determined by measuring the sun's angle at noon or by measuring the angle of the North Star from the horizon at twilight. Longitude is the problem. Galileo's method based on observing Jupiter's satellites is usually not possible, owing to a ship's motion. What is needed is an accurate marine chronometer to measure time from a fixed location. Pendulum clocks are useless at sea because of the ship's motion. Not long ago, in 1714, the government offered an award of up to 20,000 pounds, depending on accuracy, for an accurate seagoing timepiece. Up to now, no one's been able to come up with an accurate enough device. There's a fortune waiting there for anyone who can invent an accurate chronometer. Want to try your hand?"

"I wish I could. I could do with a personal fortune," Antony admitted.

"Me too," Brandon agreed with feeling. "Where are we stopping tonight?"

"I hope to reach the Bear and Beagles Hostelry on the Charmouth Road by nightfall. I sent a messenger ahead yesterday warning of our coming. Few coach companies are operating this time of the year. Only the Bear and Beagles has stabling for all our lot."

As anticipated, the innkeeper was delighted to be receiving a full house at this time of year. Business was slack. Antony did not offer his name, but by his companions addressing him as 'm'lord', he appreciated he had the status helpful to his business. He was impressed, too, by Magistrate Travallyn's command of his men. Not all guests had control of their retinue who, when their master got drunk, got drunk in turn and could do damage.

"My lady, daughter and I will have your principal room, Magistrate Travallyn your second, and Sailing

Master Pereira, his own accommodation. My retinue will have dormitory accommodation. They will have lights out by 10. They're to be served no more than three pints of ale per man per evening. Two will remain on guard in turn throughout the night on the landing and one downstairs. They're not to be served drink while on duty."

"Guards won't be necessary through the night, m'lord," the innkeeper replied.

"Those are my terms. See our rooms are warm and well lit, and our mounts are well housed and fed. The coach will be leaving in the morning. The rest will be staying a number of nights. Come up to our room in half an hour with our menu. I appreciate fresh food is difficult at this time of the year but do your best."

"Yes, m'lord." The landlord bowed, hurrying away. This guest meant business. Even if he would not be selling a lot of expensive wine and brandy, at least he would not be paying to repair the mayhem which drunken guests too frequently caused.

The principal room had a warm fire and wall lights lit when they entered. Antony was concerned for Maribel. Eleanor shifted the warming pans to one side and put her between the warm sheets. She was cold and listless but gave them a faint smile. What would he do without her? Maribel was his life. He felt her forehead. It was hot, and her breathing unsteady. "Dadda, Mamma, you'll be with me tonight?"

"We will." He held her hand. She seemed no worse than yesterday.

"I kept her wrapped in rugs all day and held her close to keep her warm," Eleanor said anxiously.

"You did well." He continued to sit on the bed and hold Maribel's hand. The innkeeper knocked and came in to describe what he had for an evening meal, looking at Eleanor curiously.

"I will require seamstresses in the morning who can make ladies' clothes of quality," he said to the landlord.

"I'm a seamstress," Eleanor reminded him.

"You were employed by us to make up table and bed linen. Your role now is to look after Maribel." He looked at Eleanor kindly. Despite his wealth and status, he was a lonely man. He needed someone warm who was wholly on his side, someone he could trust. "And I need you."

"Oh, Antony," Eleanor replied, her brown eyes swimming with tears.

After the evening meal and inspecting the guard, he asked the maid to leave, gently put Maribel on the other side of Eleanor, and cuddled up to her, head in her neck. For him, this was a luxury; real love and care was something money could not buy. He wished the night could go on forever.

At two in the morning, he was woken up by a furore downstairs. The ex-marine had shot at and wounded an intruder who had escaped. Outside, the innkeeper found his dogs drugged, twitching on the ground. This had never happened before, he claimed.

"Good job you had my guards on duty," Antony replied, annoyed to be woken up, wondering if this was something more sinister than a normal break-in. When he came back to bed, Maribel was asleep, but Eleanor was sitting up, distressed.

"I can never be a lady," she said, winding her long brown hair round her fingers. "I don't want my hair cut off and wear a wig."

"I don't want your lovely hair cut off either, but with me, you need clothes becoming your status. In other respects, I don't want you to change, just be your warm, natural caring self. Your father, as a master printer, taught you well. Though you don't know French, you can write and speak English better than most ladies I know. I don't like ladies. They've led pampered lives. They're opinionated and conceited with hidden agendas."

"That's why you fell in love with Maribel's mother."

"She was sweet, loving and, as an under-maid, led a hard life. I know, you could say I've led a pampered and privileged existence, which I once took for granted but do no longer. With you, I've found real happiness."

"Oh, Antony, I will try, but I find it difficult. I feel a fraud."

"You don't have to say much. People could think you're foreign, different. Let the maid prepare your hair in the way you like it and give it a light dusting of powder. In the morning, I've arranged a meeting with Brandon and Joao. Joao is intelligent, brave and able. Most importantly, he knows more about Barbary pirates than anyone as he was captured by them but survived for long enough to be freed by the navy, but then pressed to serve with them. Joao learned to speak English while in the navy. His speech can be colourful at times. I've ordered two seamstresses, experienced in making ladies' clothing to call. I've written a list of what you'll need. I was brought up with two older sisters, had to dress like them when I was a young child. You'll be all right. I'll see to that. I appreciate how you must feel."

"I feel out of my depth."

"Bear up, let me give you a kiss." Antony held her close and snuggled up to her, feeling he needed her more than she did him.

Once again, the morning came too soon. Not having Claude, he had instructed the duty maid on the landing to come in at dawn and rouse him, asking for a washing bowl and a barber. Though claiming he wanted to do more for the less privileged, which he genuinely believed, he instinctively used his inherited privilege and power in the cold light of day.

Outside Brandon's door, he instructed his duty maid to rouse him, saying he would meet him and Joao downstairs in an hour. Downstairs he asked the guard to rouse Joao and inform him he would meet him and Brandon in the inglenook in an hour. He then asked for breakfast, warming himself by the roaring fire, requesting the latest edition of *The Spectator*, since 1714, available in book form three times a week. Opening it, he read an article on Charles the Second and his brother, James the Duke of York's, passion for yacht sailing.

The yacht, apparently, was the invention of the fourteenth century Dutch, who initially used small, fast boats for chasing smugglers, pirates and criminals. Rich ship owners and merchants began using yachts, a Dutch word, to sail out and celebrate the return of their successful merchant vessels. It began to catch on as the fashionable thing to do. To sail such vessels, designed to sail close to the wind enabling them to negotiate winding channels, was challenging and took skill. King Charles, he read, had a number of yachts built for him and studied navigation and boat building, such was his enthusiasm for this new fashionable sport. Other rich noblemen, following the king's example, were acquiring yachts.

His father had never mentioned yacht owning, not being super-rich and having a mobility disability. The idea interested him. His reading was interrupted by Brandon joining him, tousled, sleepy and needing a barber. "I've called for a barber mid-morning; get him to shave you as well." As with Antony, Brandon liked to be clean-shaven. "Use my barber; his services will be part of the bill." Only men of resources could afford a barber or have their beards trimmed by a barber; most had to trim beards or stubble as best they could, often with the help of friends.

"Are you sure?"

"I'm footing the bill."

"Thank you."

This reminded Antony that he asked for seamstresses to make appropriate clothing for Eleanor while away with Antony where she would be escorted. A lady's fine clothes cost more than the ordinary man earned in a year. Ladies had to be escorted, otherwise they would be robbed and injured for their clothes if not left for dead. He made a list. Ladies' clothes were becoming more realistic. Mantuas were out except at court. Sack-back dresses, a la Francaise, were more informal. Antony could not see Eleanor wanting to wear hooped petticoats. She would need a small linen cap and a hat for outdoor wear. However, he knew she would prefer a hood, which would be more practical.

He finally opted for a shift, a blue casaquin dress, the very latest, embroidered with lace at the neck and cuffs, pleated skirts, a waisted darker blue day jacket, a smart double-breasted grey outdoor jacket with long sleeves and mother of pearl buttons, a fetching mid-thigh short gown and dainty blue shoes with plated silver buckles that twinkled like jewels in the sunshine. Nothing outdated or old-fashioned about that lot. He knew she did not like a maid dressing her as she was not used to it. She certainly would not like being laced up tightly at the back.

For Maribel, he ordered two petticoats of the palest shell-pink satin, quilted in small heart shapes, below a band of cream wool pleated into a shell-pink linen waistband, very pretty. Maribel would really like those. He also got her a beige dress with Pelerine, another of ivory-coloured silk and a smaller pink version of a waisted blue day jacket and a warm, double-breasted coat with a hood like her mother's but in violet, all for the next day.

That done, he waited for Joao, who arrived hungry, eager for breakfast. Antony told him to order what he wanted and, while he ate, probed him further for ideas based on his experience.

Joao repeated, in all probability, the galley was hiding up a local estuary or sound not far to the west, waiting by arrangement for a small, fast-sailing merchant ship, likely with large fore and aft triangular sails mounted on long curved yards with fast-sailing ability, particularly to windward. It would be sailing under a foreign flag to bear the captives swiftly to slave ports on the southwest Mediterranean coast. "They would go off if not transported without delay," Joao affirmed.

"What do you mean, go off?" Antony asked.

"You know, get weak and sick, lose value," was Joao's simple answer in his strange lilting English. "They forage ashore for food and water for crew and rowers, but slaves are different. They are very unhappy, soon get sick.

They're sold on to traders. The English do the same, buy blacks from traders in West Africa, then sail them to the Southern States or West Indies as fast as possible."

"Blacks are different," Antony observed. When he related this conversation to Eleanor later in the evening, she did not agree.

"We're all human," she said, "and feel the same pain. All slaves should be freed." Something Antony had not considered and realised he was not as humane and radical as he thought he was.

"So, we need to act quickly then," Brandon interjected, "how?"

"To find them, we'll need a fast sloop that can sail well to windward like a Bristol pilot with a long-luff mainsail which would catch the wind up an estuary. One that me and my boys can sail," Joao answered simply. "Lieutenant Travallyn knows how to navigate. The galley can't be far away."

"Ex!" Brandon muttered.

"When we find it, he can lead a boarding party of your dragoons. A platoon will be more than enough depending on the size of your platoons. More would get in each other's way. I'll be with the lieutenant to show him the galley's layout."

"Boarding?" Antony queried. "We've dragoons, not marines?"

Joao grinned broadly, broken teeth, black, unkempt beard and large size giving him a formidable appearance. Fingering his cocked hat, he explained that, in all probability, the galley would be hidden up a nearby estuary. They would need to purchase a suitable craft without delay to find the seized captives. Only day sailing would be possible. At night they must take shelter.

Antony and Brandon considered the plan. "What do you think, Brandon? You've probably taken part in boarding operations. I've no seagoing experience. Is the plan feasible?" Antony asked.

"On the face of it, yes. We can but rely on Joao on the way Barbary pirates operate these days. Only he has that experience."

"Right, let's go down to the Cobb as soon as we've finished breakfast. There appear to be lots of small craft lying idle at the moment, owing to declining markets. You can take two sailors if you like, but I'd like the rest left behind to provide security for Maribel and Eleanor," Antony decided. There was no time to hang around.

Down on the Cobb, within the shelter of the sea wall, they looked for and found the harbour master who pointed out an ex-mercantile sloop, converted into a rich man's yacht, impounded by court order, whose creditors could be found up at the Seal and Anchor. Despairing of ever getting a buyer, the creditors seized on Antony's offer to buy the vessel for 200 guineas. A fore and aft rigged sloop was just what they were looking for. He had no idea the worth of the vessel, but that was all he felt he could offer. To his surprise and relief, the money was eagerly accepted. How it was to be proportioned was up to the creditors. He went into a side room with Joao and the two seamen who watched him count out the guineas before it was handed over in exchange for a Commissioner of Custom's registration certificate.

Leaving Brandon, Joao and the sailors to examine the rigging of *Spray Sprite*, Antony went back to the Bear and Beagles. He ordered lunch in their room. His wound still made him tired. Eleanor said she would look at it after lunch. Antony outlined the clothes he had ordered for them. He said that before their evening meal, he had arranged a bath. He liked bathing and the feeling of being clean. He said he would like Maribel bathed. It was up to Eleanor whether she took a bath with her. After that, he would like them to try on the clothes he had bought, which had just arrived.

Eleanor said she knew Maribel would be enchanted by lovely new clothes, but she was not so sure. There would come the time when she would have to relinquish fine clothes until she could come back to the castle when Antony had succeeded to his title. In the meantime, she felt uneasy, jumped-up, an imposter in her temporary role as a lady, something Antony had not thought of. A down-to-earth, honest human being like Eleanor could not be manipulated in this manner. She was not a doll to be dressed up but a sensitive human being. Antony, considering himself something of an enlightened philosopher, nevertheless had much to learn about human nature.

The new clothes arrived not long after Eleanor had bathed Maribel and reluctantly bathed herself so as not to waste money, she explained. As a bath cost a shilling. Antony felt that was one way of looking at it.

As predicted, Maribel tried on all her new grand clothes, asking Eleanor to turn her around so she could view them from every angle in the mirror. Then she pleaded with Eleanor to try on hers. With considerable reluctance, Eleanor was persuaded by Maribel to try on the shift, then the stylish blue casaquin dress with the lace at the throat and ends of the sleeves. With her trim figure and upright bearing, she did look distinguished.

"A lovely lady, my mamma's a lovely lady!" Maribel cried. Her delight was so real that Eleanor turned about to show it off for Maribel. Finally, she tried on the dark blue waisted day jacket. Maribel bounced about in her chair, chanting, "Mamma's a lovely lady! Mamma's a lovely lady!" At that point, there was a knock and the landlord entered with maids carrying their evening meal. He was obviously much impressed with Eleanor's appearance and smiled broadly.

"M'lady looks very charming this evening," the landlord said, turning to Antony. "Shall I expect you in late?"

"Not tonight, thank you," Antony replied briefly, hoping Eleanor was taking note of the compliment.

To Antony's relief, Eleanor remained in her fine clothes, eating their evening meal, taking great care not to spill any food on her clothes, and seeing Maribel did likewise. It was only later in the evening when food and bathwater had been removed, that Eleanor took off her fine clothes and prepared for bed in her shift.

Later, as they snuggled up in bed, Antony whispered to Eleanor, "You did look adorable in your new clothes."

"I put them on for Maribel and you. Thank you for buying them for me. They must have cost a lot."

"No more than you deserve. Thank you for putting them on for us." Antony held Eleanor close to him. He did enjoy cuddling her. She smelt lovely with the perfume he had given her along with the clothes. Maribel had put on so much perfume that Antony felt she must be smelt from downstairs. It was such a refreshing change for Antony, being away from the castle with people about him genuinely on his side, people he could trust. Particularly he had grown fond of Eleanor in a way he had with no one else since Maribel's mother died. He hoped she felt the same way about him but was not so sure. He felt the difference in their status stood in the way, something neither could help, but Antony hoped could be overcome.

Once again, dawn came only too quickly. If they were to free the captives, they would have to act quickly. Now a suitable craft was found, they needed to get seeking without delay. Antony suggested that an additional bodyguard be hired to ensure the security of Maribel and Eleanor at the inn, but Maribel protested, she did not want to leave her father again, and Eleanor said she only trusted their present motley lot who were needed to crew the sloop.

Brandon, the most senior among them with sailing experience, looking at Antony for approval, said that Eleanor and Maribel could accompany them if that was their wish but life at sea, especially in winter, was cold, wet and hard. They could only light a brazier for warmth and a cooking stove at night when anchored up a shelter creek or estuary. A naked flame while underway in a wooden boat was far too dangerous. Antony turned to Eleanor. "Do you understand what you're taking on? Your role would be to look after Maribel."

Both Eleanor and Maribel chorused, "We don't want to be left behind!"

"And dangerous," Antony added.

"We don't want to be left behind!" the girls repeated.

"Very well then," Antony agreed, "as long as our captain is content." If Brandon had private reservations, he did not say.

They prepared to leave the inn. It was important to stay in a coaching inn or hostelry for the horse catering facilities. Horses, necessary for transport, were an expensive commodity. To be of use, they had to be well fed and looked after. If they became ill or weak, they needed to be replaced. Hostelries, along with roads, comprised England's transport infrastructure. They would need their horses in good condition for their eventual return, a costly expedition component for Antony to manage.

The seagoing members of their party were already aboard their mercantile sloop, *Spray Sprite*. Moored out in the sheltered harbour, they had taken in the stern kedge anchor and had raised the mainsail, seeing how the gunter spar enabled the sail to be pulled almost vertical to increase the length of the luff, enabling the vessel to be sailed fast and high pointing, experimenting with the two control lines. High pointing was something Antony did not understand but was told was most important, in fact, essential for what they wanted and needed. Eleanor carried Maribel down to the ship's boat and, along with Antony, were rowed out to their new home.

As soon as Lieutenant Commander Travallyn, advised by Sailing Master Pereira, were satisfied they had got the hang of the rig, they signalled to the harbour master for clearance, got towed out and set sail westward, assisted by a moderate south-east breeze. It was cold out on the water. *Spray Sprite*, logging six knots on the larboard tack, rising and falling in a moderate seaway, made good progress. Every so often, a burst of spray whipped across the deck. Antony, Eleanor and Maribel were assigned the former owner's cabin in the overhanging stern with its range of aft windows. Brandon assigned himself the captain's, and Joao he assigned the mate's. After half an hour, Brandon popped in to demonstrate how to rig a lee cloth to stop Maribel being thrown out of her bunk.

"What's all this about it being important that *Spray Sprite* points high?" Antony asked.

"Being able to sail close to the apparent wind means we can escape pursuers by sailing to windward to a greater degree than they can. It's also useful sailing up winding estuaries, the tall rig being able to catch the wind," Brandon replied.

"Apparent wind?"

"A fast-sailing vessel will make its own wind to some extent. We've got to get used to the vessel. We've only got enough crew for one watch with our present numbers. At our rate of sail and a favourable tide, we hope to reach the Axe Estuary by nightfall and anchor in shelter a mile upstream. In the calm water, we'll be able to light a brazier in your cabin and cook a hot meal in the galley."

"Can I lend a hand? I don't like just being a passenger?" Antony asked.

"We'll be altering course in half an hour, after which we shouldn't be catching as much spray. You can come up on deck, but you'll need to be taught how to climb the rigging."

When Antony sensed a change of course, he wrapped up warmly and went on deck. A weak sun was setting in the west under a reddening sky. Joao was up in the rigging, instructing his crew regarding its workings."

"You've set that staysail sheet too loose again, Will," Antony heard Joao call, "Do it again and I'll have your balls for—"

"Mind your language!" Antony heard Brandon sharply reprimand. "There're ladies aboard."

Antony realised Joao was parroting language he had picked up but did not understand how offensive it was.

"Your mother wouldn't like such language!" he called loudly up into the rigging in the wind.

"Querida Mae wouldn't like it?" Joao called back.

"She would find it very offensive. Don't use it," Antony called, his voice sounding eerily distorted. As Antony anticipated, Joao's mother was an important figure in his life."

"Aye aye, sir," he replied obediently, moving quickly for a big man in the heeling rigging to show Will what he was meant to do on this heading.

Back in the cabin, Eleanor beckoned Antony over to Maribel, who was lying in her bunk, kept safe by the piece of canvas tied tightly across the outer sides. Antony noticed Eleanor had on her new dress and day jacket as it was warmer than her threadbare peasant's clothes, despite her reservations about wearing lady's clothing.

"Raise your right leg," she commanded Maribel. With a great effort, Maribel managed to raise her right leg off the canvas by 18 inches. She put her hand against her foot. "Now push like you with would one of your arms." With an even greater effort, Maribel appeared to exert some pressure against Eleanor's hand. "Now, do the same against your father's hand." Antony noticed Maribel was wearing her new clothes, which she had no problem with. To Antony's delight and amazement, he felt a slight movement in her deformed leg.

"I've been trying for the last six months to get her strong enough to stand and perhaps even walk with crutches."

"That's wonderful news!" Antony threw his arms around Eleanor and gave her a big hug, then bent down and kissed Maribel. "You've kept this secret. One of our seamen, Will Worthington, is an excellent craftsman.

I'll get him to make arm crutches for her; see how she goes!"

At that point, the ship heeled further to starboard, turning to a northerly heading. Going out on deck, Antony saw Jack and Danny struggling with the wheel, the ship mounting short sharp seas, a seaman in the bow calling the depth as he swung the lead. "Keep swinging continuously, Bill!" he heard Brandon call. "We can only enter on the high tide!" Brandon turned to the helmsmen. "The narrow entrance is beneath Haven Cliff, a degree to starboard. There's a shingle bank to the west marked by withies and a pier of sorts to the east. The shingle bar is constantly changing!" Antony realised this was a tense moment.

"All sheets tight!" Joao called from aloft, his voice trailing off in the wind. "Close-hauled as we go!"

Spray Sprite heeled further in response. In the gathering dusk, Antony observed they were entering a river estuary. After being thrown violently up and down, Antony holding on to a belaying pin tightly for support, the ship turned back onto a westerly heading, and all was calm. Looking about, Antony saw they were in a narrow channel between great chunks of jumbled ice.

"Let go the anchor, the holding's good. As she falls back row out the kedge. The ebb and flow at peak runs at five knots or more. There's no room to swing, especially with these great chunks of ice extending out from the shore. The channel is only kept open by the fast tide, the rise and fall breaking up the ice into great chunks!" Brandon called to the watch.

"It looks as if we're in a glacier!" he said to Eleanor when he went back into their cabin.

"What's a glacier?"

"A river of jumbled ice," Maribel answered.

"How does she know?"

"As she can't get about, she's always reading, and she's clever," Antony answered for Maribel. "When she lived at the castle, I saw she had plenty of books. She's picked up Latin and Greek."

"Better than a lady?"

"Much better, they only know a little French, embroidery and how to play the harpsichord or these new-fangled pianofortes and perhaps sing. If she were a boy, Maribel could hold her own at a university."

"There are people cleverer than ladies?" Eleanor asked.

"Much; you are if you only knew it. Being clever has nothing to do with education. Education is learning. Maribel is self-educated and clever as well."

"You only say that to make me feel good."

"It's true, isn't it, Maribel, darling?"

"Mamma's smart," Maribel answered simply.

"Maribel must have got her brains from her father."

"Not from me. I had a tutor but struggled to learn."

"But her mother was a maid?"

At that moment, a marine came in with a brazier. "Captain says you can have a brazier now. I'll bring in a hot meal as soon as we get the galley going."

"Thank you, Jack. Give the captain my compliments. Tell him he did well to get us over the bar and in here."

When the marine left, Eleanor gave Antony a hug. She said no more. Antony was born a lord and, though claiming he wanted to help and understand the less privileged, was used to command, warmth and comfort. Now she was exposed to his lifestyle, she had to admit to herself that she appreciated a warm cabin and meal to follow, especially during these exceptionally cold winters of recent years. Her kiss and hug said what words could not convey, which pleased Antony, who needed her more than he knew.

"Shouldn't we be inviting some of the others in here in the warm?" Eleanor said."

"There's not many of us, only one watch. I expect they're gathered around the galley fire waiting for their meal."

"What's a watch?"

"Enough crew to man the vessel for six or eight hours at a time. If we were going on a voyage, we would need enough crew for three watches with one member capable of being in charge, a watch leader."

They had got themselves warm at last around the glowing brazier when there was a knock, and a marine came in with a large platter on which there was a sizeable baked cod with fried vegetables and potatoes seasoned with chopped thyme, wild garlic and scurvy grass. "The cod's just been caught," the marine announced. "There's a jar of ale."

"Smells delicious!" Eleanor exclaimed.

"Danny's a good cook for a seaman."

"Worth his weight in gold," Antony agreed. "Tell him his efforts are much appreciated."

"Very good, m'lord." The crew member saluted and went out, dressed more like a pirate than a crisp ex-marine.

Chapter Seven

Antony woke in the morning refreshed, the gentle movement of *Spray Sprite* responding to eddies in the tide through the night he found lulling. He was vaguely aware of the anchor watch coming in every hour to check the brazier. Maribel did not call for them from her single bunk, though Eleanor was restless at times in their double bunk, muttering in her sleep that she had not the experience to be a lady. Antony's response was to give her a hug and a gentle kiss.

The first thing Eleanor did when she woke up was to go over and check on Maribel, who was still asleep. "I don't think we'd have survived the night without the brazier. It looks so cold out there," she said, looking out the frosted stern windows. "What's going to happen today?"

"I think the idea is to check the estuary for a Barbary galley."

"In the sloop?"

"More likely the ship's boat. I can't see *Spray Sprite* tacking in this narrow channel."

"Why's the ice in big chunks?"

"I think it's due to the rising and falling of the tide breaking the freezing surface water into great jumbled slabs." Antony noticed that Eleanor had gone to bed in much of her fine clothes for warmth. "I'll find out before long."

"I don't know how poor people can survive these winters if they can't afford fires."

"Neither do I," Antony agreed, taking for granted no longer his privileged position in society.

They had just finished dressing when there was a knock on the door and seaman Jock McKiver entered carrying a wooden bowl of gruel and three wooden spoons. "We can't get ashore because of the ice, and Captain says there'd be no food for us anyhow at this time of the year."

"Thank you, Jock, that will be fine."

The gruel, steaming hot, looked as if it was made of last evening's leftovers, supplemented by oats and nuts and smelt of wild garlic.

"I bet you haven't had many such meals?" Eleanor remarked.

"Not many," Antony admitted. "Tastes not bad, though." He carried Maribel over and put her on his knee so she could dip into the gruel.

"Is there anything else to drink?" Maribel asked. "I don't like ale or beer."

Antony gave Maribel to Eleanor. "There's probably tea for our cabin, as long as the water's well boiled to make it safe to drink. We couldn't get spring water before we left. I'll go out and see."

When Antony returned, he said, "A pot of tea will be brought in directly. Brandon, Joao and three seamen will be rowing in the ship's boat north upriver on the flowing tide for a couple of miles. After that, the river wouldn't be navigable further for a galley. If a Barbary galley is not there, we'll need to sail west to check out the next possible place it could hide in. I'm to be left in charge here today. I've got a seaman to advise me and two ex-marines to stand guard."

"Goodie, Dadda will be with us all day." Maribel was delighted.

"I'll show your father later how you can stand," Eleanor said as she moved about tidying the cabin, hesitating as the sloop jerked at its anchors in the tidal eddies.

Antony enjoyed his day, a new experience for him. He greatly enjoyed the time with Maribel and Eleanor, at the same time appreciating being surrounded by loyal people he could trust. He was shown how, by bracing her legs, Maribel could stand with support and take a hesitant step.

Every hour the fire watch duty, Seaman Bill, checked the brazier. The watch marines Antony arranged to climb the rigging hour by hour in turn to obtain a wider view while he took bearings hourly as he was shown to record any anchor drag.

At midday, as far as they could judge by the height of the sun, Eleanor went down to the galley to see what she could devise for all left onboard. She reheated the gruel swinging in a pot, adding angelica and a little camomile to make for a change of taste. As they dipped in turn into their bowl, Antony noticed with concern from their stern cabin windows mist stealing across the water.

He went out on deck. The mist, in his mind, had a sinister quality like an evil shroud descending on the estuary. "Walk right round the deck, Mathew, so you can take in everything. Flotsam not moving much means we're low tide. The boat party should return before dusk on the ebb," Antony said to the ex-marine on watch. He observed for himself for a while, turning the hourglass before returning to their stern cabin.

"I don't like the look of it out there," Eleanor said with a shiver when Antony returned. "I hope the boat party will be back soon."

"They'll return with the ebb. Brandon said they have to work with the tide. They can't row against it. I waited on deck until the hourglass needed turning. I can't remember how Brandon said the bell code went. I don't think he wants ship's bells anyway when we're not sailing. They advertise our presence."

It was near sunset when they felt a bump alongside and a call for lines and a rope ladder. Rope squealing in blocks could then be heard, along with groaning davits. Finally, there was a great thump on deck. "I think we can take it that the ship's boat has been retrieved. Brandon doesn't want it grinding alongside all night," Antony announced.

Not long after, there was a brief knock on the cabin door and Brandon and Joao burst in excited. "We've found them, not much more than a mile upstream, a few hundred yards above the wide drying section, under a bluff on a starboard bend! The bluff is steep, almost a cliff with a few stunted trees in places. The captives are on board. We could tell by the smell that a lot of people were confined in very close proximity, also we heard the occasional faint cry in English for water. We weren't seen in the mist." Brandon was over the moon with the discovery.

"How awful for the captives!" Eleanor exclaimed.

"But we can rescue them!" Brandon turned to address Antony. "Your coastguard company of dragoons is in winter lines somewhere near Beer Head."

"There's a watchtower on the head. The galley should have been spotted going upriver – if the tower was manned as it should have been!" Antony replied ruefully. "Since regular private raised troops can't be kept in town garrisons, it's been a problem maintaining our coast guard company operational in tented lines during these increasingly cold winters."

"Why can't they be in garrisons?" Eleanor asked.

"Since the Restoration, Parliament has been concerned that the king can't call on regiments raised by noblemen to overthrow parliamentary government and exert military control, as this is what really Cromwell did. Now, much of the New Model Army, other than the Lord General's Regiment of Foot Guards, has been disbanded, and privately raised forces have to be kept in temporary accommodation when not fighting for the Crown in overseas wars. I'll see the captain of our coast guard company about a capable platoon."

"The captives have to be rescued," Eleanor insisted.

"I agree." Antony turned to Brandon. "Can you get me and the two marines onto the Beer shore in the morning?"

"We'll do that if you can scramble over the ice." Antony was not going to have a repetition of his leisurely day in the warm.

"I'll give you marine netting, otherwise you'll fall in between the chunks. They turn if you put weight on them. We've been ashore and got some bread and wine. We had to pay a lot as the locals are short of food," Brandon explained.

"Our watchtower is on Beer Head, a couple of miles to the south-west. I want to check that it's manned. Our guard company is in winter lines in a sheltered valley a couple of miles to the north-west. I'll be going there to interview Captain Harper. Unless we can hire horses, it'll be foot-slogging."

"Can I come with you, Dadda?" Maribel called.

"I'm afraid not. We won't be able to hire a carriage, and I expect there'll be only rough tracks. I'll be back as soon as I can."

That evening the wind rose, howling through the rigging, the sloop surging at its anchors. Now and then, clumps of dislodged ice, like mini-icebergs, knocked against the hull, sounding as if the sloop had been hit by cannon fire. Fire watch extinguished their brazier just in case. Maribel did not want to stay in her bunk and came in with them, which was rather a squash. But Antony enjoyed their presence. It was nice being close to those he really loved. In the morning, the wind had abated enough for the brazier to be relit in time for their getting up.

"I wouldn't have liked to be sailing in open waters in a gale like that," Eleanor observed with a shiver.

"Me either," Antony agreed.

For breakfast, as well as the usual gruel, there was fresh bread and local wine. Antony went down to the galley to see about tea, as wine was not suitable for Maribel. The cooking fire, which had been relit, was contained in a sheet iron galley stove, resting on an open-topped sandbox capped with bricks. The stove consisted of a hot water tank, two ovens with heating surfaces for pans and kettles surrounded by iron pipe railings, with an iron and copper stove pipe equipped with a damper.

It was a complicated device, and, without a specialist cook among their small crew, no one knew how to use it properly, though Danny did his best. What everyone did know, however, was that it was potentially dangerous, the fire being carefully put out before the sloop got underway. Antony made sure the water was boiling hot before making honey-sweetened tea in a pot. Life was difficult enough on board without getting an upset tummy. He took the tea carefully back up to their cabin, putting the pot on a large pewter plate.

"I've got to be off soon," Antony observed.

"Wrap up warmly, take some bread and wine with you." Eleanor got out his linen knapsack with leather strap and brass buckle.

"Do you have to go, Dadda?" Maribel put her arms out. Antony went over to her, giving her a kiss and hug.

"I'm afraid so. I'll be all right. I have Tom Tedworth and Mathew Bates with me with their blunderbusses. We're not going far, eight to ten miles at the most. We'll need to be back by dusk as we wouldn't know where we were in the dark."

Antony was not as confident as he sounded. He said he wanted to know how the rest lived and was finding out. He did not have Claude at his elbow to bring him all he wanted. There was not enough food on board for gentlemen officers like Brandon and himself to have anything different from the rest, something idealists of the civil war who wanted to change society would have approved of.

"There are bad elves and goblins in the forest at night," Maribel warned.

"You have been out of the servants' hall for long enough to know all that talk is not true. They're ignorant and superstitious. You are educated. You know the teachings of the Greek philosophers. They formulated facts."

"I know. I just get worried at times, especially in the dark."

Antony went over and picked up his daughter. Since she could remember, the conflicting uncertainties of her life would make anyone anxious. "In English folklore, there are benevolent goblins as well, but folklore is not proven facts. I'll be back before dark. If I weren't, I'd get lost; that's a fact." He turned to Eleanor, "Keep her close to you. Don't let her be on her own."

Eleanor took Maribel in her arms. "I will. God protect you, Antony." She wiped away a tear. They were all dependent on Antony. She, like Maribel, did not like to see him go.

Out on deck, Tom and Mathew were waiting for him. As usual this winter, it was perishingly cold. The ship's boat was lowered, waiting for him, with Bill and Jack at the oars. "We've only got marine netting, not scramble nets, the sloop being mercantile," Jack puffed as the rowers pulled strenuously, crabbing across the tide for a jetty on the west shore. "The last 10 feet is among the ice. We'll see if we can bridge the gap with the nets."

Very expertly, they did, hooking the far end on a cleat. "When you get ashore, secure the far end of the netting firmly on the jetty. Good luck, m'lord," Jack called.

Making sure everything on them was secure, Anthony, Tom and Mathew scrambled ashore. But for the netting, they would have fallen in, as they could feel the ice blocks churning and tumbling under their weight. Antony smiled to himself. Six months ago, he would never have thought he would be taking advice from an ordinary seaman. He had come a long way since then. Here they were all part of an expedition, dependent on each other's skills, loyalty and courage, irrespective of status. It was an eye-opener for Antony.

From where they were, they could see the watchtower on Beer Head but not whether it was manned. Ruefully, Antony realised he should have taken an eyeglass. With no prospect of hiring horses, they had to scramble up nearer, puffing and panting, none of them used to walking, until they were near enough to see clearly that it was unmanned. What Antony had remembered to take was a hand-held dry card compass and a marine chart, as they now had to find Captain Harper's winter camp to the north-west. Antony vaguely remembered the word Holyford but could not remember if it was in connection with the camp. He thought they would walk about what he felt were two miles to the north-west and make inquiries. After a short rest and a ration of wine and bread, they started off.

At the conclusion of what Antony considered must have been about two miles, they came across a small hamlet of four or five houses but at the sight of what must have looked like a strange gentleman accompanied by two brigands, everyone fled inside and shut their doors.

There was no prospect of getting directions here. In the end, they found the camp themselves. Scrambling up a ridge, they spotted it in a narrow valley about half a mile away to the north. Getting closer, they were observed, and the guard was turned out to meet them. "m'lord?" the corporal of the guard said in surprise when he recognised Antony. "I'll take you to Captain Harper. Come this way."

Within the perimeter, consisting of a wooden stockade with a fire step, the lines of tents were covered by substantial flies that almost reached the ground. Inside, Antony observed canvas floors and lit braziers.

Captain Harper's command tent even had carpets. Clearly it was not a light campaign set-up.

"Former marines Mathew Bates and Tom Tedworth, my escort," Antony explained to Captain Harper, who was eyeing suspiciously his ruffian escort who, to their credit, sprang to attention, clicking their heels.

"At your service, sir!"

"All right, you're dismissed. I'm sure you'll be shown where to wait and be given some rations while I speak with Captain Harper."

Surprised why he was being visited by the son of the marquis, Captain Harper invited Antony into his operations room, where he was invited to sit down in a campaign chair. Scones, tea and wine were called for. Antony looked about curiously at items like a powerful telescope on a stand, an assortment of coastal maps, trophy swords and campaign equipment like trestle boards to keep track of troop movement and gun positions of engaged forces in combat situations.

Captain Harper was curious and apprehensive about why he was being visited by the son of the owner, a self-styled colonel. "You may have heard," Antony said as he settled down with tea and scones, "of the 27 young people snatched by Barbary pirates from the village of Limbeley on the way to Shertonham nearby on Christmas Eve not far from the castle. What is particularly concerning is that the pirates had very precise knowledge regarding where these young people would be at that time, unescorted and vulnerable."

"I've heard rumours but not about the pirates having precise knowledge. I thought the pirates were lucky or the young people very unlucky, whatever way you look at it."

Antony frowned. He told Captain Harper all the details of how, when he went out to the village to give his condolences and offer support, he was booed. He went on to say how his father was most concerned regarding the hostility of his estate people and his unpopularity, how his father could have offered his dragoon companies to the government at profit to fight in foreign wars, but in the end had kept them home at his own expense to guard the coastline in the area of his estate for which purpose he had raised them in the first instance.

He thought the captain blanched at the prospect of being involved in bloody foreign wars. Antony added that he had spent his personal savings trying to discover how the pirates were getting their information and searching for the captives by buying a mercantile sloop, sailing it with a minimum crew and, in the end, finding the pirates and captives less than two miles away from Captain Harper's winter camp. He went on to say that, this morning, he had found the watchtower on Beerhead overlooking the Axe Estuary unmanned, not far away from where the pirates had made their snatch, obviously waiting for a runner to say that a fast ship under a foreign flag was waiting offshore to bear the captives away to the Barbary Coast for sale. At that point, Captain Harper asked if he could be excused for a minute to go out and order today's watch section to be put under guard when they returned at dusk.

When Captain Harper came back, looking very concerned, Antony said that, as the signs were a gale was imminent to mask the sound of their approach, he wanted a platoon of his men, or perhaps a few more depending on the size of his platoons, about 30 would be ideal, in a couple of days' time, to mount a rescue operation by boarding the hidden galley early evening after dark. They would be led by former naval Lieutenant Travallyn and former naval Sailing Master Pereira, who had been at one time a captive slave rower who knew the layout of galleys and the way they were operated.

Captain Harper would be guided and supported by these officers, plus by two former marines, who would be the first on deck, as they had naval experience of boarding. The idea was that they would be on the deck of the galley in numbers before the galley officers and crew were aware of their presence, and overwhelm them with minimum casualties and risk to the captives.

Captain Harper looked alarmed. He would have to have an order in writing from the marquis. His orders were to keep his men in a good state through these exceptionally cold winters, as they had lost enough expensively trained men providing escort for the wedding party through exposure and winter rhumes caught at Exeter. He said his men were dragoons, not marines.

Antony countered by pointing out it would take days to get back to the castle and return with a written order from his father. By that time, the captives would have been whisked away, and when his father learnt later that, when he had the opportunity to rescue the captives and restore his father's reputation, he had not the initiative to do so, his father would be most displeased. He said marine nets would be fixed to the steep slope above for the boarding party to climb down on, the gale disguising the noise of any dislodged rocks and stones. He wanted his most fit and intelligent platoon; there would be no time for rehearsals, but it would be explained to them in advance how the operation was going to be mounted but not where and when.

Their horses could be used to help transport the captives back to their village. Baggage train wagons could also be helpful. Outriders would be needed to inquire the way ahead as the captives would not know how to get to their village. Once freed, the former captives would be his responsibility. Lieutenant Travallyn, Sailing Master Pereira and his navy trained escort would be required to sail their minimum-manned unarmed mercantile sloop back to Lyme Regis.

"Two days from now. Be in place by dusk. Here's a chart of the galley's exact location, less than two miles away." Antony handed Captain Harper his well-thumbed chart. "Don't breathe a word to anyone about our plans. Some locals might be selling them food and could give the game away."

"No one would do that."

"Some people would sell their grandmothers, including people in high places." Captain Harper looked appalled. "Do a good job, and I could overlook the fact that I found the watchtower unmanned this morning."

"Very good, m'lord. The watch detail will be arrested on their return."

Antony felt that Captain Harper was an honest family man without imagination. He stood up to go, Captain Harper solicitously seeing him out, offering food and drink to support them on their way, a worried frown on his face.

"Good luck, we must be back by dusk, or we'll lose our way in the dark. Rendezvous at the top of the embankment above the galley. Our party will be coming upriver on the tide by ship's boat." With that, Antony left, accompanied by his escort, in failing light.

It was dusk when Antony signalled the sloop from the end of the jetty. It was a good job some people could keep a proper watch as he felt in no mood to hang about. Eleanor with Maribel were waiting for them on deck. He kissed them both, then gratefully went below, appreciating the lit brazier and a warm drink.

"It's lovely to see you back, Dadda," Maribel said, putting out her arms.

"It is indeed," Eleanor agreed, coming up to him and putting an arm about his waist to bring Maribel close to her father.

Antony's bad mood, brought on by the cold and the worries of the day, fell away. Here, tonight, he would find happiness. Though a privileged lord, he was deprived, deprived of real love and affection. Here the people about him were unreservedly on his side. What more could he want in life?

He was also learning every day what life in England was like for the great majority. His father prided himself on having an excellent table with the best food money could buy, including expensive coffee and tea and wonderful ornamental confectionery made possible by costly imported sugar and spices. Now he was looking forward to Seaman Danny's concoction. Anchor watch had caught some flounder, the main ingredient of this evening's gruel supper, the only food available for all ranks, not quite the five-course meal Antony had been used to for much of his life but which he ate hungrily like the rest.

After his meal, sitting with Maribel on his lap, he began to have doubts about the rescue mission he had set up with Captain Harper. Though his father had insisted he had some training as a dragoon lieutenant, he was an armchair warrior. He had no experience of active service. He was like an admiral who had never been to sea. The first thing he must do was to call Brandon in and tell him what he had planned.

To his relief, Brandon thought the plan was fine. He was right not to get too many men involved. Of course, he, Joao and their two ex-marines would lead the assault, taking Captain Harper with them. Antony was right; surprise was the essential element. If Antony could stay on the cliff top and direct five dragoons down at a time, they would not get in each other's way. Fifteen men in all could be enough. The rest could be employed helping the captives to safety up the cliff. If Antony could see to that side of the operation, he would be playing an essential role.

Dragoons were trained to respond to snare drum commands, but a drum could be not brought down the steep slope and would not be heard in wild weather anyway. Instead, it was agreed that a rocket would be fired to signal cease sending men down, and a second rocket that freed captives were coming up. Much relieved, Antony turned to Eleanor and Maribel, looking forward to spending the evening with those he loved.

Though the hours of darkness were more than those in the light at this time of the year, the night went only too quickly for Antony. The gentle movement of the sloop in the sheltered estuary was lulling, flickering light from the warm brazier enhancing the quality cabin woodwork. Though responsive, enjoying his closeness, Eleanor was sleepy. Antony tried to keep awake, savouring the moment, but after a strenuous day, he too soon fell asleep.

Next morning, in the cold light of day, his doubts returned.

The day was going to be used setting up for tomorrow night's operation. All equipment had to be checked out and assembled. Pistols, not used for a long time, needed cleaning and testing. Nets, ropes and torches had to be got ready, all to be taken upriver by ship's boat on the tide the following day. Antony had a gentleman's training on the use of the cutlass and rapier but decided he would not take a cutlass as he would probably trip over it, and he would not be boarding himself anyway. Instead, he would carefully clean and reprime his pair of pistols.

"What are you doing, Dadda?" Maribel asked.

"I'm going to clean and reprime my pistols. You can help me clean one, but I'd better reprime them on deck with the brazier lit here in the cabin," Antony replied. He lifted her down beside him and gave her a cloth.

"You look worried, Dadda?" Maribel remarked. She was always observant.

Antony tried to smile. "I guess it's about my plan."

"Brandon said it was a good plan," Eleanor reassured him, coming over and joining them on the form which was firmly secured to the floor. Nothing could be left loose on a ship.

"It's not the plan; it's my role in it. I know I'm used to civilian command, but I've never been involved in combat like the others. I don't want to lose my nerve when the time comes. I feel a bit of a fraud."

"That's what I said to you when you said you wanted me to dress and be your lady while we were away together."

"And what did I say?" Antony tried to think back.

"You said I was educated and as good as any lady. It was just a state of mind. I say to you that you've had military training and are as good as any officer. It's just a state of mind."

"If you think so."

"Dadda's brave," Maribel put in.

"Of course, he is. He'll be fine." Eleanor put her arm around Antony's waist and gave him a kiss. Antony felt like a child going out in the world, supported by his mother's kiss, only he never had a person he could think of as a mother.

"We'll finish cleaning and oiling the mechanism of these pistols, then we'd better go out on deck to prime them. You can't be too careful. Brandon said that those bringing powder up for the guns on rated warships have to wear soft slippers."

"We have no guns," Eleanor observed.

"We are mercantile only. Brandon says heavy guns slow a vessel up and cause it to be lower in the water and less stable. Our sloop was chosen to sail up shallow estuaries and sail fast, especially to windward."

"And does it?"

"It appears so. Like you, I've got no sailing experience. Let's collect up what we need, go up on deck, and prime the pistols. I better give myself some firing practice."

"Can I have a shot?" Maribel asked eagerly.

"I can't see why not if I put in only a little powder, otherwise they have quite a kick."

"A kick, pistols kick?" Maribel queried.

"Recoil can hurt your arm and shoulder."

"You have a bad arm."

"If Eleanor can throw chips in the water up tide, we can shoot at them as they pass by. They'll be close, so we won't need much powder. Eleanor will be with you on the bulwark. Let's go."

Out on deck, it was cold as usual, but by now everyone knew to wrap up warmly. Antony checked to see that he had primer, black powder, balls, patch lube, flint and ramrod. With Eleanor supporting Mariel against the bulwark, Antony proceeded to load the flint into the cocks. Then, with cocks half-cocked, he loaded very carefully, measured amounts of black powder down the muzzles and tamped it down, after which he primed the flash pans a third full with primer.

"Powder for a range of no more than 20 feet. The chips won't be further away than that, likely closer but moving quite fast. When the triggers are pulled, the flints hit the frizzens, creating sparks. The frizzens are designed to open the pans. When the sparks ignite the primer, the flash explodes the black powder in the barrels which fires the balls out. Pistol kickback should be small. I'll have the first go in case I've overdone the powder."

"It sounds very complicated!" Eleanor called from the stern, ready to throw overboard a number of wood chips. "Get ready! I'll throw the chips out one at a time!"

"Wait a minute, m'lord!" Joao called from where he had been tidying halyards. "I'll hold the young lady while you test your pistols. You can't fire accurately holding her, and she could be too near the flashes."

"Thank you, Master Pereira. I would be grateful," Antony agreed.

From the way Joao held and talked to Maribel, Antony could see he'd had experience of children at some time in his life. As wood chips floated by, Antony selected two, one for each pistol, and fired. He did not hit them but was satisfied that he was near enough.

What did concern him was the searing pain in his injured arm brought about by the kick or recoil. "Bloody hell!" he muttered under his breath, letting his injured arm drop to his side. He decided to put less powder in again when he reloaded for Maribel.

With Joao holding her, Maribel wanted to reload one pistol while Antony reloaded the other, carefully giving her reduced powder. Joao could see that it would not normally be enough but knew the reason why and said nothing. When the chips floated by, she took careful aim at two, squeezed the triggers deliberately, as instructed, and fired, the pistols throwing upwards, burnt powder streaming off to windward. "How did I do, Dadda?" she called excitedly.

"Quite as good as me," Antony replied, thinking ruefully he should have a lot more regular practice, hoping that tomorrow evening he would not have occasion to use them.

"The little lady could be assisted to walk," Joao observed, testing Maribel's ability to stand.

"How come?" Antony asked, pricking up his ears.

"When I was young, we lived in Brazil. When we Portuguese conquered the country, a curative glass mountain was found in the interior where the natives had gone for generations for cures. The Roman Catholic Church took it over as a holy shrine, charging for cures. When my mother fell and broke her tail bone, my father took her there to be cured."

"A glass mountain?"

"Composed of the substances glass is made of."

"And was she cured?" Antony asked, intrigued.

"Yes, and there are hot springs in the Azores that do the same," Joao added, eager to be of help.

"There're also hot springs in Bath," Antony mused, very much taken by the idea that perhaps, one day, with the help of crutches, his precious Maribel could walk. If he could not take her to Bath before he became marquis, he certainly would when he did.

"Wouldn't it be wonderful," Eleanor said, coming over and overhearing their conversation. "It's what I've been trying to do, strengthen her legs."

"Yes, I'm very grateful," Antony said, smiling and putting his arm around her. "Let's go in out of the cold."

Back in their big cabin, Antony felt he had better get gear ready for tomorrow evening as Brandon said they would be leaving at midday in the ship's boat on the flowing tide. There was a lot to get in the ship's boat along with themselves and personal arms like netting, ships' spikes, brush lights, rockets and, of course, a reliable tinderbox. As it looked as if they were in for a good blow for the next few days, it was always difficult to strike a light in wind, but essential for those first on deck to be able to suddenly light up the scene.

He was glad his role was to be on the top of the cliff controlling five down at a time, then, hopefully, seeing the released captives up into the shelter of the wagons. There was much he had to bear in mind. He had never been involved in action before other than the brief skirmish when wounded in the left upper arm. He packed his knapsack carefully, putting in only what he would personally need, a small night glass being one essential.

Back in their large cabin, the brazier was very welcome as they had got cold up on the deck. It was a luxury they were grateful for. "You did well, darling," Antony said to Maribel, taking her on his knee.

"The pistols were very heavy."

"They're not designed for children, though there are ladies' ones that are lighter, which I must get for you and Eleanor."

"Joao has a funny voice. Some things he doesn't understand," Maribel commented.

"No, he doesn't. He comes from a land far away where people speak a different language."

"Is that why he says bad things?"

"He says things he's heard but doesn't know the meaning of."

"Like a parrot."

"Precisely."

"But he's a nice man."

"I've always thought so. If you say so, he must be. You're very sensitive. I wonder what Danny has for evening meal?" Antony realised, perhaps for the first time, what it was like to feel hungry, like the majority of people on his estate. He had to admit he did not relish the experience. In the event, the meal brought into their cabin by Danny was delicious, consisting of freshly caught crab and reheated gruel garnished with edible sea wrack. Maribel dipped into their communal bowl enthusiastically, showing she was now in good health. Antony did not feel that great, indicating perhaps he was still suffering from a degree of sepsis and, though he did not know it, anxiety. But he enjoyed being away with Maribel, and Eleanor, the two people he really loved.

They had a limited supply of candles, so went to bed early in the big bunk after having sipped hot tea and honey, Eleanor making sure to empty the chamber pot to leeward. The moon rose, describing a pathway through the water. Maribel sat up between them, delighted to have her mother and father on each side of her. "Your father and I are hoping to have you walk with crutches," Eleanor said.

"Is it possible? I would like that!" Maribel said, delighted.

"While we're away, I'll ask Will Worthington to make you arm crutches. He loves making things. We'll look for suitable ash boughs. Ash is very healing for children. It has been used since early times to assist children's health and development."

"That's what my father says," Eleanor agreed.

Maribel was full of life. Having mostly to sit around while other people were active, she had energy to spare. She was still prattling away while the other two fell asleep. When Antony awoke to change the position of his aching arm Maribel was at last asleep. He gently put her on the other side of him and cuddled up to Eleanor, who sighed when she felt Antony's closeness. Like Antony, content to enjoy the moment.

Antony did not know how long he had been asleep when he was woken up by Maribel. "A ghost! The ship's ghost! Listen?"

Antony and Eleanor, who had been woken up as well, listened. They could indeed hear something. A faint light sound, quite near them. Maribel hung on to Eleanor. Antony, who was the nearest to the starboard panelling, put his ear to it and smiled. "I think you'll find it a friendly ghost. I'll go out, find it, bring it in and introduce you to it." Maribel screamed at the prospect and held Eleanor closer.

Giving Eleanor a wink, he lit a candle from the brazier and made his way to the lower deck, passing his small sleeping crew in hammocks quietly so as not to disturb them, and then to the bilge hatch. Lifting the heavy hatch with his good arm, he jammed it. Then, walking on main ribs to keep out of the fetid bilge water, aware of scurrying sounds, made his way to the starboard side of the hull. Being careful not to drop his candle where it could not be retrieved and set the ship alight, he found what he was seeking behind their cabin panelling. "Come on, silly, come to me or follow me."

Two green eyes looked at him balefully. "Come on." The green eyes followed him. At the hatch, he lifted the cat up to the lower deck. With difficulty, he scrambled up, being only able to pull himself up with his good arm. He then, as quietly as possible, closed the hatch. The cat looked well-fed, with lovely fur, feeding, no doubt, on the rats. Antony thought he knew the problem. He took the cat out onto the main deck, where it drank thirstily of rainwater in the scuppers. When it had drunk its fill, he carried it up into their poop deck cabin. "Voila! The ghost!"

Maribel was delighted. Eleanor took her out of their bunk and held her next to the cat, who rubbed itself against her legs. Maribel leant over and stroked it. The cat purred. "Can it come in with us?"

"If you want it with you, it will have to be in your own bunk. There's hardly enough room for us three in the big bunk without a cat."

"I'll go in my own bunk if the cat will stay." Eleanor lifted Maribel into her own bunk with the cat beside her, which settled down, purring loudly.

"Perhaps we can all get back to sleep again," Eleanor sighed. Antony put out the remnants of the candle before snuggling up with her back in their bunk.

He could have done without night ghost hunting as he felt tired when he awoke, but this was action day, so he could not lie in. Quietly checking his knapsack, taking his heavy cloak and pistols, he joined the others in the galley. Three seamen were staying on anchor watch and guard duties. The rest, along with Captain Harper, who they were to meet, were spearheading the boarding party. They had an hourglass hour and a half before they calculated that the flowing tide would be strong enough to bear them upstream. The ship's boat was lowered, gear assembled on deck for the assault loaded aboard, leaving little room for personnel.

There being no space for rowing, a rowlock was placed in the stern for the boat to be sculled to provide steerage way, which Jack McKiver did with difficulty. "You need to twist the oar more as you stroke from side to side," Commander Brandon advised, having seen it done before in harbours.

With increased steerage way, they made more accurate progress in the ice-free mid-channel, the rising gale masking their approach. "They're just round the next bend," Brandon affirmed. "We'll have to create a channel through the ice to beach the boat to unload. The chunks will have to be dragged out one at a time with a boat hook. Up forward, Jack, and see what you can do."

As each block was prized loose, it was dragged out to be sent floating down channel. Antony hoped the blocks were not going to create a problem for *Spray Sprite*. In this way, eventually, a channel was created on the west bank for the ship's boat to be grounded on the shore and unloaded. There appeared to be about an hour of daylight left for the assault gear to be taken to the bluff above the galley and, in the dusk, got into place, netting secured down the near-vertical cliff face.

They met Captain Harper fussing about, complaining that two of his men had sprained their ankles and another two had got sick with the cold and were sheltering in the wagons, reiterating that they were not marines. Brandon looked to Antony, who told the captain bluntly to get on with it, feeling that he had passed the first test of being in overall command, something he was worried about.

It was completely dark when the first boarding line was assembled: Brandon, Joao, Captain Harper, former marines Tom Tedworth and Mathew Bates, holding a magnesium flare, brushes, torches and tinder box. Seaman Jack McKiver had been left to guard the ship's boat. Behind them were five of the most agile dragoons, with another file of five again standing in readiness. If anything, the gale had increased to blot out the sound of falling rock and movement on the near-vertical cliff face. Antony was on tenterhooks, ready to take control of the descending files of five, waiting for the signal to go, hoping his plan would work and that he would acquit himself well.

With a jerk, he suddenly realised the first line was off. All was silent other than the noise of the wind. After counting 120 seconds, he signalled for the second line of dragoons to follow. Antony felt his heart thumping to the extent he felt others must hear it.

Abruptly there was a brilliant light from below, shouting and shots, the brilliant light dying to be replaced by streaming flares. Antony kept on counting, then motioned for the third line to follow. More shots occurred. He could hear indistinct shouting, then comparative silence. Without warning, a rocket shrieked upwards, spraying the waiting lines with sparks. "That's it! About face!" Antony ordered. "Clear the immediate area." The surprise boarding had been successful. No further dragoons were needed. He said to their sergeant standing behind that the dragoon platoon was now to make themselves ready to help weakened released captives into the shelter of the wagons, otherwise attend to their needs and be prepared to receive possible wounded members of the boarding party.

After what seemed another 20 minutes, a second rocket sizzled overhead. The dragoon platoon sergeant detailed a number of his men to go partway down the nets to assist those struggling upwards and light flares to illuminate the area.

Antony was shocked by the sight of the white-faced, frightened young people helped over the cliff face. What they had been through he could not imagine. He tried counting them to see if they had all survived but was not sure in the confusion. Before long, Captain Harper emerged, also looking shaken but appearing unhurt, to take control of the evacuation and repatriation of the surviving youngers from the stricken village. "Look after them, get them back to their parents and loved ones as soon as you can, and my father will be eternally grateful," Antony said to a worried-looking Captain Harper, who nodded in understanding.

Looking back, Antony became aware of strange-looking wild men scrambling up behind, shouting in languages he could not understand. "Captain Harper, your attention, Master Pereira must have released the slave oarsmen. See they're not armed, otherwise they'll terrorise the countryside, and you'll have more winter engagements on your hands!"

"On, no, what next?" the even more worried-looking Captain Harper complained, detailing a section to watch the crazed oarsmen disappear into the night.

The last to scramble up were Joao, Brandon and their two former marines. They all seemed intact other than Joao, who had blood smeared across his face, though he looked triumphant and did not appear bothered by his wound. Antony noticed the four were carrying what appeared to be very heavy objects for their size.

"Your surprise boarding plan went off brilliantly, m'lord, easy as pie. They were caught with their pants down. It was the last thing they were expecting on a wild winter's night! As they appeared on deck, we were there ready and took them out one by one!"

Now the tension was off, Antony felt relieved and very tired, needing to sit on a log and watch the others retrieve the marine nets and securing spikes from the near-vertical bluff face. Ghost hunting during the night and the degree of sepsis still in his wound had left him exhausted. He could barely stagger back to the ship's boat, where he wrapped himself in his cloak and shut his eyes while the ebbing tide carried them back to *Spray Sprite*.

Scrambling up the rope ladder using his one good arm was the straw that nearly broke the camel's back. Tumbling into their poop deck cabin, he flung himself into their bunk. "Oh, Dadda, are you hurt?" Maribel cried out in concern.

Instantly Eleanor was beside him, examining him tenderly. "I'm all right. The boarding was a great success. The captives were released. I just feel whacked. I haven't the strength I used to."

"Dear Antony, I was thinking of you. How did you make out?"

"I took command, my first real command, like my forebears."

"I knew you could. I'm proud of you. As you said to me, it's a state of mind. Your father always runs you down."

"There's another thing, on the way back, Joao told us that, knowing where a galley kept their Atlantic season's plundered gold, he relieved them of that burden. I've decided that we'll share it among our small ship's company in the way prize money is shared by navy ships. My share, by the look of it, will more than reimburse me for my savings which I've used to finance this mission. I'll see you and Maribel also get a share."

"Antony, that's wonderful news, but what is most important to us is your safe return." Eleanor gave him a hug and put Maribel in beside him, who snuggled close, gently stroking his brow. Eleanor stoked up the brazier and let him sleep till supper time.

Supper was delicious crab again, caught during the day by the anchor watch, with gruel spiced with dill and wild garlic, brought in steaming hot on a heated pewter plate. "Smells wonderful, Danny," Eleanor said appreciatively, "I don't know how you do it?" She gently tugged Antony awake, who sat up at table with Maribel on his lap. Antony, who had almost forgotten what five-course castle meals were like, which now seemed part of another life, ate hungrily. This one tasty course was luxury.

After they had eaten, Brandon called in. He said that high tide tomorrow was approximately midday with strong winds continuing from the south. With cliff contours and high ground to the north, they would need a good blow to get them safely over the bar and beyond the shallows into deeper water more than half a mile offshore. Food was running out, and now their mission was accomplished they should be moving on. Antony agreed, but he said that of necessity, he had to leave the time and day of leaving to Brandon's judgement as he had insufficient experience. If he advised tomorrow, they would sail on the tide.

Like the food, their night together seemed part of another life. The ship with its small crew was their castle in which all were mates. They were happy together. Antony told Maribel traditional good fairy stories, which she liked. Though highly educated, she was a child at heart. The wind sighed through the standing rigging, giving them a cosy feeling, something not part of life in a castle.

Chapter Eight

The cold light of day brought a sense of urgency. After reheated gruel was served, Joao brought them together on the lower deck. Commander Travallyn had something to say. Getting out of the haven was going to be a good deal harder than coming in. At the high tide, without the assistance of the ebb, they had to come about and instantly pick up the wind on the other tack to beat strongly out through the heavy surf. If they were caught in irons, they would be beaten back and wrecked, likely with all lives lost.

Sailing Master Pereira was of the opinion that seaman Jack McKiver and Danny, who brought them in, or the other three seamen for that matter, were not up to it. A successful helmsman had to have sensitivity and touch. M'Lord Antony and Lady Eleanor had expressed a willingness to help out as crew. He would like both of them, within the haven, to try coming about promptly and picking up the wind on the new tack at the right moment. If he did not mind, he would try out His Lordship first. Sailing Master Pereira would give the commands.

"We're doing an upwind turn as we can with a fore and aft rig, unlike a square-rigger. There's barely enough room. We need to pick up maximum way first. Once we've got that, I'll call 'Lee Ho!' As the booms swing over, there'll come an exact point, when the ship has passed through the eye of the wind, with the helm in the right position, the helmsman can feel and pick up the wind on the new tack still with way on, to beat strongly out of the bay. Miss that exact moment, caught in irons, we'll be beaten back and founder. Off we go! Maximum speed. Ready about, strongly, strongly! Lee Ho! Missed it! In irons!" Joao took the wheel.

Sailing Master Pereira looked doubtfully at Eleanor. "Your Ladyship, would you like to try?" Eleanor stepped up to the wheel. "Pick up speed. Ready about!" Joao gave the same set of commands.

Eleanor turned the wheel strongly. The booms swung over. The ship passed through the eye of the wind, still with way on. She picked up the wind on the new tack at the exact right moment, the ship springing forward like a released caged animal. Everyone cheered. "We'll try you again, m'lady, if you don't mind, in case it was a fluke." Eleanor came about three more times successfully. "You're a miracle. I've never seen a helm managed better – and a woman! We need to be at the entrance in half an hourglass hour. All stand-by."

Antony looked at Eleanor with incredulity. "I'll be beside you if you need help in turning the heavy wheel."

"Maribel can't be left below. I'll bring her up and put her in the dogbox along with the sheets, tying a piece of cork to her. She can see out through the lattice vents," Eleanor said. While they waited, Eleanor perched up on the dogbox roof with Maribel on her lap.

Observing the water where floating debris was at a standstill, Commander Travallyn said, "Bill, begin swinging the lead. Jack, give Her Ladyship the wheel. Get the ship sailing fast!" *Spray Sprite* picked up speed, water curling at her bow. The suspense was palpable.

All looked to Eleanor. "Your Ladyship, come about NOW!"

Eleanor began spinning the heavy wheel as fast as she could. Antony sprung to assist her. "I've got to decide the instant!" she screamed. "Back off!" He backed off. The booms swung over. All held their breath. The fore and aft sails picked up the wind on the new larboard tack with a bang. *Spray Sprite* surged out to sea, surf sweeping the deck. Maribel screamed from the dogbox. Brandon swung up into the rigging. Eleanor hung onto the wheel, getting soaked as did Antony, clinging onto a rat line to windward. The crew cheered as they pounded through the breaking surf, pulling on the sheets.

Once clear of the surf, *Spray Sprite* ceased to take water aboard. Half a mile out to sea Commander Travallyn called again, "Ready about!" It did not matter this time if they were caught in irons as they had plenty of sea room. "Lee Ho!" The booms swung over. Eleanor got it right once more. *Spray Sprite* was now sailing her fastest on a mid-reach up channel, heading for Lyme Regis.

"M'lord, give Her Ladyship a rest so she can get inside and change, steer 90 degrees by ship's binnacle. Jack!" He raised his voice. "When Master Pereira has finished with you sail setting, relieve His Lordship."

Starting when they did, owing to the time of high tide, they would be entering Lyme Regis harbour in the dark, tricky at any time. None had been sailing for a long time. They were just getting the feel of the vessel. They were one skeleton watch where there should be three. After seven hours without relief, everyone was tired. The only beauty was that, sharing the gold according to Royal Naval prize tradition, they were all going to get large sums. If they did not sink and drown getting into the harbour in the dark, that is.

When Antony entered their cabin, wet and cold, Eleanor ran forward and threw her arms about him. "Antony, dear, I didn't mean to offend you. I was very anxious when I helmed *Spray Sprite* out of the haven. I didn't want to drown us all. For everyone's sake, I had to get it right."

"I understand. I was only trying to support you. You have a rare skill few possess. Ships-of-the-line, square riggers, are slow turning. If taken-aback, they sustain great damage, I'm told. They can put themselves out of action. I wouldn't want to be a helmsman in one of them."

"I guess whoever's chosen hasn't a choice. You and I were volunteers; that's the difference. It's perishingly cold in this cabin without the brazier going. I'm lucky. Thanks to you, I have plenty to change into. I'm sorry I didn't seem more appreciative at the time. The thought of being a lady alarmed me. I'm trying now not to let you down."

"You've got great status in this ship, that's for sure." Antony went over to Maribel and picked her up.

"Put me down, Dadda. You're all wet. Get changed first."

Antony realised he had not as much to change into as the girls. His only other outfit was riding kit. He must still have a degree of sepsis in his arm. The dressing had not been changed for some time. It felt hot, and he felt tired. He had to lie down for a bit. Eleanor put Maribel in beside him. "When the waves swept over *Spray Sprite,* I thought we were sinking."

"I'm sorry, darling. It must have been terrifying for you. All hatches were tightly shut. Mamma's skill saved us. We all have certain skills, some we may not know about until we try. You are able to understand many things others find hard or impossible."

"I wish I knew how to walk."

"Your not being able to walk is a handicap you were born with. Eleanor and I are trying to get you help to enable you to walk, with crutches at first, perhaps. When I'm marquis, I will make it a priority."

"When will that be?"

"Only God can tell. Not long perhaps, who knows?"

Maribel gave him a supportive hug.

It was dark when Brandon knocked and entered the cabin.

"Do you mind coming on deck, Eleanor? We might have to come about in a hurry. With this gale still blowing, we're approaching Lyme Regis too fast to be able to pick out any leading lights, if there are any. My sight's not that good."

"Maribel has excellent sight. She wouldn't mind dressing up warmly and coming up to assist."

"That would be a great help. None of us have sailed for years."

Unless experienced, no one could believe how cold a ship's deck at night in winter could be. Stepping outside, the freezing wind took their breath away. Can you see the quays?" Brandon asked.

"A little to the left, Mamma. The tide's carrying us to the right, see," Maribel replied.

"I don't see, Maribel, that's the problem."

"A little more still to the left, Mamma. Up front." Maribel tugged at Antony to carry her up to the forepeak.

"That's about right," she called back, her voice trailing off in the wind.

"Still good?"

"Hold it, Mamma."

"Still good?"

"A nudge to the right."

"Get that way off, you yellow-bellied, gutless whitebait. Halliards! Faster!" Joao shouted.

"Language, Master Pereira. Respeite sua mae!" Brandon called.

"What did he say?" Eleanor asked.

"Respect your mother," Maribel replied.

"How do you know?"

"Easy peasy, what he's saying comes from one of the Latin languages."

"Amazing!" Eleanor replied.

"She's a clever girl," Antony said proudly, patting her on the shoulders, feeling weary, having stood for so long. "It's those confusing maze of shore lights," he muttered, peering ahead. "You think you've just begun to work out the detail when the moving lights of link boys escorting carriages make you realise you've got it all wrong."

Ominous shadows in the form of groins loomed ahead.

"Get way off, way off!" Joao screamed at the top of his voice.

"Pennies!" Brandon began calling left and right.

"Why is he calling that?" Maribel asked, puzzled.

"Men are sleeping in sheltered niches in the quays, waiting for payment to help with ships' berthing. Since the wars, like the Medway fiasco, there's been a lot of unemployment in these parts."

"The Medway fiasco?" Eleanor queried, turning the wheel a few spokes at a time, peering into the darkness. "Like you say, it's those confusing shore lights, making it difficult to see groin lights if there are any."

"When the Dutch occupied the Medway Towns roundabout the estuary," Antony answered, likewise peering into the darkness. "It's these confusing shore lights. You seem to be doing well."

After much shouting in the dark, warps thrown, the 'pennies', jumping on other vessels, edged and pulled *Spray Sprite* towards the eastern groin, Danny and Bill securing it to bollards. Brandon directed them to be on a two-hour berth watch, adjusting the warps in accordance with the movements of the tide. So he and Eleanor could get a good night's sleep, Antony went down to the lower deck to find and put the ship's cat beside Maribel. That being done, he cuddled up to Eleanor, making sure he did not get her pregnant as that could be very inconvenient until such time Eleanor could be established at the castle as his de facto lady.

The one watch crew were exhausted after the long afternoon passage back to Lyme Regis. Brandon let them sleep until the town clock struck nine. Then he and Brandon needed to arrange the selling of *Sea Sprite*, informing waterfront taverns and hostelries that he had a mercantile sloop for sale, fitted out as a gentleman's yacht. Antony decided that they would stay aboard *Sea Sprite* for the next two days as it was cheaper and more secure, after which Eleanor and Maribel would be lodging with Seaman Danny and his family. She would be assisting with their newly established printing business which Eleanor knew a lot about and would be of invaluable help, after which, reluctantly, he should return to the castle after successfully releasing the seized young people.

Meanwhile, having advertised as best they could a yacht for sale, they went back aboard *Sea Sprite*. Antony realised how much he would miss the camaraderie that had been built up with people from the most diverse backgrounds, utterly loyal to him and each other, so different from his life at the castle. He felt life had never been better. He had lovely nights with the girl he loved along with the company of the daughter he loved. What could be better?

For the last day aboard, Antony said the crew could have shore leave, taking turns for three to remain aboard for security and warp watch. However, before going ashore, they had to promise to have no more than three strong drinks, as a drunken sailor could spill the beans. For his part, a final day with Eleanor and Maribel would make for a perfect last time aboard. At mid-afternoon he sent ashore to a harbour inn for a special evening meal with all the trimmings. When it came, steaming in the cold air, it consisted of oleo, pigeons, sirloin of roast beef, venison, chine of mutton, turkey, snipes, ducks, partridge, artichokes and French beans, a delicious feast fit for a king. They could not eat it all and invited Brandon and Joao, and finally the crew, to finish it off.

In the evening, they played a guessing game with Maribel, ending up by dressing warmly and going out onto the poop deck to watch the activity of the town at night, which none of them had experienced before and the warp watch adjusting the securing lines. Antony observed Maribel staring ashore. "What is it, darling?"

"There's a horseman in a dark cloak looking down on us from a rise halfway up the town. I can see him outlined in carriage lights as carriages pass nearby. I don't like him. He's pointing a cutlass at us."

"You have excellent sight and observation. I've got an idea who he is. I'll ask Brandon for the watch to remain vigilant and to have someone up on the quay."

"I don't want to spend the night here."

"We'll be going in the morning. Come on in, it's getting cold."

Antony found the ship's cat for Maribel. He must ask Danny if he and his wife wanted a cat and arrange for it to go to their place for Maribel.

With the ship in harbour, the brazier made life aboard much more tolerable. Though Maribel had the cat with her on her bunk, she was restless, and she took time to go to sleep. After which, Antony cuddled up with Eleanor on the larger bunk, dreaming he was in a beautiful garden, at the end of which there was a pool. Tinkling fairy music filled the air to add to the scent of roses. It was a garden of enchantment. A gorgeous princess in flowing white appeared on the other side of the water, flew gracefully over it and came towards him. As she came closer, he saw she was Eleanor, Maribel skipping elegantly behind her, holding her train.

He was woken abruptly by the cry of *fire*. Leaping out of his bunk, he saw, reflecting in the water, that the standing rigging was a towering inferno, flames also leaping over parts of the main deck. A person or persons unknown had thrown incendiary material over the main deck and rigging and set it alight.

Chapter Nine

Antony grabbed Maribel and his waist bag, heavy with gold, Eleanor trying to seize the terrified cat. The poop deck being higher, he rushed over, climbed up on the bulwark, placed Maribel up on the groin and threw his waist bag after her, turning to help Eleanor scramble up onto the groin, the demented cat leaping up herself. He shouted to the crew to come up onto the poop deck and do the same, which they did, throwing up their gold-laden waist bags before them. Looking down, he saw rats on the opposite side jumping into the water through the scuppers, tiny V washes marking their progress.

They all stood back as the heat was so intense, finally having to move up towards the town as flaming debris began falling from the rigging over the groin. Eventually, the wooden town fire engine was trundled down the groin by eight fire fighters in what looked like civil war roundhead helmets, ready to pump the handles each side up and down. But it was obvious they could not get anywhere near the blazing inferno. Like the rest, they had no choice but to look on safely from a distance.

Finally, what was left of the flaming masts fell, hissing into the water. The remainder of the sloop heeled away from the groin into the water, the warps long burned through. At that, the harbour master, who was among the watchers, approached and told Antony he would be charged with the disposal of what was left of the hull left under the water. What he hoped he would get back from selling the sloop had turned into another expense. It was a good job his waist bag was heavy with gold. When he had paid for this disaster, it would be somewhat lighter.

Finally, the spectacle over, they began to get cold, dressed in whatever they had been sleeping in. Antony said they were all to back to go the Bear and Beagles, whose proprietor was on the groin, along with half the town, being told they would be spending the rest of the night with him. As business was still slack, he was delighted to have them back.

Without the fire, they began to shiver in the cold night air. "We've no clothes, only the petticoats you see us in," Eleanor said, shivering.

Antony, carrying Maribel, replied, "All of us will have to replace clothes. As far as you and Maribel are concerned, when you live with Danny and his wife you will need to be in clothes appropriate to your station. Danny can't afford to provide escorts for you dressed in ladies' clothes. I will buy for you and Maribel the sort of clothes you would have had when your father was a successful printer in Lyme Regis before he developed problems and you had to seek work at the castle. My father owns no properties in Lyme Regis, so his dragoons have no rights to enter and search properties in the town. Now the captives have been released, I will have to go back to the castle before long."

Back in their former at room at the Bear and Beagle, after supper had been brought and eaten, Eleanor asked what was on all their minds, "That fire was deliberate. Who was behind it?"

"The same sinister organisation who were behind the attack on me. Their leader appears to be the mounted horseman in the dark cloak, always on an eminence, looking down on us, pointing a cutlass in our direction as if directing an attack on us."

"This organisation, what might that be?"

"Lady Beatrice knows more. She's always after me and Mamma Eleanor," Maribel said with a thoughtful look in her eyes.

"Do you think she has something? Eleanor commented.

"On occasions, she has insights the rest of us don't possess. Perhaps it's her age. She may well grow out of it. She could be referring to my father and his relationship with his friend, the earl, whatever exactly that might be?" Antony mused.

"Are we any wiser for that?"

"It might be where we should be looking for a clue?" Antony went to the basin in an endeavour to wipe some of his meal off the lace at his throat.

"I'm tired," Maribel announced.

Antony lifted her into the big bed and sat beside her, holding her hand until she soon fell asleep.

"I'm sleepy as well," Eleanor yawned.

"I'll roster three below on guard and inform the rest they can sleep till 10." When he came back, the other two were asleep. Antony joined them for what was left of the night, hoping for no further cry of fire or any other emergency.

Next morning at breakfast, Antony announced that he and the escort would be leaving for the castle the following day. He sent a note to Danny saying he would need Eleanor and Maribel collected at nine tomorrow before going out to buy used clothes for himself and the girls, there being no time for a tailor or seamstresses to call and make up appropriate clothes. It was all go.

Antony ordered for their last meal together, a feast similar to the meal they had for their last one aboard the ill-fated sloop, warning the innkeeper for him and his staff to be on high alert. With the fate of the sloop very much in mind, the innkeeper set up a cordon around the inn for the night. Though appreciating his custom, Antony felt he would be glad when they had gone.

Although in many ways, he would have liked to have dined with the crew for the last evening, as he did not know how long it would be until he would see Eleanor and Maribel again, he felt he must dine with them alone. However, he arranged for Brandon to preside over a celebratory meal downstairs with a maximum of four mugs of beer each throughout the evening. As always, he wanted his men alert. A drunken escort was inviting trouble.

Their meal, much like their one on their last evening on the sloop, was delicious. They could not eat it all and sent what they could not below to add to that of the crew's. When it came to bedtime, Antony went below and observed that the innkeeper had hired a dozen armed night watchmen. Their inn, being free-standing, could be guarded on all sides. As everyone in the town had observed the fate of the sloop, the watchmen took their role seriously, being on their feet walking around, not asleep at their posts. Satisfied, he went up to their room.

Maribel was already asleep, Eleanor in her petticoat awaiting him. He felt how pretty she looked, her uncombed hair framing fine features, shapely figure and firm breasts, so different in bed from Beatrice with her shaven head, blotched features and drooping breasts after nights of heavy drinking. Arranged marriages were all wrong. He took out the only precious item he had from his secret time with Mary, a piece of torn parchment of a sketch of a girl with long ringlets on a bench with hollyhocks behind her and noted the remarkable similarity with Maribel's drawing style. After studying it a while, he quietly got in bed beside Eleanor, who gave a sigh and pressed him close to her.

Day came only too soon. While breakfasting with Brandon and Joao, Danny arrived for Maribel and Eleanor. He went upstairs and gave them lingering kisses before leading them downstairs. "I'll visit you as often as I can until I can have you permanently at the castle." Danny escorted them out a back door into back allies in their newly acquired town people's clothing. The innkeeper gave them his bill, which included the cost of the night watchmen and hire of horses. All watched carefully while the amount in gold was weighed. Then they set off for the Friar and Flagon, conscious of ambush.

All but Antony were eager to get back home and rode off with a will. The only thing he could think of was a time when he could see Eleanor and Maribel again. However, for once, he hoped his father would be grateful for his restoring the morale and approval of the residents of Limbeley. Their hostility had shocked his father to the core. Before that, though he had tried hard, his father thought his endeavours a waste of time, unbefitting the son of a marquis. He rode on with a heavy heart.

All were tired when they reached the Friar and Flagon. The innkeeper scurried to get them a meal. As they were not celebrating, two mugs of ale accompanied the dinner. Next morning, with fresh horses, they set off for the castle. As predicted, for once in his life, in his father's eyes, Antony had done the right thing. Beatrice, as usual, made no comment; Antony, in turn, gave her a formal greeting, hoping she would not want copulation tonight. He said he was tired in a discouraging manner and went to bed early, hoping she would drink with the gentlemen.

"So you're the hero now," Beatrice remarked sourly in the morning while the barber was giving Antony a shave.

For some time now, Antony had been reflecting on the simple life he had experienced among loyal people. It had been an education, including the food, one course if you were lucky, shared equally, irrespective of status, compared with the protocol, rivalries and jealousies of the castle, the only life until now Antony had known. He also set about thinking of the remarkable courage of his crew, risking their lives for others, and talents bought about by adversity like Eleanor's remarkable ability as a helmswoman and Maribel's courage and insights. He deigned not to reply to Beatrice's sarcasm.

Instead, he said to Claude, "Have my horse and my father's carriage put on stand-by."

"Where do you think you think you're going, hero?"

Antony walked out, quietly shutting the door. Entering the dining hall, his father called him over by the fire. "Have my carriage prepared, boy."

With the confidence of leadership during his time away, he replied, "Father, I request you not to call me boy in front of the servants. It's demeaning." Such was the new authority in his voice, his father was taken aback.

"If that's your wish, son."

"It is."

"We're going to Limbeley. Order a platoon of our dragoons ready to accompany us."

"Very good, sir." Antony strode off, a taller person.

Chapter Ten

The drive to Limbeley was triumphant. His father was very pleased to have back his reputation in the village, and Antony experienced a glow of achievement in the fact that his father, though not knowing the details, was very aware who had brought that about. There was a reception committee. They were offered food and drink, from which they accepted a token so as not to offend.

The days were lengthening as they drove back. His father, he felt, was immensely curious about how he had brought the rescue about. He was aware that, at some point, he had asked for the help of a platoon of his dragoons but nothing more. Knowing his thoughts, Anthony eventually said, "The young people's release was brought about by a small group of dedicated and courageous people from all walks of life who risked their lives," and left it at that.

"Our people look poor," the marquis observed on the way back.

"Believe it or not, it's due to the increasingly cold winters. Crops are failing. I'm trying to introduce crop rotation."

"Does it help?"

"The latest scientific experiments say it does."

"I've heard ships are not getting through to Greenland. Ivory is in short supply."

"That's what I was telling you." As they bumped and swayed along in the light, two-seater coach, Antony was impressed that, for the first time, his father was agreeing with what he had been saying for a long time: that climate change was a fact and of concern for all. It was the new authority in his voice and that he had been able to improve the image of his father and the reputation of the estate which had brought about the change. From now on, Antony was determined to keep it that way.

"I might have to be away again before long." Antony eventually remarked.

"Why's that?"

"On the last occasion, we were concerned to free the hostages."

"Well done." The receiving of praise was such a new experience that Antony found it hard to get used to.

"We need now to find out who is behind the Barbary pirates receiving such precise information."

"Have you made progress?"

"The clue could lie in the past."

"How's that possible?"

"Commitments, misplaced loyalties, losses perhaps?"

"Debts?"

"Possibly." Antony could not say that the idea of misplaced loyalties came from Maribel.

Though the coach was well-sprung, he could see the lurching was hurting his father's hip. "Some brandy, Father?"

"Thank you." This again was something new, being able to help his arrogantly independent father.

"How did it all go, m'lord?" Claude asked after they had arrived back at the castle and his father had been carried inside in a sedan chair.

"My Father has decided to treat me as an equal."

"Not before time, if I might say so, m'lord," Claude replied, genuinely pleased for the master he liked and served.

"It certainly makes a change."

Two weeks later, with Brandon and the same trusted crew who were with them on *Sea Sprite*, they set off for the Bear and Beagle en route for Lyme Regis. He arranged for two of his team to patrol the perimeter of the inn in two-hour shifts through the night. At one point in the night, he thought he heard pistol shots as if the perimeter patrol were discouraging shadowy figures from approaching the inn. He would inquire in the morning.

Approaching Lyme Regis, they decided to stay at another venue, the Bear and Buzzard, a small and obscure inn down a side street, Joao making the booking. They entered the inn discreetly through a back door, Joao introducing the six escorts but not mentioning Antony or Brandon, who stood in the background, organising stabling at town stables nearby.

The next day they were preparing to set off for the village of Tadingham where Maribel had become so strangely agitated at the prospect of entering the porch when Danny brought the shattering news that Maribel had disappeared. She was last seen playing in an alley with local children behind Danny's printing business. Antony, Brandon and the crew immediately began asking people on the Cobb if they had seen a child with golden ringlets being carried onto a boat. Eventually, a 'penny' said he had. He did not give the person money but continued to ask others who confirmed without payment. If it became known information was rewarded, such information would no longer be reliable.

Antony went up onto the long west outward sloping wall, took out his pocket telescope and searched the horizon to the south for a Barbary corsair lying just out of sight of land. There had been talk of a redemption fund like in Denmark to ransom ships and individuals, but it had not been taken up in England, even though the pirates had precise inside information. The feeling was that such a fund might be an inducement like buying them off.

"We'll need a longboat or something like it, a small vessel," Brandon announced, "to see if there's a xebec lying offshore just out of sight of land. If there is, we'll stealthily approach their prow and set fire to it as they did us. While they're distracted, we'll board aft near their light stern structure, cut through it if necessary, and seize back Maribel."

Antony realised a plan of that nature had inherent dangers, especially for Maribel, but for all of them if things went wrong. However, he applauded their enthusiasm and willingness to once more put their lives in danger. What more could he ask of them?

"Great idea!" Joao agreed. "I'll find out where we can get incendiary material like this newly discovered phosphorus."

"Do you know how to handle the stuff?" Antony asked anxiously.

"I'll find out." Antony realised they could not prepare for the mission at Lyme Regis where they would be observed but needed to go to Traveslington, the next village to the east after Charmouth in the same silted-up inlet of the sea as the castle, like with them the sea, now two-thirds of a mile to the south. It still had a fishing community with a few small craft for sale. As they only needed a small boat, Antony was sure they could find a suitable craft there. This obviously made sense and was agreed.

The next day they rode to Traveslington to look for a suitable longboat or perhaps a crabber. They found a longboat with a strange history. A year or so ago, it had come in on the tide manned by a number of swarthy dying men. All passed away except one. Everyone kept well clear as it was felt they might be carrying some sort of plague. It appeared they had come from far away, by the vessel's size being used for ferrying goods between islands. Perhaps a sudden great gale had swept it far out into the Atlantic. But one man survived who could not speak English but called himself what sounded like 'Eddie' who slept in the boat under a sail, the kind local people leaving him food.

As Eddie's boat was the sort they were looking for, Brandon asked Antony if he could negotiate with Eddie to see if he was prepared to sell. "Have in mind a fair price. He's no idea of English money values. Use the offer of a small house in exchange for his boat. If he agrees, buy him a small house. See it has in it what he needs. What guineas there are over indicate he needs to keep out of sight and use sparingly, otherwise he'll soon run out of money." Antony agreed, realising they must rescue Maribel as soon as possible.

"All this is going to take time."

"Which I appreciate. But Eddie can't be left homeless. The money we gave him would be taken off him in hours. While you're doing that, the rest can be getting the longboat ready for sea, checking sails, rigging, whatever."

"I can see there's no better option. It's miles before there's another port east," Brandon agreed.

"If you notice, Eleanor, this vessel has a tiller," Brandon pointed out when he returned to where the rest of the crew were, checking out the longboat on the hard.

"What does that mean?" Eleanor, their best helmsman, asked.

"It means that, unlike a wheel, which you turn in the direction of your intended new course, with a tiller you push away from your turn, so if you mean to turn to starboard, you push the tiller strongly to larboard."

"That's funny?"

"You'll have to practice it."

"I certainly will, given the opportunity, bearing in mind we've got to get to Maribel as soon as possible. I can't think of the abuse my darling must be suffering at the hands of the monsters." Eleanor could say no more, tears filling her eyes.

"We're all preparing as quickly as we can. If you notice, there're places for rowers each side to get us out of the creek and row directly into the wind if necessary, though sailing would be quieter," Brandon added. He could see Eleanor was not taking any more in, overcome with emotion.

That night, in the Bear and Buzzard's only private bedroom, Antony could see how upset Eleanor was, as he was himself, without Maribel. He felt so much for Maribel, frightened and alone, as did Eleanor. Both could only hope their daring and desperate rescue mission would succeed, immensely grateful for the others' keenness and courage, knowing they could not feel like them as Maribel was not their child.

The next morning, they were down at Traveslington early to secretly undertake the final preparations for their surprise night assault under the cover of setting fire to the foremast of the corsair.

"How are you going to get your incendiary device alight?" Brandon asked.

"A tinder box," Joao replied, a broad smile appearing on his swarthy features.

"In an open boat?"

"Sheltering under canvas, it only takes a spark." Antony only wished he shared his confidence.

"Eleanor, our best helmsman, will need to get experience in handling the longboat and going about. At least it won't be undermanned; our seamen can row us clear of the creek," Brandon remarked. "We'll need to find where the corsair's lurking just out of sight of land for our surprise setting fire to their foremast to create a distraction." He turned to Eleanor. "All right with you?"

"I can't wait to release our darling girl."

"Tonight, identifying the whereabouts of our quarry; tomorrow night, the rescue!" Brandon continued with confidence. In all, it seemed a very neat plan. Antony felt better at the thought.

As soon as dusk had fallen, they gathered unobtrusively on the hard. Compared with their former mercantile sloop, the present craft was tiny, all the better for their imminent mission, less likely to be seen. "Seamen at the oars, a marine fore and aft," Brandon commanded. "You, Joao, with your incendiary devices in the fore peak."

Having got aboard two at a time by means of their small tender, they rowed silently down the creek in the gathering darkness, Antony with Eleanor in the stern in case she needed help with the heavy helm.

Clearing the inlet, they hoisted sail, initially steering south then west, with Brandon and Joao in the forepeak. When the lights of Lyme Regis appeared, they again steered south until the lights disappeared over the horizon. After that, they began sailing a roughly reciprocal course east and west to try to make out the silhouette of a corsair, Eleanor taking the longboat about upwind. It was very difficult to see the basic binnacle as they dared not show a light. At the top of six-foot swells, in the light of a fleeting new moon, Brandon suddenly felt he could see the curving yards of a corsair, three oars a side stroking slowly to keep the vessel on station, the rest raised, 400 yards to the south-west. Satisfied, Brandon directed Eleanor to sail north-east back towards Traveslington, taking the sails down before entering the creek, anchoring in a curve for the night.

Back in the Bear and Buzzard, Antony ordered up an evening meal, neither of them feeling like eating with the others. However, if anything, Eleanor was a bit more cheerful, having convinced herself Maribel was going to be rescued the following evening, Antony sharing her optimism. Holding each other close, Eleanor cried herself to sleep; Antony felt like doing the same but could not release tension in the same way.

Next day they departed for Traveslington as unobtrusively as possible to make final preparations for the night's rescue mission. Local fishermen looked at them curiously on arrival, wondering what their activity was all about. After the horses were collected and taken back, excitement mounted. "Are you sure you can light your incendiary devices at the last moment?" Brandon asked Joao. "Otherwise, it would be better to get a fuse and light it before we finally sail off." Joao scrambled up a nearby bank to sense the wind speed out on the water.

"A fuse might be wise," he admitted.

"I'll get one from the quarry," Brandon replied. "Wind it around, leaving space between coils on a bed of sand. We don't want to set the longboat alight."

As they left the shelter of the creek, on a mound where a windmill once stood until it burnt down in a gale, Antony thought he glimpsed a mounted figure in a dark cloak sardonically waving a cutlass in their direction. His heart sank. It could not be! It had to be an apparition seen in the half-light. He said nothing to anyone, carrying on with grave misgivings.

Clearing the creek, the longboat began rising and falling on a four-foot swell, wavelets sweeping the surface driven by gusts of wind backing south-east, the moon mostly hidden in cloud. The rescue mission had begun.

Nobody expected it to be easy, like the last boarding of a galley trapped in ice beneath a cliff, but the desperate need to rescue Maribel meant they had no choice but to attempt a dangerous surprise boarding at sea. Antony was particularly apprehensive, full of foreboding. All fell silent as they neared their objective, realising the risk.

Once the lights of Lyme Regis were over the horizon, Eleanor began a three or four-mile sweep east and west, Antony marvelling at her ability to come about upwind, sensing the instant to pull back on the helm to bring the sails effortlessly over to fill with a crack on a roughly reciprocal course. This was something they could not do as they neared their target, needing a completely silent approach.

In fleeting periods of moonlight, all were tensely looking out for the sinister curved yards of a corsair.

After three sweeps east and west, for an instant on top of a wave, they glimpsed dead ahead what appeared to be curved yards. Brandon whispered for sheets to be slackened to take off way but not to the extent of letting their sails flap. For their plan to work, they needed to fire the fore yard of the galley to create the necessary diversion. Brandon instructed Eleanor to bear away and approach the stem. While doing so, a shaft of moonlight briefly lit up the longboat. While still some distance off, Brandon instructed Joao to get his fuse lit.

For what seemed an eternally long time, Joao, with his tinder box sheltering behind canvas held by Danny and Bill, attempted to get the fuse going. Eventually he did, the fuse hissing like a menacing snake, while the others, when the longboat was on top of waves, tried to keep the corsair in sight.

Now, attempting to disguise their fear, they made the final approach. Even on the height of the swell, compared with them, the corsair looked enormous. This is what they were taking on. Only complete surprise would bring about success. Eleanor approached the corsair's starboard bow, trying not to increase speed down the waves to reduce phosphorescence, intending to sheer away at the last moment. Brandon signalled for them to get ready with their personal arms, Antony cocking his pistols, hoping his powder was dry, Joao preparing to light his first incendiary device. Antony felt his heart pounding so loudly he felt others must hear. All looked to Brandon for the word to go.

Abruptly the three oars stroking slowly to keep the corsair on station stood up with the rest. At the same time, from nowhere, grappling hooks were thrown, clamping the longboat securely alongside. Only initially,

Antony and Eleanor did not realise the implication. They soon did.

Dozens of heavily armed pirates were blinding them with lanterns, commanding them to put down their arms. Some jumped in and roughly tore them off them. Their commander began to speak, Joao translating. Last time they were taken completely by surprise. Their revenge was to seize Maribel as a bait. Agents ashore were watching every move. Their desperate attempt at a rescue was fully anticipated and just what they wanted. They were bundled savagely below.

"Mumma, Dadda!" Maribel screamed upon seeing them.

There ensued a lively debate by the pirates about what they were going to do about Maribel as she was a cripple. Some said she should be thrown overboard, which caused Eleanor to scream with anguish when she got the gist of what was being said. Antony felt he had been knifed in the heart. Others, however, said that while she was young with her pretty white face and golden flowing locks, she might sell in Algiers as a beautiful live doll, the white equivalent of the decorative black boys in satin and lace, fashionable in the homes of the very rich. It seemed for the present she was going to be kept. He further gathered that a handsome English lord would fetch a good price in the slave market.

They were not going to be transferred to a foreign vessel but taken to the slave market by the corsairs as quickly as possible as their vessel was due for a refit in its own port on the Barbary Coast. That night, in the depth of despair, they felt the vessel set sail in a brisk favourable wind, for them soon to spend short, miserable lives as white slaves.

Chapter Eleven

Lieutenant Commander Gregory Mainhampton-Sutton was very proud of his first independent command, a full rigged frigate, built for speed and hardiness, used for patrol and escort, with 28 guns on a single upper deck, much more versatile and fun to handle than a ship of the line, and often given interesting missions.

His mission was a patrol around St Lucia to make sure the 1730 agreement with France that the island remained neutral territory was being observed. Having done that, and the spectacular twin Pinnacles Peaks had sunk below the horizon, his instructions were to cross a difficult stretch of ocean to Bermuda. Here he was to demonstrate that the navy was there to support the islanders since an attempt by French and Spanish forces in 1706 to oust them. There, further instructions would be awaiting him.

The voyage had begun well enough. He kept the American Colonies coast in sight, turning east-nor-east at Charleston to begin the difficult 1,100-miles passage to Bermuda. Sudden vicious squalls appeared without warning. On one occasion, a water-spout tore across the prow of the frigate, causing extensive damage to the top sails and jibs of the foremast. Commander Gregory had been told that, for his first command, with the assistance of the master at arms, he must assert from the very start firm and fair discipline. This proved very necessary during the squalls when unquestioning rapid response was needed to the sailing master's urgent directives to keep the frigate under control.

Now the problem for Gregory and his young second in command, Lieutenant Gordon Maplefield, after sailing 1,100 miles, was to find Bermuda. According to the ship's log line, dropped over the stern and let to run out for a set time by the half-minute sand glass while the knots were being counted, they were in the vicinity. The island was so low-lying it could be easily missed. Latitude, they were fairly confident of; longitude, they were not. They had been doing independent calculations which, when compared, were 200 nautical miles different. They decided to do them again. Gregory knew Gordon was a clever young man, more able at mathematics than he was, accepting that he might well be right. Evening was drawing in.

Looking at the evening sky for inspiration, Gregory noticed skuas, birds out in the ocean he had not previously observed, heading purposefully to the east. Maybe they were land-based birds. He decided to sail through the night slowly to the east, a seaman swinging the lead, a forewatch listening intently for breaking surf. At first light, he saw the skuas flying out from the east and begin fishing. He asked for more sail and continued to the east.

"What makes you so confident Bermuda lies to the east?" Gordon asked. "I've been taking star bearings."

"So I've noticed. What I'm doing is not in the Admiralty's Officers' Navigation Manual but is probably one of the ways our Viking ancestors navigated. We haven't seen those skuas before."

"Well?"

"I think they're land-based birds, spending the nights ashore."

"Are you sure?"

"Not sure, just an idea. Where do you think we are?"

"I'm not sure."

"Let's follow the birds." Gordon shrugged his shoulders. His commander was proving surprisingly unorthodox. That evening, as the skuas flew off to the east, Gregory felt he could smell the scent of land. The wind dropped to a whisper. He ordered the ship's boat to be lowered, towing them east, rowers changed every two hours, a lead line swinging. He threw straws into the water and noted their speed and direction, looking at an outdated chart of the islands, seven in all.

Gregory stayed on watch most of the night. If the wind increased, they would have to take in the boat and bear away. It did not. By morning they made out low-lying land ahead and could smell the scent of land. Now to find Castle Harbour. Gordon wondered how much of these procedures Gregory would put in the official ship's log. Boats came out from the shore, offering to assist in towing them towards Castle Harbour. Gregory gratefully accepted the offer as the increasing wind was on the nose. Their own boat brought warps which were eagerly taken up. They were carefully towed through the entrance, Gregory noticing the island's unique pines to undertake spar repairs. He did not want to bring his first command back home in a partly wrecked state.

The harbour was large, with St George up in the far corner. He let parties ashore under the watchful eyes of the quartermaster. Any seaman found drunk would not be allowed ashore again. He and Gordon were entertained by the president of the council and his lady, the president having in his possession a recent despatch saying that, after his time there, he was to sail on to the Azores. The locals, very able craftsmen, were of great assistance in repairing the rigging, the unique pines making excellent spar replacements.

Gregory also noticed how the health of his crew improved with fresh produce. On the first Sunday, a ship's detail led by Gregory in his best uniform, marched up the steep steps to St. Peter's Church to give thanks to the Lord for their safe arrival after a difficult passage, marvelling at the interior woodwork, the design suggesting the carpenters were more used to building ships than the roofs of churches.

After five weeks, with the frigate looking more like the trim vessel Gregory took command of, they were towed carefully out of Castle Harbour and sufficiently offshore to pick up the prevailing westerlies to begin the 1,900-mile journey to Horta. This being a well know route, a course was set nor-nor-east in accordance with laid down sailing instructions.

After 15 miles, the fairy isles were lost over the horizon. Overnight the seas started to build. Two days later, they were sailing under lower fore and mainsail only, breaking seas swirling over the deck. They could only but run before the storm, fortunately in their intended general direction. For the next three days, they were becalmed in confused and lumpy seas, their sails banging about. The sailing master advised furling to prevent damage, to which Gregory reluctantly agreed. Ten days later, the weather changed with blinding rain squalls. All watches were stretched to the limit.

With still another 900 miles to go, they were again becalmed. When the wind eventually returned, it was dead ahead, which meant, with their square rig, they were losing ground in a manner difficult to calculate until they could get a sun shot. Pods of dolphins appeared, riding on the bow waves, relieving the monotony.

After 25 days, according to their distance run calculations, Gregory and Gordon agreed they were in the right latitude. As usual, longitude was the problem. There appeared no other way but to sail west for two days, then east for four. Gordon wondered whether his lieutenant commander had any unorthodox way of finding these islands. He watched him looking at the clouds as if for guiding angels. "I think it's in that direction," he said, pointing east-nor-east, "that towering darker cloud, streaming away with the wind. I think that bears ash coming from Sao Miguel."

"What's that?"

"A volcano on the island of Sao Miguel. I've been interested in volcanoes since reading about Pompeii. We'll head in that direction." After a day's sail, distant peaks appeared which gradually became islands. Horta was not too hard to find. Gregory picked out what looked like some sort of galleon ahead, the first sail they had seen. To starboard, the Island of Pico was unmistakable. Horta, he knew, was on the opposite island of Faial. They had arrived at their instructed destination.

The water was deep, he could have almost sailed alongside, but common sense said that it would be best to put down the ship's boat and get warps ashore. He did not want to hazard his vessel. Tied alongside, Gregory learnt that there was a tidal range of about four and a half feet and a current from the south-east flowing at about half a knot.

On the first morning ashore, not far from the quay, Gregory and Gordon came across a group of people fervently praising a local saint for the recovery of a child found locked in a nearby sail loft, thought to have been lost in the harbour. Gordon found his commander quite taken by the scene and the child. "I would like a child, but a life at sea would mean I would rarely see it. I would need to resign from the service."

Gordon looked surprised. There was a lot he had still to learn about his commander. For his part, promotion was the goal. He did not want a wife and child. "Where do we look for a despatch? Is there a British resident, a mayor, a fort commander, a senior British ship in port? We need to find out," Gregory mused.

They never did find a despatch. While waiting, they learnt that the Flemish had settled in the area and that recently there had been an earthquake which accounted for some damaged buildings. After two weeks, a ninety-eight-gun second-rater called. Gregory asked the captain if he had a despatch for him, but the captain did not. Two weeks later, Gregory announced that they would make sail. He was not prepared to wait in Horta indefinitely.

"Where to?" Gordon asked.

"Gibraltar initially, it's spring back home after a very cold winter. We can't wait here all year."

"Are you sure you're doing the right thing?"

"Not necessarily. See that port dues are paid, and we've got aboard good stocks of food and fresh water." Gordon could only do as he was directed, wondering. Two days later, they shaped a course for Gibraltar.

Gregory and Gordon agreed it was a voyage of about 1,300 miles. Making an average of five knots they would be about 10 days at sea with a fair wind from the west. With adverse winds, they would not get anywhere. That was the nature of sailing. Their course would be due east without allowing for currents and leeway, of which their charts gave little information. They would have to throw floating objects overboard and try to calculate what way they were moving and at what speed as a means of trying to measure the amount they were being offset.

When, after 15 days, the distinctive rock of Gibraltar came into view in the dusk, they felt they had done really well. The watch cheered. They could hear the crew below clapping.

Suddenly a vessel appeared upwind, a galley, a low silhouette on the horizon rowing frantically into the wind. "They didn't like the look of us," Gordon observed."

"They certainly didn't," Gregory agreed. "They could see our high sails long before we could see them."

"We'll make Gibraltar by morning."

"Perhaps." Gregory moved aft to the helmsman, asking a seaman to tell the sailing master he wanted his presence at the helm. "We're going to alter course south-east," he said when he had him by his side at the helm. "It will be a fast point of sail for us as long as the wind holds steady. I want the maximum safe speed."

Gordon was intrigued. That course would not get them to Gibraltar. He would have very much liked to ask why the change of course but felt that it would not be in his interests to be always querying his commander's decisions. He was further intrigued when Gregory climbed the foremast and squeezed up through the hole into the foremast crow's nest, the watch looking on curiously. Hearing a muttering from one of the seamen, he called him out strongly, which he knew would meet his commander's approval.

It was bright moonlight. Gordon could make out his commander peering ahead with a night glass. A seaman in the rigging scrambled down and hurried towards Gordon, who was standing by the helm, with the message that the frigate was to be held steady as she goes. What next? Near dawn, he was to find out.

"Clear for action!" was beaten. The command caused a sensation. It could not be a drill at this time of day. There followed the gigantic hubbub of everything stored and bulwark protection stuffed into place, petty officers wives donning soft footwear, bringing up powder from the magazine to the guns. At that point, Gregory intervened, saying he only wanted the bow chasers charged and the first two guns on the starboard side. He particularly did not want a trail of powder leading down to the magazine.

As the light increased, all could see that they were bearing down fast on a galley from upwind, the galley not being able to do its usual manoeuvre, which was to row directly into the wind. Gregory went up to the bow chaser guns, rolled out, ready to fire. "When we're 50 feet from them, take out their larboard oars." Gordon observed the enthusiasm in the eyes of the gun layer. "Grappling hooks ready! Lieutenant Maplefield, assemble a boarding party, prepare to board!"

The suspense was nerve tingling. Gregory winced for his nicely repaired frigate as they crunched alongside, splintered oars spinning aboard, causing gun crews to duck. He went to the two run-out starboard guns.

"Precisely take down their masts. Don't fire until their decks are clear." After shouting, clashing cutlasses on scimitars and small arms fire, the boarding party disappeared below to emerge with white shaken figures. Gordon being hugged by a grateful woman, followed by a gentleman carrying a crippled, fair-haired child.

Chapter Twelve

"That's cheeky Sub-lieutenant Travallyn, who went along with a seaman who was overheard saying that the *Monmouth* was off Falmouth when his captain said they were approaching Benbridge Point!" Gregory exclaimed loudly for all to hear.

"I would have you know, sir, that you are addressing Magistrate Travallyn, studying law to become a high court judge," Brandon replied equally loudly. Gregory said no more. All officers knew that the whole naval system was based on patronage. When he found that the gentleman carrying the crippled child with the lovely golden tresses was a lord, he invited them into his cabin. A lord could have friends in high places like in the Admiralty. One had to be very careful not to offend.

"Come to my cabin, m'lord, m'lady, you must have had a terrifying ordeal. I'm Lieutenant Commander Mainhampton-Sutton, at your service."

"Lord Antony, lady and daughter. My lady and daughter were attempting to disguise who they were, hence their dress. Thank goodness for the navy." Antony sat down on a bench, his head in his hands, Eleanor holding him sobbing, Maribel on his lap, the pupils of her eyes dilated, strangely white and still.

Gregory could see that they were in a state of shock, especially the child. He did not know what to say. This was beyond his experience. "Can I get you wine and order up a meal?"

"The others are the crew of the small boat we were captured in, commanded by Magistrate Travallyn, a personal friend, one-time naval officer. Together we were involved in trying to find out how Barbary pirates, raiding the English south coast, were getting precise information from some traitorous person or group ashore. I had hired a longboat to search for a galley lurking just out of sight of land. My daughter was snatched to lure us into attempting a rescue to put an end to our inquiries. We had previously surprised another galley up the Axe Estuary and rescued many young people seized in an accurately targeted snatch. We would appreciate a meal and time to recover, thank you."

"Unless orders are awaiting me, after taking on water and fresh food at Gibraltar, we'll head for home. What port would suit you best?"

"Lyme Regis, Commander, thank you." Realising they were best left alone, Gregory withdrew, ordering up wine and the best meal possible while underway. He went to find Gordon.

"Accommodate Magistrate Travallyn, Lieutenant Maplefield." Gordon looked appalled. It was the last thing he wanted to do but philosophically realised the need.

"What is the galley situation? One of the captives, a big Portuguese, seemed able to communicate with the pirates and knew how to go about releasing the galley slaves, captives from many nations, no English."

"Right, leave the galley to the slave oarsmen; it's no use to us as a prize. Put the pirates, officers and men in their boat and let them take their chance. Really, we should throw them all overboard like they do."

"Very good, sir."

Gregory returned to his stern cabin. "I would like the carpenter to construct for you, m'lord, and your lady, your own area and sleeping arrangements."

"Make the bunk big enough to accommodate Maribel; she needs to be beside us. She's not well, if you please, Commander."

"As you wish, m'lord. I'm afraid there'll be some disruption."

"We'll go and check on the rest of my crew."

"They're on the mess deck other than Magistrate Travallyn, who's in Lieutenant Maplefield's cabin."

Antony was aware that legally Eleanor was not his wife or Eleanor the mother of Maribel, but while they were away from the castle, he liked to have it where their hearts lay. The good lieutenant commander would not be any the wiser. When he became marquis, he would live the life he wanted. For him, the result of the recent nightmare was to reinforce his desire to make the world around him a better place, starting with their own estate.

He talked to all of his crew who were in an equal state of shock, Joao appearing the most resilient. He had been a galley slave. He expressed to Antony what his present concern was, "Please don't tell them, m'lord, that I used to be a sailing master."

"Don't worry, wouldn't dream of it, Joao. I don't think this ship has the need of one anyway. Your being able to communicate with the pirates made our lives a little more tolerable than they might have been, for which we're all grateful."

Antony continued down below the waterline to where women were looking after the injured. None of the boarding party had been killed, but there were some badly cut arms and damaged heads. Two amputations were possible. Antony expressed gratitude regarding their courage and wished them well. Lieutenant Maplefield was walking around with a nasty abrasion on his forehead, which, to say the least, must have given him a headache from which he was likely still to be suffering.

Having witnessed the navy in action, Antony was even more acutely aware of the contrast between his pampered life at the castle and the lives of those in other walks of life. When he eventually returned to the stern cabin, he found that a rough and ready bunk had been made for them, complete with a sailcloth and flock mattress. Ever since his arm injury, he lacked the stamina he once had and lay down gratefully to be joined by Eleanor and Maribel. Having shared between them a bottle of the lieutenant commander's best wine, they fell asleep.

When they awoke, it was some time in the evening. A meal was bought in. "This is the best we can do," Lieutenant Commander Mainhampton-Sutton said. "We damp down the galley fire while underway."

"We understand. Our first vessel was a mercantile sloop. We did not serve hot meals while underway owing to fire risk. Azores biscuits and dried fruit will do fine." They tried to make conversation with the gallant lieutenant commander who had saved their lives, but it was going to be some time before they could recover from what they had been through and indulge in normal conversation. The hideous fate they had been saved from was still a constant nightmare.

"Have you spring water for Maribel? Drinking wine all the time is not good for her." Antony could see the lieutenant commander was quite fascinated by her. He was obviously fond of children by his manner and brought out a bottle of spring water from his well-padded wine store, pouring it out into a fine glass, giving it to Maribel, concerned by her still white appearance and dilated eye pupils. "And one more favour, Commander, while incarcerated, we were bitten by everything that bites. Have you a helpful balm?"

"I have from Bermuda Aloe Vera, a wonder balm, mentioned in the Bible." He went to another locker and took out a pot, gently rubbing Maribel's hands and arms with it before handing it to Eleanor to apply elsewhere. Eleanor took her behind their screened-off portion of the cabin and rubbed it all over her, as she did herself, coming out and offering it to Antony to do the same.

"If you have enough, Commander, we would appreciate all our crew using it. That would help the nasty little denizens spreading to your crew."

"The very reason I took on a good supply at Bermuda. They can be a plague onboard, bringing sickness and bad temper." With less skin irritation, Antony and Eleanor forced themselves into conversation in gratitude for their rescue. They were relieved when Gregory excused himself. He had been up practically all the night before.

Safe and secure, Antony, Eleanor and Maribel lay down on their bed – after what they had been through, a luxury. "I find it hard to believe," Eleanor sighed after Maribel had fallen asleep between them, holding them both close, "that our ghastly fate has changed. I would like a child of my own before I got too old, you being the father, but to bring a child into such an uncertain world? Will it get colder and colder? Will the scourge of Barbary pirates ever end? Can enough food be grown if the climate continues to become colder? Is it right to bring a child into such an uncertain future?"

"We certainly won't be trying for a child tonight, but if conditions improve, when I'm in charge, it might be nice if Maribel had a little brother or sister. But I know how you feel."

"What are you going to do for money when we get back? None of us have a penny? How are you going to pay the commander?"

"I don't think he needs paying. He took all the gold and coinage he could find and will be paying it out naval fashion to his crew. I left my money with the innkeeper of the Bear and Buzzard. It's what's now best for you and Maribel. I've been thinking about it. I'd like to put you where no one would think of looking, in the castle."

"Oh no?"

"It'll be spring; the new manor must be progressing. Soon members of the household will be moving in. The castle will become increasingly redundant, modified over the years as it has been from the fortress it originally was. There are plenty of places you could live quietly in it while parties were scouring the countryside, whether from the castle or the Barbary pirates' English agents. My left shoulder still hurts, and my left arm is weak from the attempt on my life.

"I know."

"I have to rest at times as if I were an old man."

"I know." Eleanor put her arm about him and held him close. It was moments like these Antony knew why he loved her for her love and compassion, something very precious.

"Tomorrow, we should go out on deck. We've been kept in the dark for long enough. It's warm in these latitudes. The lieutenant commander keeps a happy ship. He is respected for his firm discipline and consistent management. All know where they stand. He will go far."

"He's also fond of children."

"I've noticed that. I'm sure he would like some of his own. All of us could do with mixing with his off-duty crew to help us get over our recent ordeal as well as getting some sunshine and fresh air."

"I hear we'll be in Gibraltar tomorrow."

"Everyone's looking forward to that. I think this is Lieutenant Commander's first independent command. If he's left without further directive, he'll be in a difficult position."

"Is that a problem?"

"I think it poses a problem for him as to what to do next."

"He said he was going to take us to Lyme Regis."

"I don't know if this meant carrying on eastwards into the Mediterranean to show the flag or straight away. There's an island called Malta, ruled by the Order of St John. The Ottoman Empire attempted to take it in a great siege in 1565 but was unsuccessful. I need to get back to the castle."

"Must you?"

"I'm afraid so. Now we've been freed, let's enjoy our time together." Antony gave Eleanor a hug and Maribel a long cuddle to help her recover before falling asleep, lulled by the rise and fall of the ship and the sighing of the wind in the sails.

They were wakened by Gregory tapping gently on the partition. "We'll be in Gibraltar in about four hours, m'lord, if the wind holds as it is. If it changes, it can be anyone's guess."

"Thank you, Commander." Antony thought how their mercantile sloop could beat to windward. He had heard that the navy did possess sloops, but their role was fast message carrying.

"I can order up breakfast, but if the wind holds, you might be better served waiting until we arrive at Gibraltar. I'll give you a bottle of spring water in the meantime. Is your daughter a little better? She seems so pale and still, especially for a child?" "No, she's not. She's been a captive longer than the rest of us, initially on her own."

"Poor thing. Let me know if there's anything I can do?"

Fortunately, the wind held its direction. Antony could recognise the great slab of rock from sketches hanging in the castle. It looked impressive as they approached mid-morning, captured firstly by the Dutch in an audacious raid in April 1607. Sails were smartly furled, and the ship's boat launched to begin towing them into the tideless harbour to anchor. Directedly after, Gregory, in the ship's boat, headed for shore to discover whether there was a waiting directive. At the same time, boats came out laden with fruit and local produce, the master at arms calling them alongside one at a time to allow Cook to taste and bargain.

That evening they dined on deck, Cook and assistants excelling themselves in producing a meal fit for a king, Antony, Brandon, Eleanor and Maribel dining at the high table with the ship's officers. Gregory fussed over Maribel, at one point calling the carpenter over with instructions to make her crutches, her formers ones being left behind when she was seized. "I hope your daughter improves. She seems so quiet and still for a child, and her eyes look strange."

"No, she isn't. She's in a state of shock. She was a captive longer than the rest of us, initially on her own." Antony noticed how smart the officers looked in their cocked hats, smart black jackets with long white guilt lapels and cuffs ending in lace, white guilt waistcoats, black knee-length pants and white socks with gold buckles on their shoes. Both had attended barbers ashore and were, for the present, smooth-shaven, making them look younger.

The next day they went ashore with Gregory, the Union Flag flying over the naval base along with the flag of England. Gregory said the naval base should be flying only the Union Flag, but old habits persist. Eleanor could see Antony wince when he put Maribel on his shoulders, showing he was still having trouble with his injury. Antony continued to worry about how much hurt Maribel had sustained from their recent ordeal, especially being a captive longer than the others, to start with on her own. Antony, too, had noticed that the pupils of her eyes were dilated, her skin clammy, and she was unusually still. Antony patted her reassuringly and tried to make her laugh by pretending to be a galloping horse but did not succeed. He frowned. She could not smile, let alone laugh. "What shall we do to get her out of her state of shock?"

"Lots of love and tender care," Eleanor replied, reaching up and giving her a hug, "keep her warm and snug."

"Of course, at the castle, you'll be with her all the time, and I'll contrive to see her daily."

"She would like to see you daily. She needs us both."

"I would like to see you both daily. This was the problem when you were in hiding elsewhere."

"As long as it works. Life's such a worry. I'm scared every day."

"And I'm frightened for you. While my father's alive, I too would be in considerable difficulties if he knew I was hiding you both."

That evening, eating again on deck, listening to Lieutenant Gordon Maplefield, Antony realised not everyone shared his rather pessimistic view of life. Gordon was optimistic, contrasting life today with what his grandfather had told him about what life was like under the Puritans. Since the Restoration, he said people could have fun once again, laugh, throw parties, dress colourfully, enjoy Christmas. Under the Puritans, people had to work hard; they were not to celebrate saint days; there was a monthly day of fasting instead, and sports and entertainment were banned. Sunday was a holy day; people judged to be doing unnecessary work were put in stocks. It was good to be alive in this much freer age. He was sure the climate would get warmer again.

Antony had not known his grandfather. Most people did not survive into their fifties, let alone their sixties; those who did were well-to-do, enjoying better housing and food. Preoccupied with his own worries, it was a revelation to know there were people out there who thought life was good. Maybe, now freed, perhaps he should have a more positive outlook. "It was good talking to you, Lieutenant. I wish you luck."

That evening he told Eleanor about his conversation. "That's nice to know, but he's not in our position."

Chapter Thirteen

Next morning, Gregory told them he had decided to weigh anchor and make for England, having taken aboard all the supplies he needed, there being no directive to do otherwise. The ship's boat was manned at first light and, looking out the stern windows, Antony could see they were being towed into a wide bay. As the ship's boat was hoisted, sails were unfurled. Before long, they were sailing south-west to clear Vape de Sao Vicente. Underway, they could not use a chamber pot but had to carry Maribel to the heads, which clearly distressed her. "Must I go there?" Lifting her skirts, Antony observed her knees were scratched.

"I noticed that when I rubbed her with balm," Eleanor said.

"Before you were captured, I had to crawl there myself."

There were times when Antony was pleased he had a privileged status. "Gregory is obviously fond of you. I will ask him if the ship has some container with a tight lid we can use as a chamber pot for you."

Sure enough, such a container was soon found, after which they all went up on deck. Gregory came over. Maribel sweetly thanked him. "Mamma is the best helmswoman ever. Can she have a go at the helm?"

Gregory looked surprised. "She's never helmed a square-rigger, but what Maribel says is true," Antony confirmed.

To please Maribel, Gregory said he would allow her try with the helmsman standing over her. For a ship to be taken-aback was costly and devasting. Shyly, Eleanor stood up to the helm. Within seconds the ship came alive. She could anticipate the gusts and curling seas. Gregory signalled for the log and knots to be counted with reference to the half-minute sandglass. "Is there anything else your family can do amazingly well?"

"Maribel is very clever, mathematically brilliant. She could soon learn how to navigate."

"And what about you, m'lord?"

"I have no special talent." Antony, not for the first time, wondered about Maribel's real mother and her heritage, something he must find more about. Who were her parents? Watching Eleanor proudly, Antony felt the pupils of Maribel's eyes were a little less dilated, which he felt must be a good sign.

Three days later, they cleared Cape de Sao Vicente and headed west to pick up the trade winds out in the Atlantic. A pod of dolphins joined the ship, riding the bow waves, gambolling alongside, occasionally leaping high into the air and landing with a resounding slap. Maribel was fascinated; Antony held her securely on the bulwark. When he eventually tired, Eleanor explained about Antony's left shoulder. Hearing this, Gregory offered to take a turn, holding Maribel firmly but tenderly, obviously fond of her. Maribel did not mind, sensing his kindness and care.

"We need to head well out west," Gregory said to Antony. "In January, the trade winds are favourable. By

July, they're not, the Horse Latitudes moving north. In this mid-season, we need to be careful not to be caught out." It would be some time before he was back in the castle, Antony thought, wondering what he was going to tell his father. After his last success, he did not want to tell him he had been so inept as to be captured himself by the Barbary pirates.

His thoughts were interrupted by Maribel. "I like your face all smooth, Dadda," Maribel said.

"That's because we visited the barbers in Gibraltar. Ships don't carry barbers; they move about too much at sea for it to be safe to shave. I'll have to wait until we're back in England."

Gregory did his best to help Maribel. He had two light spars rigged up on deck and encouraged her to try walking, holding onto the spars to strengthen her legs, and he contrived to give her the best to eat the ship could offer. Anthony could see him leaving the navy to have and enjoy children of his own before long, whereas Gordon was very much a career officer.

After a number of days westward sailing, the frigate turned north, borne by the trade winds. The weather got perceptibly cooler. All on deck needed to dress more warmly. Gregory showed Maribel how the Davis quadrant was used when the sun appeared at its highest point. It was an arc fixed to a staff so that it could slide along to cast its shadow on the horizon vane. The navigating officer, with his back to the sun, looked along the staff through a slit on the horizon vein, sliding the arc so that the shadow aligned with the horizon. This enabled the angle of the sun to be read on the graduated staff, its accuracy depending on the length of the staff. In this way, latitude could be determined. How far east and west was the problem. At night and in bad weather, if they calculated they were nearing land, navigators had to be very careful, maintaining a double lookout or even standing off till dawn.

With all the attention and stimulation, Antony and Eleanor noticed Maribel was brightening, the pupils of her eyes less dilated. The next day when Gregory was undertaking his usual noon sighting, a sudden, out of the ordinary size wave hit the frigate, causing Gregory to nearly lose hold of the precious Davis quadrant. He staggered and danced about, trying to hold onto the device at which Maribel gave a tinkling laugh, the first heard from her since her ordeal.

All on deck were appalled – to laugh at the commander! There was deadly silence. Realising it was Maribel, Gregory gave the quadrant to Gordon, went over to Eleanor, who was holding Maribel in her arms and gave Maribel a hug. Appreciating what the laugh meant, Eleanor spontaneously gave Gregory a kiss. After a further minute of silence, those of all ranks witnessing broke into a polite cheer; never had there been such a scene on one of His Majesty's naval vessels! After that, stern ship's discipline followed for the rest of the day, signalling that this very humane lapse was at an end. Maribel, nevertheless, had won many hearts.

Of an evening, Gregory liked to be invited into Antony's half of the stern cabin, obviously enjoying family company, Maribel being the special attraction. He talked about his desire to see her walking on crutches by the end of the voyage. During his later visits, they learned they were nearing landfall, the frigate standing off during the hours of darkness.

A few days later, there was the cry of land in sight. Drawing nearer, the Lizard was recognised. They knew where they were. Gregory decided not to call in at Falmouth but to proceed up to Lyme Regis, saying Falmouth was a wild and unpredictable place. At Lyme Regis, Antony said he would like to slip quietly ashore to collect the gold he had left at the Bear and Buzzard so he could pay his crew. To his surprise, Gregory insisted he must not slip ashore, but he would have him landed with a substantial ship's escort to show the town and Barbary agents that the increasingly powerful Royal Navy was there to protect them, a force to be reckoned with. Antony, on the other hand, felt that he would be better able to uncover the person or syndicate behind feeding the Barbary pirates with precise information if it were thought he and Brandon had been captured and sold into slavery. However, he knew he had a moral obligation to go along with Gregory's wishes as, if it were not for him, he would have been sold into slavery.

A number of days later, the ship's boat towed them into Lyme Regis, eager hands wanting to earn a penny by assisting. After which, to the applause of the townspeople, a substantial armed ship's contingent landed, and Antony and Brandon were escorted to the Bear and Buzzard. The proprietor opened the door in alarm, surprised to see them, maintaining the coinage left with him was intact. Antony roughly assessed it was, leaving him with a sovereign, after which the contingent left for the quay, "Showing the Flag," as Gregory put it. Eventually, Antony realised his father would receive a garbled version of all this, wondering why Antony had a Royal Navy escort and what it all meant. Antony would have to offer some convincing explanation.

They spent the night in the harbour. Now he had money, Antony ordered from shore a substantial meal with all the trimmings, which the officers had in the stern cabin. Half of it was shared among the ship's crew on the lower deck, it being too cold to sit out on deck. The next day they were towed out of the harbour to continue the journey to Castle Creek.

As the onshore wind made anchoring unsuitable, they had the tricky procedure of losing way sufficiently for the ship's boat to be launched. Antony could see Gregory was quite upset to be saying goodbye to Maribel. Antony told him that, when he was marquis, he would be a welcome guest at the castle at any time for as long as he wanted to stay. He thanked him warmly for rescuing them and doing so much for Maribel, who shyly gave him a kiss.

The ship's boat was crowded, heaving up and down in the swell. Once in the shelter of the creek, they waited for the tide to be an hour off high water before rowing to Castle Landing, where they again waited while Antony went up to the sleeping castle to make contact with Claude through the servants' quarter.

When he had, Brandon and their crew left the ship's boat, walking silently on to Castle Inn. Meanwhile, Eleanor and Maribel hid nervously in the shadows, waiting for Antony to escort them in the darkness, via the servants' quarters, up to the unoccupied south-west tower. The ship's boat left with the turning tide.

To gain the top floor, Antony did not use the later staircases but led them to the original stone stairway in the wall, accessed from behind panelling which Antony had discovered when he was a boy. In this way, they slipped up to the top storey, their footsteps making no echoing clatter on stone steps, and enough light coming through the arrow-slit apertures to help them feel their way. On the top floor, bedding was there from the last occupants, Claude bringing up cold food left over from the evening meal. Antony decided to stay with them for the rest of the night before appearing before his father the next day.

In the event, the next day he felt tired, his arm hurt, so he decided to spend another day with Eleanor and Maribel, reminding them and himself to keep away from the windows. It being late into spring, with the sun on the windows and the conical roof, it was amazing how warm it became.

They had a lazy time, revelling in the fact that Maribel was over her state of shock, at one point walking her up and down together, hands under her armpits to try and keep up the good work of strengthening and co-ordinating her legs. That night they all slept together, Antony appreciating that he could not disappear every night to be with them.

Reluctantly, early the next day, giving both Eleanor and Maribel kisses and long hugs, he slipped down the old stone stairway within the walls, listened, and slid through the panelling, shutting it carefully after him. Then he made his way through the servant quarters, a few looking at him curiously, up to the quarters he shared with Lady Beatrice. When she eventually woke up, she found him being shaved by the castle barber.

"Where the hell have you been? You've been away for months!" She looked at him critically, noting he looked older, his eyes expressing suffering she could not understand, lean, deeply sun-tanned other than where his beard had been compared with the plump, soft-living men she knew. She even felt she could smell salt on his faded, worn clothes. In his usual manner, he gave her no answer, her maid servant quivering at the violence of her questioning.

"Carry on, Ben," Antony said to the barber who had stopped shaving him, his hands shaking.

"As you wish, m'lord." Slowly, with care, Ben continued.

Later that morning, Antony went down to meet his father in a change of clothes. His father, looking frail and older, was pleased to see him. "You've been away for months. We've heard all sorts of conflicting rumours, the last being you were seen with the Royal Navy. You look haunted as if you've seen a ghost."

"You could put it that way."

"How can you get a legitimate heir if you're away all the time?"

"I was on an important mission affecting the lives of many."

"Your duty is here, looking after our lands and people."

"That I intend doing, but first Magistrate Brandon and I wish to put an end to the scourge of the Barbary pirates receiving precise information from an informer or informers."

"Have you made progress?"

"We're getting nearer," Antony replied somewhat untruthfully.

"Leave that. Stay here where you're needed or I'll stop your allowance."

"The Royal Navy is actively looking out for and hunting down Barbary pirates," Antony commented, changing the subject.

"About time. Make sure you're at evening meal," his father said, indicating he was about to rest by the fire.

Three days later, when Antony contrived to slip up and see Eleanor and Maribel, he said, "Why don't we disappear for a few days and give ourselves a little time together without any other commitment or involvement?"

"Would that be possible?" Eleanor asked.

"Wonderful!" Maribel called. "As long as those terrible Barbary pirates have no way of finding out."

"Not possible this time. No one will."

"Where are we going?"

"Not far, into the forest on foot. My horses won't be gone. Only Claude will know we're away, and he won't know where so that it could never be got out of him."

"So where?" Eleanor and Maribel asked together, intrigued.

Some time back, riding alone, I came across a pair of charcoal burners. They are generally solitary men, but this was a man and his wife who supplied charcoal to our blacksmiths. I never knew they existed in our forests, nor does anyone else. They've been forgotten. We could stay with them for three nights while the days are still warm. It would be primitive, but we've got used to basic living. How about it?"

"Just ourselves and the couple, no escort?"

"Just ourselves and the solitary couple."

"Dare we?" Eleanor queried.

"Why not."

So it was agreed. Two days later, they slipped out through the servants' quarters with Claude's assistance while the castle was still asleep. Outside, between them carrying Maribel and her crutches, they made their way into the forest at first light. Coppicing had not been done for years. The forest, thick and dark, was a mysterious place with no discernible pathways. They only knew their way by the distinctive suppressed combustion smell of charcoal burning not far to the north.

"Goblins and sprites!" Maribel said, knowing her father did not like her saying such things.

Antony was not going to get into an argument with her. "Only good fairies inhabit our woodlands."

"Are you sure?"

"Positive."

"I think I can feel their presence."

"Smell the suppressed wood burning."

"Funny smell."

"I have to put Maribel down," Eleanor said.

"Of course, I'll take her," Antony responded. "There's no hurry. We're not being followed."

Half an hour later by the sun's inclination, in a clearing made by the falling of a large tree, they heard an exclamation and a firearm being cocked. Antony called out who he was.

"Welcome, m'lord." was the reply. Leaving his pistols in their holsters, Antony went to meet the surprised charcoal burner and his wife. "You gave us a fright. Since the forest has been neglected, we see no one." He put aside his blunderbuss.

"When the economy improves, we'll coppice again. If you don't mind, we've come to stay near you for three nights." He gave the charcoal burner half a guinea. "My Lady and my daughter," he went on, introducing Eleanor and Maribel. "We've been under a lot of pressure of late, and we want to get away from it all for three nights. No one must know."

"We are honoured, your Lordship, but our living conditions are far from what you're used to."

"That we understand. We're experienced in living under campaign conditions."

"In our tiny wattle cottage, there's only room for the two of us."

"I was looking to construct a bower for us in the lee of your stone kiln. That should keep us nice and warm."

"It won't keep out the rain."

"The weather looks settled for the next two or three days. If it changes, we'll go home. Your names are?"

"Robert and Shelley, what are you going to eat, m'lord?"

"I was hoping you and Shelley could provide for us." He showed them another half guinea.

"Not what you're used to eating, m'lord."

"We understand. Just make sure nobody knows we're here."

"Nobody comes this way." Looking very puzzled, Robert and Shelley went into their hut, amazed and a little alarmed. But as the day wore on, bewitched by the charming smiles of Eleanor and Maribel, they relaxed, and a bond was formed.

A stream from the hills where there were no habitations gurgled nearby, bringing lovely, sweet drinking water. They drank to their hearts' content. "I'll make our bower," Antony said enthusiastically, picking up a hand axe. He loved making things but was rarely given the chance. "While Maribel sits by me, seeing how many birds of the forest she can count, perhaps you could collect dried moss for me, please, Eleanor."

By mid-afternoon, up against the kiln on the lee side, Antony had completed his bower. It was nice and warm owing to the proximity of the kiln, which needed constant watching over by Robert or Shelley.

After a snooze in the sun, Antony said to Robert, "Fancy a bit of poaching for trout for evening meal?"

"Poaching, m'lord?"

"One of our dragoons, a former poacher who would have been transported had I not felt he could be more useful employed by us, explained to me how it was done. You go to a bend in the stream on the outer, deeper side, under the shadow of which trout migrating upstream to spawn rest. Very gently and slowly, you put your hand in the water until you feel the tail of a trout. Even more gently, you begin rubbing its tummy. Suddenly, with a finger each side, you dart your hand upwards into its gills, pushing the nose of the fish into the bank. Then you drag it upwards and throw it over the bank onto where you're lying. Shall we try?"

"What on earth are you doing, Robert?" Shelley shouted when she came out to attend the kiln.

"Poaching, His Lordship showed me. Look. I've got two trout for evening meal!"

"Well, I never. What next?"

"Can Dadda be poaching on our own land?" Maribel asked.

"He can't be personally, though his father would be outraged if he knew what he was doing, particularly showing others," Eleanor observed.

"Dadda's like that."

"He's liberal and controversial," Eleanor said.

"My Dadda's a good, kind man." Maribel dragged herself over and gave him a hug.

They had delicious hot fish cakes for the evening meal.

Before turning in at nightfall, Antony suggested they rub themselves with aloe vera to deter midges and other biting things. With the warmth from the kiln, they slept well though their bed creaked. Next morning, they woke up to enjoy another day under the green wood. Antony and Robert went up to another bend in the stream to find more trout under an overhang until Shelley called Robert back, saying she was not going to attend the kiln alone, maintaining it was a man's job in any case.

Eleanor stayed alongside Maribel in the clearing, telling her the names of some of the birds about them, like blue and great tits, fantails and, of course, robins. She said if Shelley gave her a few crumbs of bread and she was still for long enough, she might get a robin to eat out of her hand. Maribel was fascinated as a robin came increasingly near, looking at her sideways with bright, inquisitive eyes. Later she began to draw birds in charcoal on discarded kiln stones.

On their last day, the sky began to cloud over. They said goodbye to Robert and Shelley, with whom they had become good friends. Antony said when he was marquis, he would invite them to the castle. They went down to the edge of the woodlands where they had to wait until nightfall. In the gathering darkness, they approached the castle. Antony went in to find Claude. While dinner was being served, employing many staff, Eleanor put a shawl over her face, Maribel doing the same, after which Antony carried Maribel through the servants' quarters up to their tower, Eleanor following.

After a quick change of clothes, Antony went in late for evening meal. Next morning, in their quarters, Lady

Beatrice woke up while Antony was being shaved. "Where have you been? Your father is cross with you missing again," she said, looking at him critically. "You've got bits of twigs in your hair."

"I've been on a little holiday."

"I don't believe you."

"Please yourself," Antony replied and left it at that.

Chapter Fourteen

Lady Isabella paced the great hall beneath the flags of her ancestors. She was recently widowed, known for her intelligence; she could speak four languages, and had amazing mathematical ability. She was bereft, not for her husband but for her coach driver, her secret lover, who had gone off to fight for the king; seeing cavaliers as dashing and romantic.

News of the how the struggle between King and Parliament went filtered down slowly to rural communities away from larger towns, the versions being more to do with the sympathies of the teller than actual facts.

Suddenly the grim reality was brought to East Oxendon. The day had begun foggy, but when the fog lifted, the thunder of artillery and staccato of musket fire rang out a mile or so away, terrifyingly near and threatening. At her orders, the doors of her ancestral home were swung closed; no flags other than their household flag were flown to show they were neutral.

Near the end of the shattering day, her personal maid burst in to tell her that her young man, a former household footman, had staggered in a side entrance wounded, saying the king had lost the nearby battle at Naseby. Roundheads were out looking for and rounding up any escaped survivors to exact retribution. Her young man needed to go into hiding immediately.

Lady Isabella did not hesitate. She donned her maid's clothing and ran to the scene of the conflict, easy to find owing to the pall of smoke. There were bodies closely packed everywhere, dead and dying, evidence of hand-to-hand fighting, wounded crying for help. Among them, roundheads were moving, seeking out those cavaliers likely to survive and rounding them up. Desperate women were scurrying around, looking for their loved ones, being roughly pushed aside by the victors.

Isabella went to where cavaliers lay in great heaps, obviously their last stand. She tried to look at faces, pulling heads up of those facing down, a terrible and frightening sight. A particularly flamboyant body caught her attention. She turned him over. It was her Amis. Though still, he did not appear badly injured but concussed. Under the cover of drifting smoke, she pulled off his outer clothes and dragged and rolled him to a line of hedges. There she pulled brush over him and ran back to her castle home, entering by a side door. Inside she had hardly time to change out of maid's clothing before roundheads began banging at the front door, demanding to be let in. She commanded her steward to let them in to search her home, which they did, causing damage by pulling off panelling in places to see what was behind.

Early next morning, she demanded from her chamberlain all the guineas he had, put on a maid's going out clothing, having instructed a donkey cart to be ready, loaded with straw. Taking a pair of pistols with a supply of black powder, balls, patches, flints and ramrod, she slipped out a sally port. Using concealed lanes to get to the recent battlefield, she found Amis where she had left him, slipping in and out of consciousness. She implored him to get up and roll into the cart, which he eventually did with difficulty. Brushing insects off him, she kissed him tenderly, put a rug over him and then straw.

What next, she could not take him back to the castle?

As in all wars, lanes and highways were packed with displaced people. She had in the cart bread and wine, but at nightfall would need shelter. Before that, she urged Amis, who was experiencing longer periods of consciousness, to get into a set of her footman's going out clothes his size, which he did with difficulty, stumbling about. She then told him to get into the cart and lie down, covering him with straw. Bumping along obscure lanes, she made her way from the battlefield. She could not take him back to the castle but needed by nightfall to find an inn.

Going south by the sun, she eventually came to a highway which she followed. Near despair, she finally came to a shabby inn with peeling paint as night was falling. She did not like the look of it, but there was nothing else. She hitched her patient donkey, got Amis out and knocked at the door. An exceedingly tall innkeeper with a dark pointed beard and of enormous girth answered her knock. "Fifteen shillings a night. Show me you can pay." Isabella showed him what she knew as a sovereign, increasingly being termed a guinea as the gold came from the Guinea region of West Africa.

"I'll be needing stabling for Ned." She indicated her patient donkey. He could be stolen."

"Two shillings." The innkeeper looked curiously at her. Who was she, in poor clothing but with a refined voice, obviously used to giving orders and being obeyed? He ushered her in, observing the man with her seemed to be a half-wit. Amis being in no condition to eat in the inglenook, Isabella ordered a meal in their room, needing to half feed Amis. When the meal was cleared away, they got out of their outer clothes and prepared for bed. It had been a long day. Cupping the candles, something she was not used to doing, she fell into bed.

But try as she may, she could not fall asleep; cuddling up to Amis, who fell asleep as soon as his head touched the pillow, made no difference. It was the enormity of what she had done, leaving the security of her ancestral home, taking to the roads without an escort, that kept her awake. Her guineas would not last indefinitely. What would they do then? When would this seemingly endless civil war draw to a close? She tossed and turned. In the early hours, she sensed a thin knife lift the latch from the outside and a tall figure enter, carrying a lantern. Isabella sat bolt upright, cocking her pistols. "Get out immediately!"

"I'm sorry, Madam, I thought I heard an intruder."

"You're the intruder!" The innkeeper backed out, obviously intent on searching for more guineas.

To Isabella's delight, in the morning, helped by a warm bed, Amis awoke free of concussion. He had no memory of the ferocious battle or that the king had lost. All he could remember was lining up, ready to charge.

In the morning, breakfasting in the inglenook, the innkeeper was in for further surprises. The half-wit had changed into an attractive and articulate young man. The woman, he now knew, was in possession of a pair of pistols of a quality he had not seen before, which must have cost a fortune. He looked at her again, noting her beautiful fair flowing locks. She was obviously a woman of high rank. Why was she in disguise driving a donkey cart? He deduced correctly they were a product of the civil war.

Out on the road, they decided to drive to the warmer and more populated south. In a lonely section, they came across a number of oafs bent on mischief. Isabella, sitting in the cart, produced her pistols, and they melted away. Later in the day, they met a particularly persistent group needing Amis to fire a warning shot to show they meant business, after which he reloaded the discharged pistol.

They continued to move slowly south together, hoping to learn that the conflict had been resolved and Isabella could return with Amis back to her ancestral home. At an inn, they learnt that King Charles had surrendered to the Scots Covenanters rather than Parliament. What did that mean? Not long after that, Isabella informed Amis she was pregnant. Under their present circumstances, this was going to make life even more difficult. Near her time, they would need to find a hospice. They zealously guarded their concealed guineas. They were not going to last indefinitely. At some point, they would have to turn back for her home, hoping the occupation had ended. In the meantime, what were they to do?

The Knights Hospitallers had long gone, but for the last hundred years, the concept of a holy mission to give care and shelter to the sick and dying had taken their place. Isabella knew there were hospices in France but not in England. Near her time, they would need to seek out a local midwife who was prepared to take her in, if such a person could be found. It was all very worrying. They went on south to slightly warmer climes.

Amis could now observe Isabella's pregnancy was becoming very obvious. Childbirth was dangerous.

Many mothers-to-be died in childbirth. They needed to stop where they were and make inquiries. After much asking, they were directed to a Mistress Stowbury who lived in a timber-framed cottage with chimneys at each end set back from the road. Mistress Stowbury looked at them dubiously, travelling in a donkey cart. "A guinea, a further guinea if you want to stay."

"I need to stay, Mistress." Isabella's refined voice and assured manner caused Mistress Stowbury to look at her closely as Amis handed her carefully out of the cart. Supporting her to the door, he gave her what additional clothing she had and one of their pistols and the materials for reloading. "Dangerous times," Isabella observed.

Mistress Stowbury looked at her even more keenly. A pair of such pistols was worth more than she earned in a year. Obviously, she was dealing with displaced quality, perhaps nobility. On that basis, she wondered whether she was at risk by taking her in. Then her humanity took over. She could not refuse a lady in time of need. She had no idea what she might have suffered in disguise on the roads.

Amis kissed Isabella tenderly. He so much hoped she would be safe. "I won't be far away." He watched anxiously as she was helped inside and the door closed. He was conscious of the need to guard their remaining guineas so that Isabella and their child, if a baby was delivered safely, had enough guineas to take the stages back to her ancestral home as life on the roads was no place for a countess with a baby.

In case of watching eyes, he drove back along the road the way they had come, stopping and constructing a frame of fallen wood on the cart over which he tied a piece of tarpaulin. After that, from a public house, he bought a bottle of wine and a loaf of bread. When it was completely dark, he came back and drove into a dense copse near Mistress Stowbury's cottage, where he stopped, hitching Ned to the cart. As best he could in the dark, he felt to see that the remaining pistol was ready to fire.

It rained heavily in the night, which would keep any prying locals indoors. Amis slept fitfully, cold and uncomfortable, praying Isabella would not succumb to sepsis. In the light of day, he listened for a sound from the cottage. None could be heard. He tied Ned to the other side of the cart to give him new grass to feed on, waiting about, hidden in the copse, fretting. During the course of the day, he drank the wine, ate the bread, and by evening, felt hungry. At night he tried to keep warm under straw, wrapped in the one rug.

The next morning, at first light, he heard the crying of a very young baby. His heart jumped, hoping Isabella had survived. Amis left the cover of the coppice and ran over to the cottage, knocking on the door. A smiling Mistress Stowbury let him in. Isabella had survived – for the present at least though sepsis could set in later. He ran towards her. "It's a girl, Amis, who I would like to call Mary."

Amis gently hugged her, peeping at the swaddled baby. It was a miracle, a lovely baby girl who he hoped would eventually have long golden locks like her mother. He had fair hair to make the chance more likely. They would need to find an inn for the night. Mother and child required a warm bed. They asked for the nearest, which was the Hare and Hind in the straggling hamlet.

As usual, the innkeeper, small, white-headed, and dressed in black, was dubious of custom arriving in a donkey cart and had to be shown a guinea before they were admitted. To their relief, he appeared kindly. Amis was pleased as they would like to stay a number of nights. Fortunately, the innkeeper had no other custom to complain of a baby crying. Warm water was provided, as was a room fire. Isabella gained in strength and remained well to Amis' great relief.

Chapter Fifteen

Antony was kept busy for the next few months overseeing the building of the baroque manor house on behalf of his father, which was making progress during the summer months. During that time, he noticed his father was becoming increasingly frail. The supervision took so much of his time that he could not see Maribel and Eleanor every day, having to leave the devoted Claude the task of surreptitiously taking up food and emptying the chamber pots in the southwest tower.

When he did manage to pay Maribel and Eleanor a clandestine visit, he became increasingly aware of Maribel's concern regarding Antony leaving her, which he put down to the horrific ordeal she had been through, leaving her with anxiety and insecurity. He thought the fact that he had been ambushed and wounded might also be preying on her mind. He assured her that he had no need to ever take that route and go to that place again as she was now secretly with him at the castle.

He had provided Eleanor with linen to make new table napkins with the embroidered motto, *Ut Vivat Hodie, Cras Consilium*, To Live for Others, which, when he was marquis, was going to be the estate's new motto. When he could, he smuggled Shakespeare's plays up to Maribel, which she particularly liked. He thought these might take her mind off her worries.

But Maribel's anxieties did not lessen. In the end, he decided to disappear up into the south-west tower for a night to spend time with her and, if he possibly could, find out what might be bothering her the most. He brought with him a game of chess which she easily won. He thought that playing games might give him some sort of clue. Other than the fact that it once more demonstrated she was much brighter than either of them, it provided nothing new.

When the long late summer day ended, they prepared for bed as they dared not show a light but, before doing so, stood at the window watching the moon and stars, Antony holding Maribel close to show his love for her.

In the night, Antony and Eleanor were woken by Maribel having a terrifying nightmare. They held her close, gently shaking her awake. "It's all right, Maribel dear, we're with you," Antony murmured reassuringly. Before Maribel was finally woken, looking dazed and terrified, Antony thought she uttered the words, 'the porch'.

What did she mean by that? Antony wracked his brains. Eventually, it occurred to him. He remembered how distraught she was when brought near the church porch at Tadingham. There had to be some reason. No other church had that effect on her. Although very busy with the new mansion and generally running the estate in lieu of his father, he felt compelled to find out what may have occurred there.

To that end, he rode up early one morning to see if Magistrate Brandon happened to be in residence at Castle Inn to ask if he could borrow his escort for four days. He knew his father would not authorise a detail of the household's dragoons to provide an escort as he did not want him away.

"Not for the next four days, but why do you want them?" Antony explained the circumstances, reminding him what they had all been through and the devastating effect it had on a child who had been held captive the longest. Brandon was sympathetic. "Poor Maribel, of course," was his answer.

He told Maribel he had to be away for four days pursuing estate affairs but nothing more. He did inform Eleanor, however, of his real mission.

Antony and his escort stayed the night at the Friar and Flagon, acquiring fresh horses before riding on to Tadingham church vicarage the next day.

Before he knocked, he asked his motley escort to stay well back as he did not want to alarm the vicar. Checking they were, he knocked, calling out who he was. He was aware of being checked out through a spyhole. He stood back to show his gentleman's clothes, lace at throat and cuffs.

"What gives me the honour of a visit from you, m'lord?" the vicar asked with deference, opening the heavy door.

"I would like to speak to you privately." He paused, looking at the inquisitive and rather dominating woman peering over the vicar's shoulder.

"Leave us, my dear." The woman, who Antony took to be his wife, stamped off in a huff. Antony was ushered inside. "Do sit down. Can I offer you tea and cake?"

"No, thank you, what I've come for is to ask if you know of a tragedy associated with the porch of your church." The vicar sat down opposite, taking time to reply. He said that was what he was going to tell

Antony he had learnt from the housekeeper of the previous vicar.

He proceeded to inform him of a call one afternoon, as described by the housekeeper, of a distinguished lady to the vicarage who referred to herself as a countess, with a man and a very young baby. The countess implied they were escaping from the consequences of the Battle of Naseby. She said that the guineas they had were running out and that she had just enough left to get herself back to her ancestral home. The highways were no place for a woman like her with a very young baby, saying babies in arms were not charged for on the stages, hoping that the hue and cry for escaping cavaliers had died down by the time she returned. She asked the then vicar if he could open his church that night for her man to sleep in, as it was the convention that wanted combatants from either side could not be touched in a church. After that, Amis would endeavour to make his way back to her in the donkey cart, undertaking casual work on the way, staying in churches overnight for protection.

The vicar said that, though his bishop said he could not, he would do so on this occasion for her man. The countess noticed that the vicar had two letters, one in Spanish and one in Portuguese on his desk. She offered to translate them for him, writing the translations out in a flowing hand. The callers subsequently left, thanking the vicar most sincerely. The account was they said a tearful goodbye to each other in the church porch before reluctantly going their ways. After 20 yards, the countess looked back to see a number of renegade roundheads rushing towards Amis. She gave a cry of warning and tore back to him for both of them to be hacked down mercilessly. Their newly born baby was found unhurt between the slain couple after the assassins had left.

The vicar and his housekeeper took the baby in, hiring a wet nurse. The baby turned out to be a highly intelligent girl with long golden tresses. They became very fond of her. She brought them joy and happiness. When she grew up, she married a local yeoman. The vicar said the married couple lived with them in their large, rambling vicarage as there was more than enough room. It was not long before the girl became pregnant.

Sadly, the girl died giving birth to a daughter who survived. The daughter, in turn, grew up to be an intelligent girl like her mother with long golden hair. Eventually, her yeoman father remarried. His new wife became very jealous of this lovely girl. She said she wanted her out of the house, making her life a misery. With great reluctance, her father gave her to the former vicar's now elderly housekeeper who lived nearby in an almshouse.

By the time the girl was 12, the housekeeper knew she was dying and made arrangements for her to work as an under-maid at Antony's castle, where Antony fell in love with her. The vicar said he had found in the vicarage the two translations of letters from Spanish and Portuguese the countess had undertaken during her call, written in a distinctive hand, which Antony noted was not unlike Maribel's style of writing. He said Antony was welcome to them. Now, for the first time, Antony knew the ancestry of his lovely, intelligent daughter. He thanked the vicar warmly, carefully putting away the written translations.

Two days later, he crept up to Maribel and Eleanor's hideaway at the castle late in the evening. They were delighted he had returned. In the morning, he told Maribel where he had been and what he had found out, showing her the translations. "A countess, how tragic. I felt something awful had happened there," Maribel said.

"A very clever countess, who could write and speak at least two foreign languages and who, by her own account, ran her ancestral home as her husband had died. It was so sad how she was brutally slain saying goodbye to what must have been her lover in the porch of the church at Tadingham after rescuing him from the Battle of Naseby. Fortunately, their very young baby survived. That baby has to be your grandmother. As I've told you before, Eleanor, who you feel to be your mother as she is the only mother you know, is not your birth mother. That girl, sent to our castle home at the age of 12 to be employed as an under-maid, gave birth to you at the age of 15, fathered by me, something I was not supposed to do. I loved your birth mother very much. Now I love Eleanor and, of course, you, my darling daughter. It was what you sensed at that church porch at Tadingham that made me want to find out more."

"The baby's my grandmother?"

"Her ability has been passed down through the generations. You don't get your brains from me but from your under-maid birth mother." For a long time, Maribel said nothing, taking it all in. Then she turned to Eleanor and gave her a hug and kiss as if to say the information made no difference regarding her love for her, which met with Anthony's approval. She was a loyal girl.

"Why have you been away for four days at the Castle Inn when your father needs you here?" was the first thing Antony heard from Lady Beatrice when she woke up to find Antony being shaved in their apartment, Claude standing by with a towel.

"If you think I was staying at the Castle Inn, you were misinformed," Antony replied.

As usual, Lady Beatrice appeared much concerned regarding his whereabouts and what he was up to. Why was that? Not because she was worried about his welfare. Could it be that he might find out something she knew about or had suspicions of that she did not want uncovering? Then there was her ambivalent attitude towards the Barbary pirates targeting young people to be sold as white slaves. Everyone else in their court seemed genuinely outraged, particularly his father.

Also why did the earl, his father's oldest and closest friend, want him to marry his daughter, giving his father a substantial dowry? There must be something in all this that needed digging into, which perhaps could be linked to the person responsible for giving the Barbary pirates precise information about the whereabouts of saleable young people. As he could not constantly be away from the castle, he would express his concerns to his friend, Magistrate Travallyn.

To this end, he sent a note to him via Claude, saying he wanted to meet him at their usual rendezvous at a convenient date and time. Brandon would know he meant the fishing lodge. A week later, he received a note: *At midnight the day after next*.

After evening meal on the night arranged, Antony slipped silently out of the castle on foot, following the gurgling tidal creek down to the fishing lodge. There he fumbled for the key, helped by a break in the scudding clouds. Sitting facing the open door, cocked pistols at the ready, he waited. He was beginning to get cold when he heard a rider approach and stop, feeling for the hitching post. "Brandon?" he called softly.

"M'lord."

"Thank you for lending me your crew. Maribel now knows of her birth mother's heritage; quite revealing. It was Lady Beatrice's reaction on my return that got me thinking. After the Castle Inn, she did not know where I went, which seemed to bother her, as if I might find out something she did not want me to know. For the present, I can't leave the castle for long periods. I suggest you look into the background of the earl, my father's best friend, what he and my father got up to when they were together in the Lord General's Regiment of Foot Guards, and whether the earl lost money in the South Seas Bubble?"

"You think it might be significant?"

"Someone who lost a lot of money in the South Seas Bubble could be tempted to restore his fortunes by selling precise information to the Barbary pirates."

"You've got something there."

"See if you can track down a surviving officer senior to the two young men. Just an idea."

"I'll take it up."

"I'll help if I can."

"I'm determined to bring the person responsible to justice, especially after what I've suffered myself. Where do you think the guards' headquarters are?"

"Likely somewhere up in London. You'll need to make inquiries."

Chapter Sixteen

At end of their road, instead of turning left for Lyme Regis, Brandon and his motley escort turned right for London. By mid-afternoon, they found themselves riding through an extensive dark forest. Suddenly, without any warning, a cavalry company with shining cuirasses appeared out of the trees, surrounding and heavily outnumbering them. Only Danny, a reluctant rider languishing far behind, saw them, turned around, and bolted for home.

In the Castle Inn, Danny waited for Claude to appear for his two hours off for a gossip and a pint of ale, knowing him to be a go-between. On hearing what happened, Danny said Claude drank up quickly, hurried back to the castle, and indicated to Antony that he needed to see him urgently in private.

Concerned and intrigued, Antony heard what he had to say behind the panelling leading to the south-west tower internal wall staircase. What he heard greatly alarmed him. He knew he needed to interview Danny in person. Excusing himself from evening meal with a note to his father saying he was unwell, he hurriedly had his horse got ready and headed for Castle Inn, taking with him a handful of guineas. There he indicated to the landlord he needed a private room where he saw a very upset Danny.

Practically in tears, Danny told him what he saw, saying he was very lucky to have escaped but had no money for staying on at the inn or getting himself back home to his wife and business in Lyme Regis. Antony realised from the livery he described that Brandon and the rest of his escort had been captured by the earl's calvary company. The earl, he knew, was far too shrewd to detain them himself but would have them incarcerated in Newgate Prison for trial at the Old Bailey on some trumped-up charge.

Antony gave Danny enough guineas to stay for another night or so at Castle Inn and to buy a horse or, beyond the estate road, catch a stage for Lyme Regis. The fact that the earl had detained Brandon and his escort proved to him that he, through agents, was the person responsible for giving the Barbary pirates, at a price, the exact information needed to be able to seize vulnerable young people at will. But he had to find evidence.

He deduced that the exchange would probably take place in or in the vicinity of Lyme Regis. When this happened, there were bound to be witnesses, probably not knowing what they were witnessing. These proceedings would likely take place in the secluded inglenooks of inns like many business agreements. Any investigation would need time and resources. It might also be the reason for Lady Beatrice's behaviour. The arrangement whereby the earl and his father's children marry along with a hefty dowry might be a way of bribing his father without his realising, thinking it was due to their being such close friends and going through a lot together while in the Lord General's Regiment of Foot Guards.

A month later in late autumn, Antony received a sealed letter. It was a modest seal but definitely intact. Who could be sending him a sealed letter? It was not the earl or a legal representative; the seal was far too nondescript. He opened the letter carefully in private. It was from Danny, the only member of his loyal crew who was not in prison. He had arrived safely in Lyme Regis, sold his business, and bought a similar one in a different locality, informing no one where he and his family were moving to.

In the letter, he was told that his new assistant's friend, working in the Pigeon and Petrel, said he saw two foreign-looking men handing over large amounts of gold to two Englishmen when the group were alone in the inglenook late in the evening. He said his friend, a waiter, and his colleague, were not observed hovering in the shadows. This may be the breakthrough he was looking for if the two Englishmen, under oath, were found to be employed by the earl. He also learnt that Bandon's and his crew's indictment was that they were harassing and accusing a member of the House of Lords with a heinous crime they had no evidence of. In 1731 the role of a magistrate was not defined in the way it was to be later. If he could get these waiters to give evidence, he would have at least enough defence for the earl to drop the charges and, at the same time, convince his father of the earl's true character.

Contrary to his father's wishes, Antony concluded that he must once again leave the castle and go up to London. He would engage a barrister of high reputation for the defence of Brandon and his crew, who had risked so much for him. As his father would not provide a dragoon escort, he would have to do what Brandon did and hire suitable out-of-work men. He observed how Brandon had hired ex-navy men as, having been in the navy as a junior officer, he was taught how to manage crew and get their respect. Antony had spent much time recently on navy ships to observe how to go about managing seamen. The first thing he did in Castle Village was to put it about that he wished to hire four ex-seamen.

Within hours he had more ex-seamen than he wanted. In the end, he hired an ex-petty officer and three able seamen, giving the impression that he had once been a navy officer. He gave each a guinea, saying they would be paid monthly subject to good order, discipline and sobriety. After lunch, he said they must be on their way, seeing they were all suitably mounted, equipped with cutlasses, aiming to see how far they could get before looking for an inn for the night. By dusk, he found one, a lord and his retinue being welcome, giving his usual order that not more than four ales be served to his men through the evening.

Daily they pressed on, arriving in London after eight days. There he set about making inquiries regarding a suitable council, eventually hiring Sir Montague Gramble, Barrister of Lincoln's Inn Fields, to whom he outlined the case against Magistrate Travallyn and his retinue, saying he had two credible witnesses in their defence. Until called to make a sworn statement, they would remain in hiding; otherwise, he knew they would be eliminated. He also went on to say that he wanted Sir Montague to look into the earl's financial affairs, whether he, like many other famous figures, such as George I, had lost a fortune in the South Seas Bubble. If he had, this would be a motive for him to strike a deal with agents of the Barbary pirates to supply the exact whereabouts of groups of vulnerable young people at a substantial price.

A week later, he and his retinue arrived back at the Castle Arms. Leaving the Castle Arms late in the evening, he walked to the castle, entering through the servants' quarters, and made his way via the wall stairway up to the top of the south-west tower where Eleanor and Maribel were delighted to see him. He said he would stay with them for a day before leaving for what he hoped would be the last time for Lyme Regis for four or five days. He was very tired, and his arm was hurting. Eleanor could see he was white and weary, suffering from she did not know what. She held him close, knowing that having her with him lessened his anxieties. What he had done was all new to him and had taken its toll. She agreed he had to do all he could to rescue Brandon and his crew, who had put their lives on the line for them,

She also said how frightened she and Maribel were much of the time, staying illicitly at the castle. Antony pointed out that Lady Beatrice, with his father's permission, was employing platoons of their dragoons to scour the countryside for them, so they were safest where they were. She obviously would not be doing this if she knew that they were hidden in the castle. He said that, as usual, he was followed partway to London. He said that he and his retinue hid in the trees until their follower was alongside, then persuaded him it would be better for his health to turn back and report to Lady Beatrice that he had lost them.

With that, Antony sunk onto their bed. Concerned, Eleanor went down beside him, holding him close.

"What is the matter, Dadda?" Maribel asked, stroking his forehead.

"London is a huge place, so many people. I got a stomach problem, became weak, and my arm began aching. I found it difficult to sit my horse coming back." Realising he was whinging, he said with a wan smile, "But I'll be all right after a good night's sleep. I found sleeping difficult. I guess I missed you both." Eleanor realised that through all their other trials and tribulations, she was never far away.

"Sometimes, Antony, you say the nicest things." Eleanor was concerned for him. Unlike his father, Antony was sensitive, not the heroic type. He liked a quiet life, making and creating if he got a chance, but had been forced into actions which he was not comfortable with. He had lost weight. She knew why he needed to go back to Lyme Regis, a particularly dangerous place. If only she could help him.

Claude was surprised to see him when he brought up their food next morning. "He's only here for a day or so. He's not going downstairs. He's got to be away again. He's not particularly well," Eleanor said.

Antony spent much of the day resting on the bed. He said he would need to be away before daylight the next day so as not to be seen leaving. Maribel showed him how she could walk with support. Antony was delighted. True to his word, Antony left before dawn the following morning for the Castle Inn, where he picked up his retinue before heading for Lyme Regis, their destination, the Pigeon and Petrel.

Two days later, he arrived at the Pigeon and Petrel, where he announced himself to the owner, saying who he was. He then asked if he could interview two of his waiters, the two who had witnessed the handing over of a large amount of gold late one evening recently by two foreigners to two Englishmen in the inglenook. This was nervously granted, the owner not wanting trouble. Antony found the two waiters, Nick and Tim, to be very attractive fellows who could have been brothers but who were not.

He explained that he would pay them 200 guineas each if they were prepared to be witnesses at a possible trial at the Old Bailey, enough between them to purchase an establishment of their own. In the meantime, they would need to stay with him at his castle for their own protection as, though they did not know it, they were in mortal danger. They agreed at the prospect of owning their own business and, if they were in danger, would value his protection, working for him for a guinea a week, food and lodging being part of the deal. On the way back, Antony began wracking his brains as to what capacity he could persuade his father to employ them.

Antony found the solution on the way. He had not been feeling well when he left for Lyme Regis and was finding the journey back an ordeal. He discovered Nick and Tim to be very caring by nature, always beside him when he came to mount or dismount to give him a hand and being on hand to help him in many other ways. His father's physician, Horace, was getting old himself and was not really able to care for him properly. Nick and Tim were a very attractive pair and extremely caring by nature. He would introduce them to his father as personal helpers who could assist him in bathing and getting up in the mornings. Though his father might resent them at first, they had many winning ways.

Antony was sure they would soon win him over, much better than trying to install them in an unoccupied tower where they would get bored and be noticed at the windows, putting at the same time an additional strain on Claude.

His assumption proved correct. His father resented the idea at first, but he soon found their presence entertaining, helpful and good company, insisting they take time off one at a time.

His father, however, was very cross about his being away again, asking how Lady Beatrice could ever become pregnant if he was never about. He thought to himself that he would do his best that this never happened. He wanted Maribel as his heir, mistress in her own right.

However, he had to admit that his father's insistence on good quality, well-cooked meals made of the best seasonal foodstuffs, along with more rest, began to make him feel better.

Disappointingly his feeling of increasing well-being did not last. Two days later, he received the news that at Traveslington, the next coastal village east, there was to be a great, late harvest festival on the thirtieth of November. Many of the young people of the castle were going, like cousin Deidre, nephew Bruce and his favourite young cousin Marigold. This was just the sort of exposed assembly of young people within easy reach that the Barbary pirates would target, being informed by the sinister syndicate he and Brandon had been working to uncover and eliminate.

However, if the Royal Navy could be informed in time, the pirates ambushed on landing, they would never trust inside information again, and their threat around the English south coast would be eliminated forever. He now had an ambitious young lieutenant commander friend who would be delighted to do just that. It was a matter of getting the information to him in time, something Antony felt impelled to do.

He knew the nearest major naval base was at Portsmouth to the east. With luck, he would find him there. He must get to Portsmouth and tell him without delay. With that in mind, he paid Nick and Tim six month's wages in advance, informed Eleanor, Maribel and Claude what he intended to do, and set off before first light on foot to the Castle Inn to pick up the escort he had engaged to go with him up to London. With them, he set off eastwards to find his way to Portsmouth.

They were a number of days on the way when at the Hare and Hind hostelry, Antony became critically ill. His eyes were dilated, he was trembling, and he had muscular weakness amounting almost to paralysis. He could not speak coherently to give instructions. What were his escort to do? The ex-petty officer decided to leave the innkeeper with 10 guineas and ride back on his own with the rest of his guineas to the Castle Inn to wait for Claude's visit to seek advice.

When Claude appeared in the evening, he told him what had happened, gave him the guineas he was carrying belonging to Antony, and asked him to inform the marquis of his son's critical condition. Claude, in turn, knew better than approach the marquis but took the information and the guineas up to Eleanor.

She did not hesitate. She took the guineas plus some Antony had left her, told Maribel to take her crutches and warm ladies' clothes, put a shawl over her head, and asked Claude to take her through the sleeping servants' quarters along with Maribel, partly carrying her, to the Castle Inn. There she asked for a strong horse to carry her and Maribel back to the Friar and Flagon to see whether once again she could hire Henry and the ruby coach, then to double back east to pick up Antony and carry on to Portsmouth to inform Lieutenant Commander Gregory Mainhampton-Sutton and his frigate to ambush and eliminate the Barbary pirates for good on the thirtieth of November, which date she was sure would be conveyed to the Barbary pirates by the sinister syndicate Antony and Brandon had been working so hard to uncover and eliminate. This had been Antony's mission – and hers now for that matter.

Chapter Seventeen

The innkeeper of the Friar and Flagon knew who Eleanor was when she arrived on horseback with Maribel but was surprised to see her on her own. She told him that Sir Antony had become critically ill at the Hare and Hind to the east, and she was going to pick him up. She said that he was on an important mission, and she would see that this was carried out. He was in no fit state to sit a horse and would have to be transported in an enclosed carriage such as the ruby coach Antony hired last time. She would also hire cushions and rugs as before. She hoped in time Antony would recover. From his reported symptoms, she felt he had been poisoned, which would fit in with his important mission that a sinister party was trying to disrupt. She and Maribel intended to drink only spring water in which poison could not be disguised. She asked for two more guards to sit outside in the rear position, making three in all. She had the guineas for an extended hire. This was agreed.

Henry felt he knew his way to Portsmouth, which was a relief. They had with them a pair of pistols each and reloading materials like primer, black powder, balls, patch lubrication, flints and ramrods, which Antony had taught them how to use. Maribel complained the pistols were heavy, which was understandable in her crippled state. However, she had proved in the past that she was an extremely good shot. All this paraphernalia had to be carried in a knapsack and a change of warm clothes in another. "We've got to look and act like real ladies while we're away to carry the authority, not like scullery maids. Your father would expect it, though I find it difficult."

"We've done it before, Mamma. I like our nice clothes."

"You do indeed, and your father has found out you have aristocratic heritage. We've got to carry this through for your father, and to save a lot of innocent young lives."

"We'll do it, Mamma."

"You're a brave girl, Maribel."

"So are your Mamma. You read and write better than most ladies."

"That's because my father was a printer."

"Shall we go down to dinner?"

"We'll order up water for a bath first; we haven't been able to have one hiding in the tower. Then we'll think about how we'll have an evening meal. I'm starving."

They had their hot bath, being waited on in a manner they had learnt to expect. "I feel tired, Mamma. After the hot bath, could we eat in our room?"

"A good idea as we'll have to get going first thing in the morning. We can't afford to lose a minute." The meal that followed fitted their status, which included pigeon, roast beef, turkey, duck, and partridge, followed by sweetmeats. Eleanor carefully smelled what was claimed to be pure spring water, but as the landlord could not produce evidence of where the spring water came from, she felt they would be safer drinking champagne.

Last thing that evening, they checked their pistols before putting them on tables each side of the bed, having previously asked that the wall candles by the door be renewed so that they would see anyone entering.

The next morning it was raining when they left, which made progress on the poorly cared for roads slow. About midday, with the rain really chucking it down, their coach got stuck in a mire. Eleanor went to adjust the leather curtains covering the gilt-edged windows to stop the rain from coming in. It was at that point she noticed a sinister mounted figure wearing a dark cloak on a knoll. As she watched in increasing alarm, the figure waved a cutlass, pointing to the coach. At this, riders on horseback appeared from the trees on each side, cutlasses drawn, and moved in to surround the coach.

Somehow, Henry, his postilion and the rear guards had contrived to keep their powder dry. With their short-range spraying blunderbusses, they shot down most of them, the assailants' horses bolting in alarm. Four assailants remained, who the sinister figure urged to close in while the guards were reloading in the rain, two on each side. "Keep your pistols inside!" Eleanor hissed. "Or their recoils will break your wrists on the upper window edges!"

With a look of triumph, the remaining horsemen attempted to storm the coach. At point-blank range, Eleanor shot dead the two on her side and Maribel the other two, still complaining the pistols were heavy. "Reload!" Eleanor insisted, which they did as quickly as they could. They waited, breathing heavily in suspense.

"Well done, Your Ladyships!" Henry shouted down from outside. "They didn't expect that!"

"How did you keep your powder dry?"

"Our weapons were kept secure in lockers under our seats."

"I don't like shooting people," Maribel complained. "My wrists hurt."

"None of us do. It was them or us. Pistols are heavy. Let's hope we don't have to use them again. Just reload. Don't cock them."

"How long is it till a lunch stop?" Maribel asked. "I'm cold and shaking."

"Wrap yourself in the rugs. The wheels will have to be levered out of the mud first. The coach won't stop until we reach a place with wide views or at a tavern or inn."

After much tugging and levering, taking care not to damage the spokes, the wheels were prized out of the clinging mud as if from the jaws of a subterranean demon.

The wheels free, the rear guards cautiously looked at the men lying in the road, their blunderbusses at the ready. "A vale of horror," Maribel said with a shiver, looking out at the scene.

"A vale of sorrow," Eleanor added. "You can see they are poor men, expendable in the eyes of that evil figure sitting his horse on the rise. Some mothers, wives and children will miss them terribly and likely starve as a consequence."

"It's sad, Mamma."

"That conspiracy is what your father and Brandon in prison are trying to put a stop to."

"And we are."

"Yes, we are. Cuddle up under the rugs and keep warm. We're lucky to be in a guarded coach."

The coach did not stop until they came to a hostelry at dusk. Eleanor asked the landlord if he had heard of an ill nobleman at the Hare and Hind. He said he had, the Hare and Hind being two horse changes to the east. Eleanor was relieved to know he was not far away, impatient to leave in the morning. As usual, Eleanor made sure the landlord noted their pistols either side of their bed as a sign they were not going to be taken advantage of. Like Antony, she told Henry he and his guards had to restrict themselves to four ales over the course of an evening. She was paying for no more. Drunken guards were worse than useless, exposing them to danger.

Next morning, they were up early, Eleanor leaving Maribel on her crutches waiting at the main entrance. When she finally came out, Henry and the guards behind her, she found Maribel, holding from under her shawl cocked pistols saying to the landlord, "Mamma said our guards were to load the coach."

"Control your daughter, m'lady; she's right dangerous."

Eleanor looked around swiftly, noticing that the landlord was trying to conceal a knapsack very like the one their guineas were in, which he was no doubt hoping to swap full of small stones, obligingly loading their assembled baggage into the coach. "I gave you clear instructions that my guards were to load the coach. Lady Maribel was ensuring this was carried out. Well done, my dear." Looking sheepish, the landlord stood back.

In the coach, Eleanor said, "The landlord thought he could be well away before we were aware of the swap. It did not happen, thanks to you, my dear."

"Pistols are heavy."

"Especially to you, standing on your crutches. I'm proud of you. So will your father be when I tell him."

"Do you think Dadda will be all right?"

"I'm sure he will," Eleanor replied, sounding more confident than she felt.

Two days later they arrived at the Hare and Hind, the landlord pleased to see them. He was middle-aged, balding on top, with a large dowdy wife who appeared fussy at first meeting but who proved quite efficient. Eleanor wondered if they were complicit regarding the poisoning of Antony, if indeed he was poisoned. The three loyal, remaining escort members were obviously very relieved to see them. Eleanor and Maribel were led upstairs.

They found Antony sitting in bed in the best room. He knew who they were and was obviously very pleased to see them. He tried to speak but appeared partly paralysed; his eyes were dilated and his heart rate slow. He tried to put his arms out to them but winced at the pain."

"Has he always been like this? When did it start?" Eleanor asked.

"On his first night here, he appeared fine," the landlord replied. "He had the evening meal we all had. We found him like this in the morning, paralysed, trembling, incapable of speech or movement. He has improved since then. His men have been very good to him, going out and getting water from the Ferniricay Springs, seeing he drank plenty."

Eleanor did not know what to think. "He hasn't taken henbane, mandrake or moonshade?"

"We don't use such plants. Aren't they the plants made into balms that old ladies accused of being witches use to give them the sense of flying?"

Eleanor thought, for a landlord, he knew a lot about herbs which confused her even more about what to think. In the end, she considered the best thing was to get Antony out of the Hare and Hind and take him in their coach to Portsmouth as fast as possible. She hoped to catch Gregory's frigate, if it was still there, to persuade Gregory to ambush and annihilate the Barbary pirates as they landed. Hopefully, this would foil their plan to seize the young people undertaking a joyous late harvest festival at Traveslington on the thirtieth of November.

Not wishing to try his meals, she said she would leave with Antony straight away. His three loyal sailor escorts were given the choice of either accepting enough guineas to take them back to the Castle Inn or continuing in employment with Eleanor to help guard the coach. In view of what they had experienced, additional guards might well be a good thing. With the three sailors electing to continue employment with Eleanor, they pressed on towards Portsmouth, not finding a hostelry until after dark.

When they did, the landlord, dressed surprisingly in blue satins, seemingly rather a dandy, was concerned at their numbers, saying he could only supply a limited meal at this hour and would have to call up more horses for the morning change. That agreed, they all trooped inside, being led by m'lady, Antony being carried in on a stretcher. Eleanor explained that His Lordship was unwell with palsy, allaying the landlord's fears that he might be infectious. Eleanor said they were on an important mission and that two of their guards would be on stand-by in rotation on the landing and one downstairs through the hours of darkness. Intrigued, the landlord agreed, probably speculating what might be their important mission.

Their meal was sparse, not what they were used to, but understandable in the circumstances. What was important was that Antony seemed to be responding to the attentions of Eleanor and Maribel. He seemed to understand all they said but found it difficult to communicate as his speech was blurred as if he were drunk. He was also moving his arms more. They both hoped that before long, he might be able to walk with difficulty. They lay beside him, Maribel stroking his forehead.

"What happened to you, Dadda? Do you remember?" Maribel asked.

From what they were able to understand, he had gone to bed feeling all right at the Hare and Hind on his first evening but woke up in the night not being able to move. He appeared to like their touch and closeness, finding it soothing and gave them a faint smile. The next morning, he attempted to struggle onto his feet but fell back onto the bed. But it was an improvement.

Their men carried him onto their ruby coach, propping him up on the right side with rugs and cushions, supervised by Eleanor, after which she ordered their men to load the coach. She stood by, noting the landlord made no tricky move to interfere with their bags and that their changed horses were of good quality.

"Shouldn't we ask where we can get a physician to examine Dadda?" Maribel asked.

"Your father doesn't agree with the four humours. He says they're not scientific in this age of enlightenment, though you could say he is phlegmatic and melancholic."

"He's paralysed as if he's been knocked unconscious," Maribel insisted.

"Somebody in the Hare and Hind could have been bribed to poison him. I don't feel it was the landlord as he wouldn't want the reputation of poisoning a lord of the land, bad for his business."

"The man on horseback in the dark cloak waving the cutlass and pointing?"

"He's likely one of the principals involved," Eleanor agreed.

Antony looked interested, and Eleanor told him all about the desperate ambush incident as they drove along. He appeared to understand and eventually croaked he did not believe in the traditional humours. There was not a lot of room in the coach, so Maribel sat on his lap.

"Dadda's getting better!" she said excitedly as Antony moved his position.

"I think he is," Eleanor agreed.

They came to the next hostelry as night was falling. Antony walked in supported by two sailors, Eleanor explaining to the landlord that His Lordship had had an accident. As he did not smell of alcohol, the landlord readily accepted the explanation. Downstairs was not well lit with dark shadowy corners. "Goblins!" Maribel muttered.

"You know your father doesn't like you repeating the superstitions, as he calls them, of the servants' quarters or countryside."

"Sorry, Mamma. It's just the dark corners seem spooky."

"Maybe they do, but I need to make arrangements for our overnight stay."

As with the last landlord, Eleanor said His Lordship was on an important mission and that two of their guards would be on the upstairs landing and one downstairs on rotation through the night, to which request the landlord agreed. Before they went to bed, they reloaded their pistols, Antony watching but not trying to intervene, which Eleanor assumed meant that they were doing all right. By morning his paralysis had continued to improve. He was able to walk downstairs, supported by two of their sailors.

Before they left, Eleanor asked regarding the whereabouts of local assizes, as public hangings in larger towns were very popular, drawing large crowds, blocking roads and impeding traffic. They were gruesome spectacles which none of them wanted anything to do with and would give Maribel disturbing nightmares. She and Anthony agreed that Maribel had experienced enough disturbance already in her short lifetime.

After one more overnight stop, it was Maribel, looking about her, who cried out that Henry had misread the sign at a crossroad and was heading for Gosport rather than Portsmouth. She was right; he could barely read. Eleanor ordered him back to the crossroads. Wheeling around, Eleanor noticed the remains of a pirate high up in a gibbet. Maribel, on the other side, noticed instead what appeared to be the same sinister horseman in a dark cloak on a rise looking down at them. "Look, the horseman, are we going to be attacked?" Maribel cried in alarm.

Antony looked out to where Maribel indicated. "We've got three additional outriders from the number your mother said she had last time. There's no tree cover hereabouts. We can't be surprised." At an order from Henry, the coach stopped. All who had firearms, including Antony and Eleanor, produced them. At the sight of which, the figure on horseback gave a sardonic flourish of his cutlass as they started off again on the Portsmouth Road, making no further move.

"We're being watched," Eleanor observed.

"As always," Antony agreed. "Until we eliminate the treacherous syndicate. I feel it won't be long now."

"I do hope you're right," Eleanor sighed.

"Dadda's right." Maribel maintained. Antony and Eleanor looked at each other significantly, knowing Maribel's uncanny insight.

"What I don't like," Eleanor observed, "is that our guineas originate from pirate gold, which they got by seizing and selling fellow Britons."

"We'll be doing our people good forever if you and Dadda can get rid of them permanently," Maribel responded simply.

"I hadn't thought of it that way," Eleanor replied on reflection. By late afternoon they had reached the Portsmouth turnoff, noting the Portsmouth Royal Dockyard was about another four miles to the south. Eagerly they urged their horses forward towards the lodge in the surrounding brick wall, requesting entry for His Lordship and his retinue, and being directed to the terrace of houses for senior offices. Here they learnt that Lieutenant Commander Gregory Mainhampton had left for the quay, his frigate about to leave on the ebbing tide. Urgently they made for the quay where they could see moving topmasts.

Riding alongside the ropeway, mast pond and house, they turned onto the quay to see the frigate. With its 28 guns on a single upper deck, it had become a familiar sight. But it was being towed away from the quay by its ship's boat. Desperately, Eleanor and Maribel bundled out of the coach, waving frantically, Maribel's golden tresses blowing in the wind, Antony stiffly following.

Suddenly they saw the glint of light reflected by telescopes. Only officers used telescopes. They were observed. Knowing how fond Gregory was of Maribel, the sight of her in a pretty dress was something he could not resist. He signalled for the ship's boat to tow the frigate back and shore warps to be brought back aboard. Gregory stepped ashore. They ran to meet him.

When Antony caught up, he explained that at Traveslington, the next coastal hamlet from their castle after Charmouth, there was to be a late harvest festival on the thirtieth of November. Many young people from the castle would be there and many more from the surrounding districts. He said he was sure the sinister syndicate he and Magistrate Brandon had been working so hard to uncover would be informing the Barbary pirates. However, if they in turn could be ambushed and eliminated, their menace would be finished forever.

Lieutenant Commander Gregory Mainhampton-Sutton agreed, as did his second in command, Lieutenant Gordon Maplefield; very good indeed for career prospects and promotion. They were welcomed aboard, their seamen escort needing to return with the coach to hand back their horses. As before, Gregory insisted they share his stern cabin, ordering the previous partition to be reconstructed and set back in place while they went out on deck to watch the frigate leave port in the dusk.

Chapter Eighteen

With the ship's boat aboard and shore lights fading, the frigate rising and falling, heeling in the wind, they were invited back to the stern cabin. Gregory had found for Maribel a recently made corn dolly which he said, in his village, was given to the prettiest girl at the time of the harvest. The compliment went not unnoticed. Maribel gave Gregory a shy kiss, stroking the dolly's pretty dress made from fragments of lace and ribbon. For a moment, Gregory's cheeks went quite red. Antony could see he was very pleased to have her aboard.

Eleanor then gave Gregory more details regarding Antony's mission, which he had just succeeded in accomplishing with the frigate turning back for them. She told him how she'd received a message that he was lying ill in a hostelry then, without the marquis knowing, setting off on her own to locate, look after him, and continue his mission. She felt that he might have been poisoned with hemlock but was not sure. He had some of the symptoms, like being initially paralysed. Fortunately, he seemed to be well on the road to recovery.

She went on to confirm the account of the young people of the castle and from the surrounding districts, making arrangements to have a late autumn harvest festival on the thirtieth of November. Like Antony, she felt sure this would be conveyed to the Barbary pirates by the sinister syndicate Antony and Magistrate Brandon Travallyn had been working so hard to uncover. She pleaded for Lieutenant Commander to reach Traveslington in time, adding that Magistrate Travallyn and his retinue were currently being held at Newgate Prison for trial at the Old Bailey for a trumped-up charge brought by the marquis's friend, the earl.

Gregory said he would try, but the prevailing winds were often south-westerlies and that it would be hard to beat westward along the coast in time. He said he would do his best, engaging local pilots on occasions to help him work the tides. He made it clear, however, that in the end, the weather would be the deciding factor. He agreed on the importance of wiping out the Barbary pirate menace once and for all.

They stood by the starboard rail as the frigate was navigated carefully down the West Solent, Gregory pointing out features in the moonlight. With the Needles abeam, it was late, and they were invited back into the now reconverted double cabin.

The following morning, Gregory reported that the wind was backing quickly, and lightning was seen far out to the south-west. The indications were that a severe storm was imminent. They could make it down the Swash Channel into Poole Harbour for shelter but could end up being storm-bound in there for days. To reach Traveslington in time, they would need to clear Anvil Point so as not to be embayed and head out to sea in the hours of darkness, clawing westward as best they could. They would come back in daylight hours to sight land to see where they were, but it would be a rough passage. Antony and Eleanor said that if they were to save the young people of Traveslington and surrounding districts, they had no choice but to carry on. Gregory agreed.

"What are those blazing fires along the coast in places?"

"Sadly, they're windmills. If their sails are not taken off them in time, they turn faster and faster until the wooden gearing catches fire with the intense friction. Such a shame. The millowners will be without a living, insurance being too expensive for most."

With the frigate shuddering at the shock of heading straight into mounting seas, spray sweeping the deck, they continued their journey. Next day a cold breakfast was available. Gregory advised them to keep to their bunks, using the lee cloths, so as not to be thrown about and injured.

This they did for much of the time but felt compelled eventually to go out on deck with care, holding onto a line rigged between the main and mizzen mast, extending to the binnacle. Here they found Gregory standing next to the helm, wearing a piece of canvas stained yellow with linseed oil over his uniform. "Every so often, the rain comes in sheets. When it does, you'll be soaked in seconds. I think that high land you see is the Purbeck Hills. I'm trying to clear Portland Bill before dark while we can still see it. The storm-force winds are continually backing. When we can, we're taking advantage of them, running to the west as fast as we can under lower mainsail and staysails. Portland Bill is the big danger. Once we clear that, we've got a chance of getting to Traveslington by the twentieth."

"Where's Portland Bill?" Antony asked, swaying on the handline.

"You must be feeling better, m'lord."

"It's that sweet water you've taken aboard."

"Lovely spring water, isn't it? Here, take my telescope. Be careful not to drop it. It's on the horizon far out to the south-west. It looks like an island. We mustn't get embayed."

Antony glanced up into the rigging to see the sailing master with a number of the watch urgently adjusting sails and securing damaged flailing canvas and splintered spars. "The rain's coming again. You better get inside quickly!" Gregory warned.

Later that day, feeling better and restless, Antony made his way to the forepeak on the lower deck. Here the noise of the prow hitting the oncoming seas was incredible, the timbers shuddering and groaning, beads of water welling through the timbers at the shock, running down into the bilge. Antony felt that if the frigate was not relatively new, it would not have withstood the battering but broken up. As Gregory had advised, for safety, they spent the late afternoon and evening secured in their bunks, their evening meal consisting of rather stale bread, nuts, dried fruit, cheese and yoghurt. "To help, m'lord," Gregory said, indicating some items they were not familiar with.

They spent a restless night holding on to each other; on occasions, periods of lightning turned night into day. When would this storm end? Gregory said it was turning out to be the storm of the century. Antony became concerned about the extent of the damage ashore, hoping his estate was not taking a battering.

Next morning Gregory came in exhausted, clad in his pieces of canvas stained yellow with linseed oil. Maribel said he looked like a sort of sea sprite thrown up from the depths. Antony smiled. She always did have a fertile imagination. Gregory said from a latitude point of view, they had cleared Portland Bill and, when the churning wind was favourable, were running as fast as they could to the west. They were going to stay out to sea today, out of harm's way but close to the coast tomorrow and would appreciate it if they would help him identify the coastline to determine where they were.

The day seemed very long. They were no longer taking the seas head-on, but immense combers were striking broadside, causing the vessel to heel over so that, on occasions, the yards touched the water. Gregory ordered the guns to be double secured as a loose cannon could demolish the ship. Later in the day, patches of clear sky were showing to the west, a sign perhaps that the storm was diminishing. During the night, Antony wondered what was worse, pitching or rolling. In the end, he found rolling worse as he began to feel seasick, as did the others.

Dawn saw the wind diminishing in strength at last but seas remaining high. Antony felt the ship turning west-nor-west, the quartering seas making uncomfortable sailing. By mid-morning, land was in sight, Gregory and Gordon busy with their telescopes trying to identify where they were in relationship to the charts.

"Somewhere in Lyme Bay," Gregory muttered. "Norwest," he commanded the helmsman. "I reckon I can make out the church tower at Bridport." Gordon aimed his telescope in the same direction.

"The charts say it's a prominent landmark," Gordon agreed.

"Sailing Master, lower and uppers, two foresails and the spanker. With the wind dropping, we'd better get going. What is the date?" Nobody knew. Antony and Eleanor joined him by the helm, Maribel struggling after them on her crutches. Gregory smiled at her approach.

"The thirtieth of November," Maribel said.

"How do you know?" Gregory asked.

"I keep a diary." Maribel produced it from under her shawl. "Not in my best writing as I couldn't write well owing to the movement of the frigate, look."

"I'll take your word for it," Gregory replied, not wanting to pry into a young lady's private affairs. "We'll close the coast to half a mile or less, swinging the lead as we go. By mid-morning, we should, with your help, have identified this..."

"Traveslington." Maribel confirmed.

"Our castle and Traveslington, in the past mainly a fishing village, were in an inlet, but coastal erosion gradually silted up our inlet," Antony added, "according to my forebears, both places now being accessible by tidal creeks."

"Thanks, we'll have to work out high tide. That'll bound to be known by the Barbary pirates. They'll aim to go up on the tide. If we can get this right, hugging the coast, we'll surprise them as their boats are setting out for the shore, getting between them and the mother galley. I'll get the guns sponged out with fresh water, grapeshot to starboard, round shot to larboard, no elevation."

"At last!" Antony exclaimed. "This time, the Barbary pirates should get the message that their agents' information can't be relied on and that they are losing more trying to raid our coasts for white slaves than they were gaining."

"That's the idea," Gregory agreed.

"Against the cliffs, it's difficult for them to see us. The low ground of the former inlet is another matter. We'll stand out, but if we get the timing right, the boats taking the raiding party ashore won't stand a chance. We'll be on them before they know it," Gordon added enthusiastically.

"Before we leave the shadow of the cliffs, we need to get the sailing master, quartermaster and gun captains together," Gregory commanded. Antony observed that Gordon appeared not to see the need for his master's cautious preparations, but Antony agreed. Attention to detail was important, what he needed in administering his own estate.

"For this specific action, standard procedures will need to be modified," Gregory continued after the specified personnel had reported to him. "Sailors who ascend to the cross trees for sniping need only be those who cover the larboard side. Those there for sail alteration should report as normal. Larboard deck sand can be reduced, but canvas magazine curtains should be well doused as usual. The stove fire has been out since the gale, but canvas fire buckets filled with sand and water should be in place as usual. Netting constructed above deck with hammocks stuffed into it need only be undertaken on the larboard side. Splintered pieces of wood are hardly likely to flail about to starboard. It's to larboard we need to prepare for incoming fire. We won't beat to action stations which could be heard; a bosun's whistle will have to do. Three good broadsides from both sides should do the job. Gun Captains, we'll fire on the roll. I'll give the signal. Let's go!"

"I can see water flashing on oars and the round towers of our castle beyond in that ray of sunshine coming from a break in the clouds!" Maribel called out excitedly.

"If you take your family to the sickbay below the waterline, they should be safe there," Gregory said quickly to Antony.

"Oh no!" Eleanor exclaimed. "After all we've been through to put an end to the Barbary pirate menace, we want to take our chances with the rest!"

"As you wish but stay near me at the wheel. You can't move about in shoes when gunpowder is coming up for the guns. Quartermaster, actions stations! Sailing Master, fast sail, helm, steady as you go."

Organised chaos began as the frigate was prepared for action in accordance with the recent briefing. Ten minutes later, all were standing by at action stations, listening to the clanging and banging as the frigate rolled. Antony could feel the suspense.

"I said steady as you go, Helmsman. You're letting the rollers knock you off course. How can guns be laid accurately if the course is not absolutely steady?"

"With respect, Commander, I'm doing my best. In the shallow waters, the combers are immense."

"Damnit! Anticipate, man!"

"Can I try?" Eleanor offered shyly.

"The miracle helmswoman. Irregular. I'll stand by you if the wheel proves too heavy."

Eleanor took the wheel, feeling the wind in the sails, studying the troughs between the huge waves generated by the recent storm. "Perfect."

Antony observed that they were coming up quickly on three boats rowing hard for the shore. "Hold it, good, we're coming up to the right angle, ports open. Starboard guns out. Fire!" Gregory lowered his cutlass.

As they were recovering from the roll, smoke blowing away on the breeze, there was a thundering to larboard accompanied by an awesome banging on the hull, tearing and splintering. "Larboard guns ready with ball shot!" Gregory called. Chivalrously, he stood on Eleanor's left to protect her, which made Antony quite jealous though he appreciated why. "That's great. We're coming up level and steady, ports open, larboard guns out, fire!" Smoke wreathed around the guns, shredding in the breeze. Gregory looked carefully around. "One more each side should do the job, providing the ship's held steady."

"Will I be able to helm like Mamma?" Maribel asked.

The middle of a battle was hardly the time to reiterate that, though Maribel loved Eleanor as the only mother she knew, she was not her birth mother. Maribel had inherited incredible ability from her birth mother; helming was unique to Eleanor. Antony replied by saying. "Hang on to me. You're a wonderful, brave girl."

"I don't like the noise."

"None of us do. At least we see what's going on out here. Block your ears."

"The ship's rising to starboard, guns firing grapeshot, ports open, guns out, fire!" Gregory called. Antony and Maribel blocked their ears. They knew this was to be directed at the boats or what was left of them. The noise was shattering.

"Larboard, all guns, firing round shot!" Gregory went through the procedure again. They blocked their ears, Antony holding Maribel. When the smoke cleared, they saw the galley low in the water, sinking.

"Mission accomplished!" Gordon shouted in triumph.

"Launch our boat immediately. We're almost on the beach. No room to wear ship. Fortunately, the wind's still backing, the tide's in early flow. Take the anchor out as far as the line will allow; we'll wind ourselves off!" Gregory commanded urgently, his brow wrinkled in anxiety. "Sailing Master, the rig, quick!"

Immediately there was a mass of activity aboard as all hands rushed to comply. "What's happening?" Maribel asked as the duty helmsman took over.

"We're far too close to the shore," Antony explained. "We don't want to be wrecked on the beach."

As soon as the anchor was dropped, its line was attached to the windlass and all available crew members were called to lend their weight, the frigate rearing up through the head-on combers. "We better get inside quick!" Antony said as waves began sweeping the deck, gurgling out through the scuppers.

Further out in deeper waters, the waves, though large, were not as daunting. Antony Eleanor and Maribel were told that they would be rowed up to their landing on the high tide. Gordon would need to stay with the ship, anchor off with an offshore wind, sail away and come back at first light with an onshore wind.

The well-practised boat crew were waiting at the stern. Maribel was attached to a short line and then swung outwards on a derrick. As the boat rose on a wave, she was released and grabbed, her crutches thrown after her. Eleanor, Antony and finally Gregory went through the same procedure. In the ship's boat, they appreciated how large the waves were. In the troughs, all they could see were moving wave mountains; on the crests, they could see for miles.

Near the shore, they observed the amazing skill of the boat's rowers. Holding the boat pointing shoreward by quick bursts of rowing on one side or the other, they picked their wave and began rowing frantically towards the shore, surfing on the wave, avoiding broaching by holding their oars in the water on the side threatening to turn away.

Finally, at the end of a terrifying wave top ride, they were precipitated into the calm waters of Castle Creek, being rowed leisurely upstream on the flowing tide. "The boat's crew has done this before, Lieutenant Commander," Antony commented.

"Indeed they have, in many parts of the world, but perhaps not in such high wave conditions, m'lord."

With everyone now relaxed, breathing a sigh of relief, Lieutenant Commander Gregory, Antony, Eleanor and Maribel sat back as best they could to enjoy the ride up Castle Creek to their landing in the late afternoon. Suddenly Maribel cried out, "The tower flags are being lowered."

"So they are," Antony agreed. "They generally forget to take them down at dusk."

"They're stopped at half-mast?" Maribel queried.

"Your father has died!" Eleanor cried. "You are the marquis at the very time you've solved and put an end to the Barbary terror!"

"With the help of the Royal Navy," Antony added.

At the sense of excitement, the boat crew quickened its stroke, arriving at the landing at the top of the tide. Gregory ordered the boat crew to take their cutlasses from the stern locker, the cutlasses looking a little rusty, despite the oil on them, owing to the storm.

The first person he saw was Claude, always on the lookout for his master. From him, he learnt the recent events leading up to the death of his father. The marquis had ordered the castle company to guard the young people at the harvest festival at Traveslington as he did not want a repetition of what happened to the youth of Limbeley. He thought the company was well on its way in advance of the starting of the harvest festival when he saw the captain in the great hall. In a tremendous rage, he demanded to know why his order had not been carried out, to be told the captain had been requested to stand down by Lady Beatrice, assuming the order had come from the marquis. Fuming, the marquis had struggled to his feet, shouting, did he have to lead the company himself when he fell down and died.

Learning of events, Antony decided to make a formal entry with Antony, Eleanor and Maribel in front, followed by Lieutenant Commander Mainhampton-Sutton and the boat crew. Lining up, they marched under the former portcullis, into the courtyard, through to the main hall where the boat crew lined up on each side under the family heraldic banners, cutlasses pointing downward, tips resting on the floor.

The effect was sensational, the whole household running in to see, including many of the servants. When they were all assembled, Antony said in a loud, clear voice with the authority of the experiences of recent years, "I want everyone at evening meal. I have some important announcements to make, including funeral arrangements for my dear late father. Make sure you are all there."

He turned to Gregory. "I'll arrange for the boat crew to be accommodated in a disused tower and a meal brought up to them, and you, Lieutenant Commander, I'm sure would welcome a bath in my quarters to get the days of salt off you. I'll be doing the same."

"I'd be very grateful, m'lord."

Antony did not have to introduce Gregory to Lady Beatrice as there was no sign of her. What he did see was a letter addressed to the marquis. Opening it, he found it was from Sir Montague Gramble, Barrister of Lincoln's Inn Fields, defending the earl's case against Magistrate Travallyn and his retinue. It said that the earl had dropped the case of unsubstantiated charges against a member of the House of Lords, knowing that, not being able to eliminate the witnesses, he would lose it. Magistrate Travallyn and his retinue were to be released. Good news indeed.

At eight, the great gong sounded for evening meal. Lady Magdalene, Antony's elder sister and senior woman, entered the dining hall, sitting by tradition at the head of the table, Antony following, by tradition, at its foot, accompanied by Eleanor and Maribel. As an important guest, Lieutenant Commander Mainhampton-Sutton was assigned a seat near Lady Magdalene.

Contrary to tradition, Antony stood up and addressed the hall in a purposeful manner. "Now I've inherited my title of marquis, there are going to be changes. My consort will be Eleanor, who I love, who brought up Maribel, who she feels is her mother. Mary, her birth mother, who worked here as a maid, as it happens, had aristocratic lineage. Eleanor has no title, but she will be given the respect of my consort. When the time comes, I intend my lovely daughter, Maribel, to inherit the estate, mistress in her own right.

"We are going to have a new motto: *Ut Vivant Hodie, Cras Consilium*. To Live for Others. To do good in the world and especially to look after all on our estate, irrespective of status. Is that clear?"

An astounded silence followed. "The financial oversight of the estate will be undertaken by Maribel, who has wonderful arithmetical ability. The chamberlain can continue here if he chooses, as can Lady Beatrice, who was trying to protect her father. Finally, I don't expect Barbary pirates to terrorise the South Coast of England in future, owing to the heroism of a number in this hall today and the many others of our dedicated fraternity. I wish you all good luck, health and happiness."

You could have heard a pin drop.

CPSIA information can be obtained
at www.ICGtesting.com
Printed in the USA
LVHW040325080922
727813LV00005B/216

9 781803 812120